Chez Stinky

Susan C. Daffron

An Alpine Grove Romantic Comedy

Book 1

Published by Magic Fur Press
An imprint of Logical Expressions, Inc.
311 Fox Glen Road, Sandpoint, Idaho 83864, USA

Chez Stinky

ISBN: 978-1-61038-019-5 (paperback)
    978-1-61038-020-1 (EPUB)

Chez Stinky is dedicated to my mom, Margot Daffron who lost her battle with cancer a few weeks before this book was published. I wish she'd had the chance to read it.

Like all my other books, this novel is also dedicated to my husband James Byrd, my best friend and biggest supporter. Thanks for everything!

Chapter 1

This is Your Life

Katherine Stevens yawned at her monitor. The document on the screen blurred as she squeezed her eyes shut. She was supposed to be writing a technical white paper, but it was painfully dull. What her colleagues in the other cubicles didn't know was that instead of writing, she was thinking about the old black-and-white TV show "This is Your Life" with Ralph Edwards. The show was from the 50s and she'd only seen reruns a couple of times. The looks of horror the guests of honor inevitably would get when Ralph appeared and outlined all the most intimate details of their life in front of a live audience were definitely memorable, though.

If they showcased my life, that show would have been canceled after one episode due to terminal boredom. When Kat was a kid, she wanted to be Jo from *Little Women*, writing fabulous tales of action and adventure from her garret. Or a princess, since everyone knows princesses get to wear fabulous floaty clothes, live in a castle and ride ponies. Of course, you probably also had to marry your ugly third cousin, so as a career choice it did have some limitations.

She looked at the clock on the wall. Only two more hours to go.

No, Katherine Stevens wasn't a princess. Far from it. She was a technical writer and tales of action and adventure were few. Her acts of daring sometimes included proofreading parts lists to make sure they had the right number of resistors and capacitors. At this point in the mid-1990s, the biggest high-tech innovation of the year was the invention of the Wonder Bra. For all the talk of progress, technology had not moved much beyond asset-boosting underwear.

The company's lead salesperson, Chris Granger, walked up to Kat's desk, breaking her reverie. "Hey Kat, are you being followed by a moon shadow?"

She mentally rolled her eyes. Yes, her nickname was Kat. Mom had a fondness for 70s folk singers and a cute sense of humor. Chris never tired of the joke. "No Chris, I'm not. No moon shadows for me. What do you want?"

"I need you to edit my proposal. And I need it by Monday. John Horne is coming to talk to us. He is a super, super important guy, so the proposal needs to be really, *really* good!" Chris fluttered his long lashes for emphasis, which along with his habit of repeating adverbs was an affectation Kat found annoying. To be fair, he did have dazzling teal green eyes and dark good looks, which probably helped his sales. Like most handsome men in California, he'd bought some hair gel, slicked back his hair and done a stint in Los Angeles as an actor/waiter. When that career choice ended in destitution, he opted to go into technology sales instead.

"Chris, you do realize that the proposal is 400 pages long, right? You were supposed to give it to me last month," Kat said.

"I know, but I was *so* busy. You can do it over the weekend, right? It's not like you have anything to do anyway. I'm going to be flying out to Aspen with Mandi, so I'm not really going to be available to talk about it with you. You'll figure it out."

"Okay Chris, but I need to talk to Mark about this."

"Whatever. I'm headed to the airport now. See ya!" Chris turned around and smoothed back his dark hair with his palms. As he walked off down the corridor, he patted the tops of the cubicle walls.

Talking to her boss Mark would be an exercise in futility. Most of the time when Kat ventured to his office to talk to him, he seemed a little surprised she worked there, even though she'd been with the company for more than a year. His unique ability to make her feel invisible grated, particularly since he had a habit of calling her at home on the weekends to discuss trivial things like comma placement. But given his offensive comments about other women in the office, it could be worse. Fortunately, she wasn't his type. With her petite frame and wavy dark hair, Kat didn't have the Malibu Barbie looks Mark tended to find intriguing. Kat often reminded herself that you don't have to *like* the person who signs your paycheck.

Since Mark tended to disappear early on Fridays, Kat needed to get the conversation with him over with. She looked at the posters she had hanging on her cubicle walls. Half Dome in Yosemite, Glacier National Park, and Jackson Hole in Wyoming. Covering up the Steelcase gray partitions with beautiful scenery did help sometimes. But today, the images mostly just made her want to head to the airport, step on a plane, and get away. She sighed, got up from her chair and went down the hallway to Mark's office.

Mark Spencer sat behind his large mahogany desk looking down at his fingernails. He had his feet up on the corner of the desk. His amphibious utility sandals had some mud caked on the soles. Maybe he'd gone out for a run with his jock buddies at lunch. Kat knocked on the partially open office door. "Hi, Mark. Can I talk to you for a second?"

"Hey Kat, I'm pretty busy, but I've got a couple minutes before I head out."

"I just wanted to check with you about Chris's proposal. He was supposed to give it to me last month, but he just handed it off to me and says he needs it edited by Monday. That means I'm going to have to work on it over the weekend."

"Hmm, that's interesting," he said looking up and pointing his nail clippers at Kat. "I've been thinking about gingko lately. It's an herb, you know. Do you think it makes me smarter? I've been taking it and I think I'm getting smarter. What do you think?"

"Well, Mark, I'm not sure. You seem the same to me. If you start getting dumber, should I let you know? So, about that proposal…"

"Oh yeah, work over the weekend, but you're on salary, so there's no such thing as overtime."

With a flourish, Mark flipped his sun-bleached auburn hair and gave a sidelong glance at the mirror on the wall. He pulled a strap tighter on his Teva sandal and then put both feet on the floor with a stomp. "Wow, I really gotta go. Candi is waiting at the Beach House. We're celebrating my new BMW. Did I tell you I got a rag top? It's just so cool."

Kat stared at him. "Okay, 'bye." It was interesting that most of the men in the office had a preference for tall bleached-blonde women whose names ended in "i." Maybe the ladies signed their names with cute little hearts, too.

Kat returned to her cubicle and stared up at Half Dome. The John Muir quote suggested that she go climb a mountain. Maybe that wasn't such a bad idea.

~

Although climbing a mountain had some appeal, it definitely wasn't going to happen this weekend. Kat stood up and headed for the office kitchen. A bit of restorative chocolate was in order to help her make it through the rest of the long afternoon. To raise money for the school band, an enterprising child of one of the other writers had strategically placed chocolate bars in the high-traffic area. A little bit of sugary philanthropy might help her mood.

Maria Rossini poked her head out of her cubicle. "Hey Kat! I heard about the proposal. Chris has such a big mouth and thanks to his damn speaker phone, we all know his business whether we want to or not. What are you going to do?"

Kat detoured into Maria's cubicle and replied, "What I have to do. If we don't finish the proposal, we can't submit it Monday, and we have no funding for next year. Then we all lose. Way to plan ahead, Chris."

Maria shook her mop of dark curls. "Well let me know if there's anything I can do. I'd like to have this stinkin' job next year. I can't believe Chris sat on the thing for so long. Mark is such a weenie. Why does he let that guy get away with this stuff?"

"Who knows? Chris is a pretty man who sells stuff to other pretty people. Mark likes money. And let's face it, this place needs money to keep going. All I know is that this weekend is going to be long and boring. But I'd like to have a job when January rolls around, too. Want to come over tonight for a Wine and Whine Party?"

"Sure. You can evaluate how bad the proposal is and I'll drink. You might edit better with some adult beverages."

Although her editing skills were rarely enhanced by the addition of alcohol, Kat nodded at Maria and smiled. Maria was Mark's secretary and on her best days she looked like a somewhat shorter and stouter (Maria preferred the term *Rubenesque*) version of Sophia Loren. Today was not one of her best days, however. Maria took the concept of casual Friday seriously. There's a fine line between comfortable slacks and sweat pants and today Maria was on the sweaty side. On Fridays, Maria often didn't use the expensive hair products that kept her unruly curls under control, so today her normally big hair was downright enormous. But Maria was one of those friends you could count on to be sympathetic, particularly about work-related idiocy. This evening's bitch fest could be amusing. Undoubtedly, it would be the best part of the weekend.

A phone rang and both Kat and Maria turned their heads to look over at Kat's workstation. "I think that's yours," Maria said.

"Probably Chris with more bad news." Kat rushed back to her cubicle and said over her shoulder, "I'll talk to you later and we can work out the time to get together tonight."

Kat grabbed the phone and said "Hello?" with a great exhale of breath, so her greeting came out as more of a shout.

"Hello, is this Katherine Stevens?"

"Yes. I'm sorry, I just got back to my desk; I didn't mean to bark in your ear like that. May I help you?"

"My name is Larry Lowell and I'm a lawyer in the town of Alpine Grove. I'm afraid I have some bad news."

Kat nodded. How could this day possibly get any worse? "What news?"

"Your great-aunt Abigail has died. I'm very sorry for your loss."

"Aunt Abigail? Really?" Kat flashed on a memory of a thin white-haired woman wearing a floppy peasant skirt. "Wow, I haven't seen her in years and I think my mother lost track of her. What happened?"

Larry cleared his throat and said quietly, "I'm not entirely sure of the precise details, but I know she was ill. She was an 'unusual' person, but smart and funny, even right before she passed away. I talked to her just a few weeks ago. She came into my office to talk about her estate."

Kat raised her eyebrows, "Her estate?"

"Yes, you are named the principal beneficiary of her estate. You have inherited all of her assets up here in Alpine Grove."

"Assets? What exactly do you mean by assets?"

Larry cleared his throat again. "She has a home up here, but it's not in the greatest shape at the moment. With a little TLC, you could fix it up. However, there are a few stipulations, as well."

What was this? Twenty Questions? Getting information out of this guy could take a while. Fortunately, as a technical writer, Kat had years of practice extracting information from recalcitrant people.

"Mr. Lowell, what exactly do you mean by 'stipulations'?"

"It seems, Ms. Stevens, that there are some animals residing on the property. Abigail loved her babies, as she called them, and she wanted to make sure that they would be well taken care of after she was gone. She remembered that you love animals, and that's why she wanted you to be their new mom as she would say."

Their *mom?* This guy had to be kidding. Maternal she definitely was not. "So Mr. Lowell, what type of animals are we talking about here? I mean, I don't know anything about cows or chickens or ducks or anything. I have one cat and I live in a 950-square-foot apartment."

"Please call me Larry. We'll probably be talking to each other a lot over the next few weeks. It would be best if we could meet in person. Would you like to set up a time to talk about this matter and go over the details?"

"Okay Larry. You can call me Kat. So how many animals are we talking about?"

"Abigail had four dogs and a number of cats. When I went to the property, I don't think I actually saw them all, so I'm not entirely sure. But we think at least five cats. Abigail left detailed descriptions of the animals, but people had a habit of dumping stray cats out at her place when they no longer could take care of them, so I may have missed some outside barn cats."

Once he finally spit it out, Larry could share some serious facts. After digesting the lawyer's information dump for a moment, finally Kat said, "I think you're right. We should talk about this in person. Could you give me directions?"

Larry related how to get to his office in Alpine Grove and agreed to meet Kat on Saturday afternoon. They would then drive out to the property. He promised to explain the rest of the details when they met.

Kat hung up the phone and stared blankly at her Half Dome poster again. Her quiet and slightly boring life was about to get a lot more complicated.

~

After the conversations with Mark and the lawyer, it was clearly time to go home and enjoy a little feline companionship. Kat had had enough of the humans of the world. She picked up the three-inch binder with the printout of Chris's proposal and grabbed an assortment of red pens from her desk. She stopped by Maria's cubicle on her way out and poked her head in the doorway.

"Hey Maria, I've gotta take a rain check for tonight."

Maria looked up and gave Kat a questioning look. "What happened? Chris didn't do something even dumber, did he? Maybe we need one of those industrial-size boxes of wine."

"No, it's nothing like that. I can't really talk about it right now. I'm tired and I have to get up early in the morning, so I'm just gonna go home, feed Murph, and go to bed. It's been a long, weird day."

Maria nodded her head. "Okay, so now I'm totally dying of curiosity. If you decide to share, give me a call."

Kat promised to fill Maria in on the details. She sighed as the tension left her body. It was a relief to open the door and exit the building.

Later, Kat opened her apartment door and was greeted by a rotund black-and-white cat who loudly expressed a compelling need for dinner.

"Well, meeeee-yow to you too," Kat said as she picked up the cat.

"How's my little Murphee cat?" she said, snuggling the wriggling feline in her arms.

Murphee wormed out of Kat's embrace and jumped to the floor. The cat turned around and glared at her with a look of disgust.

"Sheesh, everyone wants something," Kat mumbled as she walked to the kitchen. Grabbing the bag of outrageously expensive cat food from the pantry, she walked over to Murphee's cat food dish as the cat continued her monologue about the merits of speedy service and fine feline dining.

"All right, all right, I'm working on it!" Kat said as she poured the food.

Murphee's prominent belly swayed as she rushed to the bowl. She started gobbling down the food, but stopped to look up lovingly at Kat for a moment. Now that her obvious starvation had been addressed, she was feeling more congenial.

Kat placed the proposal binder on the kitchen table and opened it to the first page. Several typos leaped into view. She sat down, grabbed a pen, and started marking up the text as she listened to Murphee begin her post-feeding cleaning routine.

From below came distressingly familiar noises. "Urrk, aaack, hrrak, yurk!" Without thinking, Kat leaped up, grabbed Murphee out from under the table, and ran to the bathroom, holding the alarmed cat in front of her as foam oozed from between Murphee's lips.

"Barf on the tile! Barf on the tile!" Kat yelped as she placed the cat on the bathroom floor and slammed the door.

The sounds of "Hack! URRRK! Blaaaap!" came from behind the door as Murphee finished the process of purging the contents of her stomach and a little extraneous hair from her system.

Kat sat back down and looked at the proposal. *Yeah, that's pretty much my response, too.*

~

The next morning, after enjoying a vomit-free feline feeding experience, Kat drove out to Alpine Grove. The lawyer had said *four* dogs? *Five* cats? She'd never thought of herself as an animal person, per se. Sure she liked animals, but she also liked to think that she wasn't the clichéd weirdo cat lady living alone talking to her cat. In fact, Maria liked to tease her about her early days with Murphee, which didn't exactly do much for her status as a cat lady.

Kat had found the tiny kitten one evening when she was taking out her garbage. As she opened the lid of the huge green Dumpster to throw in the plastic bag, a little mewing noise came from behind one of the Dumpster's back wheels. When she crouched down to investigate, she found a very disheveled-looking black ball of fuzz. Kat ignored the pungent smell of the garbage around her as she cautiously picked up the kitten and brought her inside her apartment.

Gender identification on young kittens is difficult for experts and Kat was definitely no expert. She had assumed the kitten was male and named him Murphy in honor of Murphy's Law, which seemed appropriate for a cat that had obviously had a little too much of that law in its short life.

Kat went to the store for kitty supplies. Within a couple of days, it became obvious that kitten-proofing the apartment was going to be vital for the kitten's safety and Kat's sanity. Murphy was everywhere and into everything. In the first week, the tiny animal managed to break two vases and chew up the afghan on the sofa. It was hard to believe something so small could be so destructive. But as the kitten grew, Kat started to appreciate Murphy's independent spirit and zest for life. Watching the kitten zoom around the apartment was endlessly entertaining and having a cat made her apartment feel more like a home. It wasn't as quiet anymore and when she came home from work, she could depend on Murphy to be there to welcome her. Or at least to request dinner.

One day a few months after she'd brought home the kitten, Murphy started yowling a new and peculiar yowl. It almost sounded like the cat was screaming or in pain. Alarmed and worried that there might be something really wrong with her kitten, Kat called the veterinarian and made an appointment.

At the veterinarian's office, the vet gave Kat a sympathetic look and said, "This is your first cat, isn't it?"

Kat nodded. "Yes, why?"

"Well, for one thing, Murphy isn't a boy."

A slight flush rose on her cheeks and Kat replied, "Well I wasn't sure how you tell and I didn't want to get all personal with him…or her."

"For another thing, you really need to get her spayed. She's about to go into heat. That's what all the yowling is about."

Kat shook her head at the memory. No, she wasn't exactly an animal expert, but after getting the kitten spayed, Kat did change the spelling of Murphee's name, so it was a bit more feminine anyway. Maria had thought Kat's lack of knowledge about cat physiology was hilarious. Every time Maria came to Kat's apartment, she picked up Murphee, held her in front of her face and said, "So are we having gender identity issues today?"

~

Kat found the lawyer's office in Alpine Grove and parked her car by the curb. Alpine Grove was a small town about two hours away from the city. As its name suggested, the town was surrounded by many evergreens. The big local attraction was the fall logging festival with tree climbing, log rolling, and exhibitions with burly men wielding large chain saws.

Kat had visited her Aunt Abigail in Alpine Grove when she was a little kid. According to family lore, Abigail had moved to Alpine Grove and married a man she referred to as the Lumberjack. The couple had big plans to drop out of society and become self-sufficient. They were going to build their own house from trees harvested from the land, grow their own food, and raise their kids on the property located outside of the small logging town. Unfortunately, about halfway through the construction of the dream log cabin in the woods, the Lumberjack decided that he'd had enough of the whole back-to-the-land idea and left. Abigail never said much about him and Kat only knew about the Lumberjack at all by piecing together her mother's oblique references to him over the years.

Apparently, Abigail had been a resourceful person and found a way to finish off the house so she didn't freeze to death the winter after the Lumberjack went on his permanent road trip. Kat knew that Abigail had loved her little bit of paradise in the woods and had managed to create the little farm-ette she wanted. Kat had fond memories of sitting in the warm kitchen with soup, made from some of Abigail's many canned goods, bubbling on the old white propane stove.

Kat walked toward the lawyer's office. How had Abigail managed to survive all these years? (Not to mention feed all those animals!) Her family had lost touch with Abigail for reasons unknown. It was probably one of those terrible family secrets that her mother liked to keep. For whatever reason, Kat hadn't seen her great aunt since she was about seven or eight years old.

Kat opened the door to the Law Offices of Lawrence Lowell and found a slender well-dressed man sitting at a desk.

"Mr. Lowell? I'm Kat Stevens."

The lawyer looked up from his pile of papers, "Oh, like the musician? The one who converted to Islam?"

Kat sighed. "Yes, just like that. Except I spell my name with a K. And I don't plan to change my name to Yusaf any time soon."

"Sorry, you must get tired of people asking that. How are you? Was the drive up here pleasant?"

"I'm fine; thank you for asking. Can you tell me more about my aunt?"

The lawyer shuffled through the papers on his desk and extracted a folder from the bottom of a stack. "I have the information right here. Please have a seat."

Kat pulled the chair closer to the desk and sat down. She watched as the lawyer rummaged through the folder. He was wearing a nice suit and was a fairly attractive guy. With his short brown hair, he seemed to be going for the clean-cut yuppie look, which was probably a novelty in a town like Alpine Grove, where flannel shirts and jeans were the norm. He glanced up at Kat and she scanned his face. His dark eyes were unusually close together, which made his long face seem even longer.

"As I told you on the phone, your aunt Abigail decided to leave her property to you. Her main concern was that her animals be taken care of and live out their lives in comfort. She has named Louise Johnson the executor of her estate. Louise will determine if you are fit to take care of the animals."

"But what if I don't *want* to take care of her animals?" Kate said. "I do have a life elsewhere. Am I supposed to just drop everything, quit my job, and take care of my aunt's animals? How would I earn a living?"

"Well, you may not know this, but your aunt was very—shall we say—cautious with her money. She had a considerable amount of savings amassed and led a simple life. She didn't spend much. Apparently, she had an inheritance from 50 years ago and she invested wisely. She never touched the principal, so now it's a rather large sum of money."

Kat stared at the lawyer and noticed his cuff links had green and red stripes on them, like an Italian flag. "You have got to be kidding me. What you're saying is that Abigail was a cheapskate and it paid off for her financially?"

"Well, no one really knew about the money. She never even told her ex-husband, which was probably a good thing."

"You know about the Lumberjack?"

"Yes, Abigail told me about how she ended up living here in Alpine Grove. She was a wonderful storyteller, and I handled her affairs for a number of years. We became quite good friends. I miss her."

Kat ran her fingers through her hair, pushing it away from her face. "You probably knew her a lot better than I did. I think the last time I saw her I was eight years old. I used to love coming up here. She was always the fun relative. I never really understood why I couldn't come back."

"Your aunt certainly remembered you. She always said you had a kind heart. But she was also a smart lady and knew that she hadn't seen you in a long time. So that's why she has put the money into a trust and enlisted her friend Louise to monitor the situation."

"What situation?"

"You have to make a choice, Kat. Abigail realized that you may have other things going on in your life. If you opt to live here in Alpine Grove at the property and take good care of her animals, you get all the money and obviously the property, too. If not, you can find the animals good homes and sell the property yourself. The money that is in the trust will be disbursed to a number of charities that Abigail supported. And every new home you find for the animals must be approved by Louise. To be honest, Abigail loved her dogs and cats desperately. They were her family; she wanted someone she trusted to take care of them, so they could all stay together."

"So why doesn't Louise take them? She and Abigail were friends, right?"

The lawyer shifted in his chair. "Louise is allergic to anything with fur. Although she and Abigail spent a lot of time together, Louise almost never went out to the property."

Kat was at a loss for how to respond to all this new information. She looked into the lawyer's dark brown eyes. "So what's next? I honestly don't know what to do here."

"I can take you to visit the property. You can see it and meet all the animals. I haven't been out there in a few years, so I'm not sure what condition it is in."

"Condition?"

The lawyer nodded his head. "Do you remember anything about the place? It may not be in exactly the same shape it was the last time you were there. Abigail was not well for a while and Louise told me that although she had assistance, the place was getting to be a bit much for her."

Kat shrugged her shoulders. "Okay, you're right. It definitely sounds like I need to go out there for a visit." Kat looked out the front window at a happy-looking couple holding hands as they strolled down the sidewalk. The serene picture seemed a stark contrast to the sick sinking feeling she had in her stomach. What on earth was she getting herself into?

~

Kat got into her car and waited for Larry to pull out into the street. A dented, salmon-colored, 60s-era Dodge pickup pulled out from an alley in front of her. She was surprised to see the lawyer at the wheel. Who would have thought Larry would be a truck owner? Certainly not the owner of a light-pink truck. He seemed like more of a BMW kind of guy. Who knew?

They drove out of town and a few miles down the road, Larry turned down a smaller, winding dirt road. They passed a red barn with a huge white J on the front and what a tour book might call the 'remains of a historic homestead,' which more accurately could be described as a log shack with a caved-in roof.

The salmon pickup turned right down an even narrower road. The two vehicles continued down the road and the trees became so thick the canopy almost made it seem like they were driving through a long green tunnel. Kat turned the steering wheel to dodge a gigantic crater in the road. It was entirely possible she was completely destroying her car. The poor little Toyota wasn't exactly accustomed to this type of off-road activity. Maybe the lawyer was smart to have that beater pickup after all. Driving on these roads, a BMW would probably leave a trail of 10,000 tiny expensive German-engineered parts.

The trees opened up into a clearing and Abigail's house came into Kat's view for the first time in 20 years. The house was set into a hillside and was made of logs sitting on top of a concrete daylight basement. The house was rustic to say the least and quite a bit smaller than Kat remembered. It was also clear that home maintenance may not have been Abigail's forte.

Years of dirt, weather, and possibly mildew had given the logs a two-tone effect like an old classic Chevy. The logs were significantly darker brown on the top than on the bottom. Below the logs, the concrete daylight basement walls were covered with somewhat shredded tar paper, which gave the house a dingy, ruffled, unkempt look. Clearly, it was not a candidate for one of those luxury-log-home magazine photo spreads.

Kat parked and stepped out of the car. The tinkling of wind chimes and the rustling of leaves from the breeze through the copse of aspen trees were the only sounds. Kat looked up into the tree tops and smelled the sweet fragrance of warm pine trees that wafted from the forest surrounding the house. Abigail's home may have been out of the way, but it was located in an incredibly peaceful spot.

Suddenly, the tranquil moment was interrupted by a mighty "WOOF!" Something that looked like a cross between a horse, a bear, and a wookie barreled toward Kat. The muscles in her body clenched in fear as her brain scrambled to figure out where she could hide.

Before she could make a move, the beast ran up to her, stopped, sat, and began wagging, creating a little tail angel in the dirt. Kat's racing heart started to slow down a little. The giant furry thing was actually a dog and not Sasquatch.

Larry said, "That's Linus, one of your aunt's dogs. She used to call him Hairy Mess...I think you can tell why."

Kat said shakily, "Oh my God, he's HUGE." The large brindled brownish-tan dog shook his furry head, which caused his ears to flap and his tongue to wave from side to side.

"Yes, he's big, but he wouldn't hurt a fly," Larry said.

Kat reached out her hand toward the dog, who sniffed it and moved his head under her hand so she could more easily scratch his large, floppy ears. She obliged. "Hi, Linus. How are you?"

Linus moved closer and started to lean on Kat's side. She hoped he wouldn't knock her over, since she was pretty sure the dog outweighed her by a considerable amount. Thank heavens he was friendly.

A large, egg-shaped woman came out of the house and stood on the stair landing outside the front door. Seeing Linus, she said, "Linus, don't you want your breakfast?"

Linus perked up his ears, looked up at Kat, and then turned and began trotting back down the hill toward the back of the house.

Kat noticed that although the woman's skirt fluttered in the breeze, the somewhat bluish curls piled on her head were completely motionless. The woman held up a Kleenex, sneezed into it, and then said, "Hello, I'm Louise. You must be Katherine. Your aunt spoke highly of you." She waved the tissue frantically and then sneezed again. "Ugh, I can't handle all this hair! It's in my nose, on my clothes…everywhere! I'm going to have to take my pills. I hate that; they make me so sleepy."

Kat raised her hand and waved slightly. "It's nice to meet you. I'm sorry you had to come out here. Have you had to take care of the animals since my aunt died?"

Larry interjected, "No your aunt's estate has been paying for pet sitters to come up here three times a day and tend to the animals. Louise is here because I called her this morning to let her know that you might be coming out."

Louise nodded. "Yes, and I wanted to make sure all Abigail's critters are happy, too. Everyone seems fine as far as I can tell, although they do seem a bit confused. Would you like me to show you around?"

"If you wouldn't mind," Kat replied. "I haven't been here in a long time. It all looks so…different."

"Well, your great aunt was not feeling well for a while before she died, so she was moving a bit more slowly than the last time you saw her. Some things have fallen through the cracks over the last few years. But she hadn't lost her marbles; she was still smart as a tack, right up until the end. I saw her the day before she died and she was talking about planting some things in the garden again."

Kat looked around and didn't see anything that looked like a defined garden area. "Where is the garden?"

"Right over there," Louise said, waving her tissue toward a welded-wire fence that surrounded six-foot-tall grasses. Swaying in a small gust of wind, they looked like they were trying to escape their confinement.

Kat said, "I guess it needs a little work."

"Oh with just a little rototilling, it would be fine," Louise said.

The lawyer peered at the area, looking dubious. There seemed to be more weeds inside the fence than outside of it.

Louise turned toward the door. "Let's go inside and see the house."

Kat and Larry headed toward the stairs. The steps leading up to the front door were made of plywood that had been covered with what looked like mud-encrusted blue shag carpeting. Kat stepped up on the first stair and the plywood creaked underneath her weight. Hopefully, Linus the gigantic dog didn't use the stairs much. She turned to say to Larry, "You might want to wait a second before you get on these stairs; I'm not sure how much weight they can hold."

Louise was wrestling with the front door latch trying to get the door open. She cocked her head, looked over her shoulder, and said, "Oh, I'm sure they're fine. Abigail used them for years and there's not even a handrail. She was a wiry old bird."

Kat walked past the heavy rough wooden door and her nostrils were assaulted by a strange and decidedly not good smell. It certainly wasn't the warm smell of simmering soup from her childhood memories. The odor was something more earthy. Maybe cow manure with a hint of antique skunk mixed in? Whatever it was, the scent was revolting and omnipresent.

Turning to look at Louise, she asked, "Do you smell that?"

"Dear, I can't smell anything," Louise replied, shaking her tissue in front of her face.

"What about you, Larry? Do you know what that smell is?"

Larry shook his head. "I'm not sure. But I doubt it's a good thing, whatever it is. Maybe something died in the walls?"

Kat groaned, "Wow, how gross is that?"

Larry said, "That type of thing can be dealt with fairly easily. Exterminators and those animal people that trap things are experts at finding and getting rid of problems in buildings."

Kat moved from the entryway, past the stairwell, into the kitchen. The old propane stove looked more or less like she remembered. She bowed her head to get a closer look, touching the black charring around the burners. The stove may have experienced a few fires in the past 20 years. Cooking could involve a bit more excitement here than in her apartment.

The kitchen opened up into a large room with a high cathedral ceiling and picture windows that faced to the south. Because the house was set into the hillside, from upstairs the panoramic view of the forest outside made it feel like a kid's tree house. Kat stood at the window and gazed at the branches of a cedar that swayed as a puff of wind passed by the massive tree. The squirrels here obviously enjoyed some rather stellar vistas.

Kat turned around and faced the kitchen again. She yelped at the same time, as a large orange cat leaped up and squalled because she had stepped on its tail. Her gaze locked with the cat's for a moment, then the cat stalked off under the table.

"That's Louie," Louise said. "He's one of the house cats. Dolly Mae and Tripod are probably here somewhere."

"Tripod?" Kate asked.

"Yes, the poor little fellow only has three legs. He's a very sweet cat—extremely affectionate. Abigail just adored him. She called him her lap buddy."

A crashing noise came from downstairs and Larry said from below, "It's okay. I think I found Dolly Mae. She's down here."

Kat leaned over the wall that surrounded the stairwell and peered down the stairs into the dark basement below. "Are you okay?"

"Yes, I just tripped on Dolly. She's fine, too."

Kat turned on the light and ventured down the stairs. At the bottom, Larry was sitting in the hallway on the gray concrete floor with his legs splayed out in front of him. A long-haired brown tabby cat milled around his black loafers. He looked up at Kat. "Hi. Meet Dolly Mae."

As she bent down to pet Dolly, Kat felt something wet caress her ear. She leaped sideways, turned her head, and found herself nose-to-nose with a furry black-and-white dog panting in her face.

Kat stood up straight, wiped the dog slobber off her ear, and said, "That's the first time I've gotten a wet willy from a dog. Ewww! That's disgusting."

"That's Lori. She is probably part retriever and part border collie. So that means she's smart and loves everybody," Larry said as he stood and brushed dust, hair, and other debris from his suit.

The hallway in the basement had several closed doors that presumably went off to other rooms. Kat remembered sleeping in one of the bedrooms down here long ago, but if the hall was any indication, Kat wasn't sure she wanted to find out what lurked behind those doors.

As Kat was taking in the dark, dusty ambiance, Lori ambled over to Dolly Mae and gave the cat a good solid nose poke in the butt. In response, Dolly Mae sat back on her haunches and waved her paw at the dog as if to swat her.

Kat looked over at Larry. "So do they get along?"

"I think so. Most of the time, anyway. Abigail never really said anything about it," Larry replied.

"What are you guys doing down there?" Louise called from the top of the stairs. "If you two are canoodling, please do it later. I need to finish showing you around, so I can get home and take my pills!" She then punctuated her statement with a loud sneeze.

"Canoodling?" Kat whispered as she felt a slight flush rise on her cheeks. She raised her eyebrows and gave Larry a conspiratorial look. "Really? Do people even say that anymore?"

"Apparently so." Larry replied with a grin. He turned and Kat watched him go upstairs. When the lawyer smiled, it completely transformed his face. Maybe he was better-looking than she'd thought.

Louise proceeded to hurriedly walk them through the rest of the upstairs, which consisted of a sparsely furnished bedroom and a small bathroom. On a decorating show, they might refer to the decor as "country kitchen," but the style might be better described as vintage yard-sale rejects with a fine patina of dog hair.

Louise said, "You both have already seen the basement, so I'll take my leave now. Please call if you need anything."

She rushed down out the door, down the front stairs, and hopped into her big yellow Buick station wagon. Gunning the motor to encourage it, she then rumbled off down the driveway.

Kat turned to Larry, "I need to get out of here. The smell is getting to me."

"Let's go outside. I can show you the outbuildings."

Kat stepped out onto the front stair landing and felt the platform wobble. "So, why is there carpet on the stairs?"

"Well, they are made of plain old plywood and it's probably pretty slippery when it rains or gets icy, I'd guess."

Kat shrugged. "Yeah, I guess."

The pair went over to an old barn and found a medium-sized golden retriever in a chain-link enclosure. The dog was obviously extremely happy to have some company and was barking furiously. The animal seemed almost to be levitating, and its ears shot straight up in the air with each bound. "Should we let him out?" Kat asked through the din.

"Better wait for the dog walker to do it. I don't know much about this dog, actually." Larry shouted back.

As they walked around the rest of property, Kat clenched her fists, digging her fingernails into her palms. It was just so much to take in; at this point she just wanted to leave and go someplace quiet and think. Somewhere without giant dogs, barking, and bad smells.

"So, what do you think? Have you made a decision?" Larry asked.

Kat said, "I need to get back home. I have a proposal I have to edit or everyone at my company is going to lose their jobs. I'm really far behind as it is because of coming out here. I'll probably be up all night."

The lawyer looked down at the ground. "That's fine, but I do need to know what your plans are."

"I know. But honestly, I just can't spend any time here with that smell. Can you do something about it? Then I can come back and look around again. I need to think about all this. And I really need to drive back to the city now."

"Okay. I'll call an acquaintance of mine to see if he can do something about the smell. He's a bit of an all-around handyman person. I think he may have experience with this type of situation. I'll give you a call on Monday and let you know."

Kat shook hands with Larry and walked over to her car. Linus was lying near the driver's side door in the shade, looking relaxed. He gazed up at her with a questioning look on his face. As Kat reached down to pet his huge head, she looked into his deep-brown eyes. "I'm sorry big guy, but I have to go now." Linus looked at her for a second, stood up, and padded toward the house. He stopped and looked over his shoulder.

"It's okay. Go on home, now."

Kat felt like she should tell him that she'd be back, but she wasn't sure. He was just a dog, anyway. He didn't know that part of her wanted to run away from this complicated, stinky disaster area and never, ever come back. But as she looked up into the canopy of trees and listened to the birds twittering, another part of her felt an oddly comforting connection to this place.

Chapter 2

Wine & Whine

As Kat pulled the car into her parking space in her apartment complex, she looked up at the door of her comfortable little apartment. Everything here was so easy. One hungry but otherwise not terribly demanding cat. Functional appliances. No mysterious smells.

After greeting and feeding Murphee, Kat settled into her favorite blue chair and picked up the phone.

"Hi Maria. Are you still up for the Wine and Whine?" she asked.

"Hey girlfriend! I may have to cancel that hot date I have with Richard Gere. But that officer and gentleman is just going to have to wait to enjoy the fabulousness of me."

Kat laughed and said, "Great. Come on over. I've got stories to tell you."

"Coolio! See ya in a few."

After Maria arrived at her apartment, Kat poured the wine and related the events of her day out in Alpine Grove. In the retelling, the whole experience seemed surreal.

"It's cool that I have an inheritance," Kat said. "But I don't think I'm really the live-out-on-the-farm country-girl type. I'm a tech writer."

"Let me see if I'm getting this straight," Maria said. "If you live at this place that smells like a sewer, you get the

27

property and gobs and gobs of money. But if you find homes for the dogs and cats, you only get the place that stinks." Maria raised one eyebrow, a move she called her Mr. Spock look.

"Yes. I get Chez Stinky either way. But what my aunt really wanted was for me to take over her life and take care of her dogs and cats. It's weird because the last time she saw me I was eight. How did she even know that I like animals at all? I could be some creepy fuzzy-bunny-hater for all she knew."

"Chez Stinky? Oh yeah, baby, you know I'm not gonna forget that. Your new homestead is forever etched in my little brain as Chez Stinky. I wanna make a big sign for you as a housewarming gift. You can put it over the door!"

Kat giggled and took a sip of her wine. "The lawyer knows a guy who can get rid of the stink. Or I hope so anyway. I'm not sure I want to know what he needs to do."

Maria said, "My uncle Bruno had a bad problem like that, and he said that if it's a dead animal, you wanna get to it before it liquefies into the wall. If that happens, you might never get out the smell. The goo gets into the drywall and you have to do sawing and cutting and stuff."

Kat lowered her head and put her hands over her ears. "That's just too gross to even contemplate."

"Yeah, you don't want those liquid dead bodies, you know. Bruno is the type of guy who knew about dead bodies."

Peering over her wine glass, Kat said, "So what does Uncle Bruno do anyway?"

"He's never been exactly clear on that. But he has some pretty nice cars. When I was a kid, he let me ride around in his fine, fine convertible Corvette. I was looking hot in that 'Vette. Even if I was 10. I was still hot."

Kat laughed. "Yeah, I bet you were."

⌒

The next morning, Kat was sipping coffee and leafing through the Big Bad Proposal, as she'd come to think of it. The pounding in her skull suggested that perhaps the Wine and Whine last night may not have been a great idea. With the proposal binder laid open on her table and red pens strewn about, Kat attempted to concentrate and move into work mode. It was slow going and Kat had the sinking feeling that she wasn't going to finish editing it before Monday morning rolled around.

The phone rang, jarring Kat from editorial tedium. She leaped out of her chair to answer it. "Hello?"

"Hello, Ms. Stevens, this is Larry Lowell. My apologies for calling so early. Do you have a moment to talk?"

"Sure. I'm awake, and I've had most of my coffee, anyway."

The lawyer cleared his throat. "I talked to my friend about the odor at your property and we went to take a look yesterday afternoon. He thinks he can address that issue, but there may be other difficulties with the structure."

Kat sighed. Maybe Larry had some kind of sinus problem. He spent a lot of time hemming, hawing, and clearing his throat. "Difficulties? What type of difficulties?"

"The main dwelling may not make it through another winter," he replied. "The roof was not constructed the way most contractors would do it today. The roof metal was laid directly upon the roof stringers with just a layer of plastic between the metal and the insulation. That's typically how you roof a barn, but not a home that is heated. For a house, generally you would have a layer of plywood sheeting and tar paper under the metal. The trusses also aren't close enough together, so ideally you would remove the roof, add more trusses, tar paper, and the wood sheeting. As it is now, you have issues with condensation, and over the years the plastic has decomposed, so there are just little pieces left. There may be other issues as well, but going up into the attic revealed that the roof is definitely a problem now."

"I don't know what a stringer is, but it all certainly sounds expensive to fix. Is repairing the house something that the estate could pay for? If I sell the place, I can't sell it if the roof is about to cave in. I think that's the type of thing anyone buying a house would want you to disclose."

"Stringers are the strips of wood that hold the trusses together. The roof metal is attached to them. And yes, the money is available for repairs if you opt to live at the property yourself. If you are going to sell the property, it may be more cost-effective to tear down the house and just sell the land."

Tear down the house? That seemed extreme. And it felt wrong, like she was throwing away all that her aunt had worked to create her entire life. Plus, what about the animals? It was their home, too. But making Chez Stinky *her* home seemed like an extreme step. Kat liked her comfortable life. Sure, her job might not be the most interesting one in the world, but it paid the rent on her apartment.

"How soon can they get rid of the smell? I think I need to go back up there and talk to your friend myself," she said.

"If I have your authorization, he can start today."

"Will the smell be gone by next weekend? Right now, I have to work and I have a big deadline."

"Yes, I'll tell him your plans."

Kat thanked the lawyer, hung up, and turned back to the dense text of the Big Bad Proposal. Some of her most vivid childhood memories centered around the house and the land surrounding it. She spent long summer days hiking with her aunt through the trees and helping Aunt Abigail in the gardens around the house. Kat figured she probably wasn't much help, but her aunt spent hours patiently explaining what all the herbs, vegetables, and flowers were and why she had planted them. Kat had asked a million questions, but Abigail loved to talk about growing things. She had shown Kat how to plant seeds and cover them with soil. Once the seedlings took root, Abigail also showed her how to identify the bad weeds from the good plants.

Kat shook her head. "What am I doing? I have less than 24 hours to edit 350 pages." She picked up her red pen and set to work.

～

On Monday morning, Kat was exhausted. For the first time since college, she had pulled an all-nighter. Back then, some of her classmates seemed to be able to thrive on less than eight hours of sleep, but Kat was not one of them. The process of dragging herself into the office felt like she was slowly swimming through molasses. But the good news was that after editing all night, the Big Bad Proposal was marked up. All she had to do today was put the changes into the computer. Kat yawned mightily and went to the office kitchen for another cup of coffee.

Maria walked up and did a hip bump against Kat. "You look like death, girl."

"Why thank you. I feel lovely today as well," Kat answered with a smirk. "I'm guessing your Sunday was better than mine."

"Yeah baby. I got a new magazine, and I followed the instructions for one of those home spa days where you use up all the stuff in your refrigerator as natural beauty products. I made a mask out of mayonnaise and a hair gel out of honey."

Kat looked at Maria's hair more closely. Her normally bouncy curls were oddly stiff with a crystalline sheen as if her hair had been frozen in a sugar storm. "I'm not sure you're supposed to leave that type of thing *on* your hair."

"Well, I didn't finish the article."

Kat raised her eyebrows and said, "You might want to wash your hair when you get home." She headed back to her cubicle and sat down just as the phone rang, making her jump and jarring her dulled senses. All the caffeine was making her twitchy, but it wasn't doing its job to keep her awake.

"Hello, this is Kat."

"Hiya. My name is Herbert Fowler. I'm a friend of Larry Lowell. But you can call me Bud. Everybody does."

"Larry Lowell? Oh, are you the person looking at the house in Alpine Grove?"

"Yep, that's me. And I gotta tell ya, that's one bad smell you got there, lady," he said with a snort.

"Yes. I noticed. Can you make it go away?"

"Yeah, but it's gonna cost ya," Bud said with a slurp. It sounded like he was shifting chewing tobacco around in his mouth. Finally, he spat out, "I gotta find the varmint and then cut out the wall and then dee-spoze of the thing in a sanitary way."

Considering how disgusting she found chewing tobacco, Kat hated to think what Bud would regard as sanitary disposal. She didn't exactly have a lot of options. "That sounds like a good plan, Mr. Fowler. Did you talk to Larry about this? I need to know the cost as well."

"Yep. He said that I need to talk to you 'cuz you gotta come up with the money for the dee-spoz-al."

Kat said, "I think Larry is supposed to take care of it with the money from Abigail's estate."

"Nope," Bud said with an emphatic slurp.

"I'd like to know how much this will cost. And can you take a credit card? I need to have the smell removed so I can spend some time there this weekend."

"Nope. I deal in cash. I'll know what it costs when I do it."

Kat rolled her eyes. "All right, please call Larry with an estimate, so I have some idea. I'll talk to him and he can get the money to you. But you promise to get rid of the smell, right?"

"Yep, no problem."

Kat hung up the phone and laid her head down on her desk. How could getting an inheritance be so expensive? Just bulldozing the place and forgetting about it was looking appealing.

∽

Kat awoke with a start and looked up. Chris was peering over her cubicle wall down at her. He thumped the top of the wall with his hand. "So, are you having tea with the tillerman or what?"

Kat blinked a few times at him trying to think of a suitably snotty retort to his latest musical reference, but she was too tired to come up with anything. How long had she been asleep? "No Chris. What do you want?"

"How's my proposal? I need it, you know," he said, tapping his index finger on the cubicle top again for emphasis.

"We already *had* this conversation Chris. I know. I'm working on it."

Chris nodded and continued tapping the cubicles as he wandered off down the hallway. A quiet non-flattering expletive was uttered by the editor in the next cubicle as Chris walked by. Sharon loathed Chris with a fierce passion that was a little scary.

A few years ago Kat had read that the secret to technical writing is an ability to tolerate boredom. Yes, her job had many boring moments, but this was the first time she'd literally fallen asleep at her desk. How embarrassing. With any luck, Chris wouldn't blab to Mark about it. Finding a job as a writer wasn't easy, and she'd had to take a pay cut to get this one after she'd been laid off a year ago. Glancing up at the clock on the wall, she pressed her lips together. It was already midday. Sadly, napping tended to cut down on editorial productivity. There was no way she could finish the proposal by herself. Time to call in reinforcements.

She strode to Mark's office and faced the back of his big leather chair. It looked like Mark might be observing something out the window or maybe playing with the toys on his credenza. Kat was sure she didn't want to know. She knocked on the door to get his attention.

Mark spun around and gaped at Kat with sheepish look on his face. "Oh, hi."

Kat raised her eyebrows. What exactly *had* he been doing? "Hi, Mark. I need to get help on this proposal. I made all the edits on the paper copy, and I think that if we divide it up and several people put the changes into the file, we can get them all in and make the deadline. Can you get everyone together and tell them this is important?"

Mark nodded his head and looked down at his fingernails. "Didn't I tell you? Over the weekend, I went out for a beer with one of my buddies at the agency. He gave us an extension. We don't have to have it done for another month."

Kat's eyes widened. "And you're just telling me this *now?*" she fumed. "Why didn't you tell me this earlier? Like when I came in after getting no sleep last night. Or even better, you could have called me over the weekend. You have my number. It's not like you don't call me with meaningless drivel all the time. You must have me on speed dial. Whenever you have one of your brilliant ideas, you call me."

Mark brushed a lock of hair off his forehead and looked out the window. "I had stuff to do. I was busy and forgot."

"And I *didn't* have stuff to do? I just found out my aunt died!" Kat spun around and stomped out of the office. She was *so* outta here. Clenching her fists, she stopped and said over her shoulder, "So did you let Chris in on this little tidbit of information? Maybe you should. Oh and by the way, I'm taking the afternoon off."

Kat marched down the hallway back to her cubicle, gathered her belongings, and left the building. Wound up on caffeine and fury, she was practically vibrating. Gripping the steering wheel in her little Toyota, she replayed the conversation with Mark in her head. Yes, she needed money to pay her rent, but being jerked around by that self-absorbed idiot was no way to live her life. She was smart and willing to work hard. Why was she settling for this?

Back at her apartment, Kat flopped down onto her bed. As if she could sense Kat was mentally and physically exhausted,

Murphee didn't complain about food. Instead, she jumped up on the bed, curled up by Kat's side, and started purring. Kat stroked the cat's long black fur and her body started to relax. Maybe she should fix up Chez Stinky after all.

∼

Kat was jolted awake by the sound of her phone ringing. She couldn't think of anyone in the world she wanted to talk to right now, so she rolled over and put her pillow over her head to shut out the noise. Murphee leaped off the bed with a disgusted meow.

"Sorry Murph," she mumbled. The answering machine could take the call. That's why she had one, after all. Kat just wanted to get some sleep.

When she woke up several hours later, Kat walked over to her answering machine and noticed that the red light was blinking. She pressed the play button.

"Ms. Stevens," the voice on the machine said, "This is Jean Hartland. I'm the apartment manager for this building. I'm calling to see if you got the letter we sent you. Just in case you did not receive it or haven't had a chance to read it, I'm informing you that the apartment complex has been purchased and the new owner will be converting the units to condominiums. You will need to find a new place to live and move out of apartment 152 within three months, so the new owners can begin remodeling the units. I'm sorry for the inconvenience and thank you for your cooperation. If you are interested in purchasing the apartment, please give me a call. We can offer you advantageous terms if you would like to stay here."

Kat's jaw dropped and she gaped at the machine, as if it might magically give her more details. *You have got to be kidding me.*

Kat had never considered buying a condo before. She loved the cozy nest she had created here, surrounded by all her favorite books and knick-knacks. Renting had certainly been convenient. Her apartment was close to work and when the hot water faucet on her kitchen sink stopped working for no apparent reason one day, all she had to do was make one phone call and someone came in to fix it while she was at work.

Kat had always been a renter. She liked not having to worry about repairs herself or deal with complicated financing and mortgages. Her mother said she was being a fiscal idiot to throw money down the toilet on rent, as she put it, but Kat had never had the money or inclination to buy her own place. Owning a home implied settling down and a level of permanence that she didn't want. Committing to one place with a mortgage would tie her down. What if she wanted to take off to Peru? Not that she ever *had* taken off to Peru. But she could!

Within the last three days, Kat had gone from a quiet and more-or-less worry-free, flexible existence to being essentially homeless with a bunch of tough grown-up decisions to make. Should she look for a place to rent somewhere else? Buy her current apartment? Buy a different condo? Fix up Chez Stinky? The options seemed overwhelming.

When Kat didn't know what to do, she liked to write things down. Maybe it was a tech-writer thing, but she always felt better when she made lists. Writing out pros and cons or brainstorming ideas on paper tended to help her think. She went to her little wooden desk and pulled out a yellow legal pad.

She sat down and considered the events of the last three days. Job, work, home, family had all become complicated. Time to write down whether the options were good or bad.

- ✓ Inheritance money: good
- ✓ Proposal not due for another month: good
- ✓ Boss is a jerk: bad
- ✓ Inheriting house: good
- ✓ Chez Stinky falling apart: bad
- ✓ Linus the sweet giant dog: good
- ✓ Spastic golden retriever: bad

Kat continued the list and then put down her pen and sighed. It wasn't getting her anywhere. Every good thing on the list seemed to have a corresponding bad one. So much for analysis. She was still confused.

~

The next morning Kat drove to work, still reflecting on her list. As she walked through the doorway into the office building, she knew what she needed to do: take a vacation!

A vacation would give her time to get over her anger about the Big Bad Proposal snafu and being so furious with Mark. And she could spend some time in Alpine Grove figuring out what to do about Chez Stinky. Kat knew that the only way she could decide what to do about her inheritance was to spend some time in the little town. She'd always considered herself as more of a city girl, and she wasn't entirely sure she was cut out for small-town life. So it was time to find out! Alpine Grove might not be Peru, but while she still had flexibility, she could just grab Murphee, lock the door of her apartment, and take off.

Excited about her conclusions and finally making a decision, Kat practically skipped into the office. It was a relief to finally have a plan of action. She dropped her belongings in her cubicle and went to talk to Mark.

She strode into his office and stood in front of his desk. "Hi, Mark."

Mark looked startled to discover Kat standing there looking determined. Sure, he might think of her as a geeky vanilla doormat, but today she didn't care. Tearing his gaze away from his nail file, he said, "Hey. What's up? How's the proposal coming?"

"Nice to see you too, Mark. Did you forget to take your gingko today? I hope not, because I need to talk to you. Since the proposal deadline has been pushed back, I'd like to take some of my vacation time. I've already done the editing on the proposal; someone else can put the changes into the computer file while I'm gone. I have some personal things I need to deal with." She paused for a moment, considering other options. "Maybe it could even be longer than two weeks, too. What do you think about the idea of me telecommuting?"

Mark wrinkled his nose and brought his brows together. "But what if I need you? There could be...stuff...that happens. I need you here. I read about telecommuting and no one does that. I don't think that idea works. I like to see my people working at their desks."

Kat mouth tightened. "Whatever. We can talk about the concept of telecommuting later. Like I said yesterday, my great-aunt died and right now I have family stuff I need to do out in Alpine Grove where she lived. I'm sure someone will figure things out here while I'm on vacation."

Mark studied her face to see if she was really serious. "Alpine Grove? But, that's the middle of nowhere. You can't go out there! It's two hours away. What if something comes up? And you haven't taken a vacation in ages. Why now? You know we have the important proposal."

"That's why I was suggesting telecommuting. We have e-mail here. It doesn't really matter where I am as long as I can get an Internet connection. And you're right. I haven't taken a vacation in a long time. In fact, I have so much time stocked up, I think I'd like to start my vacation today. 'Bye!" Kat gave Mark a slight parade wave and sauntered out the door.

Frowning slightly, Mark mumbled, "Umm. Okay. Fine." He shrugged his shoulders and looked down, returning to his fingernail project.

Kat almost skipped down the hallway back to her cubicle. Two whole weeks away from here! She was giddy at the prospect of not hearing Chris blathering away on his speaker phone or smelling the lingering scent of years of burnt microwave popcorn that permeated the place.

～

After Kat got home, she called Larry Lowell to let him know that she was coming back out to Alpine Grove and asked if she could meet with him again.

"Larry, I'd like to go out to the property again tomorrow, if that's okay," she said. "I know the smell probably isn't fixed yet, but I didn't see all the dogs and cats. I'd really like to meet them and talk to the pet sitter who has been working with them since my aunt died."

The lawyer cleared his throat, "Yes, I'd be happy to meet you there. I'll give Cindy a call and see if she can meet with us as well."

"Great! Oh, I have one other question. I can't stay at Chez, um, I mean my aunt's place, because I know I can't handle the smell. But since I will be up there for a while, I'd like to bring my cat. Do you know of any pet-friendly motels where I might be able to stay?"

"Yes, the Enchanted Moose allows pets. It's an older RV park and motel off the highway. It's not perhaps the nicest place in town, but they do have little kitchenettes and it's quite affordable."

"I won't be there for long, I hope," Kat replied. "I'll give them a call. "

Kat hung up the phone and pondered how best to deal with Murphee, since she was determined to drive out to Alpine Grove today. The first trick would be to get the cat into her travel carrier. To say Murphee was not fond of it would be an understatement. The cat clearly believed that the carrier was an evil agent of doom. It didn't help that most of the cat's experience with the carrier involved trips to the veterinarian. Kat had read all the books that extolled the idea of letting the cat get used to the carrier by leaving it out in a high-traffic area of the house, so it became just part of the furniture. The idea was that the cat would be curious, go in, and take a nap in the nice snuggly little plastic box. However, Murphee chose not to use the carrier as a bed. Instead, after a particularly traumatic check-up at the vet, she apparently viewed it as a litter box. The cat expressed her enthusiasm by relieving herself on the evil carrier when it was sitting in the middle of the living room floor.

Obviously, with Murphee the classic advice from the cat-care books wasn't going to work. Kat needed the element of surprise. Food might help, too. Kat tiptoed around the apartment to determine where Murphee was currently napping. She found the cat quietly snoring on the bed and closed the bedroom door to keep her confined. Carefully opening the closet door, Kat quietly pulled the kitty carrier down from the top shelf where she had hidden it after the last excursion.

She brought the carrier to the living room and set it on end on the living room floor. Reaching down quietly, Kat opened the metal mesh door, trying to avoid any jarring clanging noises that would alert the feline. Returning to the bedroom, Kat opened the door and said in a sickly sweet voice, "Hi, Murpheeee....how's my little lovey cat? Are you sleepy?" The cat raised her head, cocked one ear, and looked at Kat dubiously.

Kat gently picked up the cat around her middle and tucked Murphee's body under her arm, so she could grip the front paws with one hand and the scruff of her neck with the other. With as much nonchalance as possible, she carried the sleepy cat out to the living room, pretending not to notice the suspicious plastic box in the middle the floor. But Murphee's gaze latched onto the dreaded carrier immediately and she tensed in Kat's arms. Kat knew she'd have to act fast.

As it dawned on Murphee exactly what Kat was up to, the cat went into full power-kitty berserk mode, paddling all of her legs and extending her claws. Gripping the cat's scruff more tightly, Kat bent over the carrier, attempting to dump the cat nose-down through the door into the box.

She had been *so* close. But with a mighty squall of anger, Murphee braced her front paws on the sides of the carrier doorway. At the same time, the cat was using her rear claws to scratch anything in range, which included Kat's arms. Kat struggled to dodge the razor-sharp flailing talons and shove the rotund black body down into the carrier.

At last, one of Murphee's front paws slipped, and she fell down into the box. Kat slammed the metal door shut and let go of the breath she'd been holding. *Mission accomplished.* She checked her forearms, and it looked like there had been minimal collateral damage.

Kat turned the carrier so it was flat on the floor and peered in the doorway at Murphee, who had her ears flattened back on her head and a look of rage in her squinting eyes. Kat threw a kitty treat in through the wire mesh door. "Good kitty," she said. *I'm lying, you nasty cat! I hope we don't have to go through that again for a while.*

After packing her luggage, Kat strapped the kitty carrier into the front seat of her Toyota with the seatbelt. Murphee was decidedly not amused by the impending travel plans and began meowing quietly when Kat started the engine. As Kat backed the car out of her parking space, Murphee increased her volume, to make sure Kat truly understood the gravity of her unhappiness and how very wrong car travel was. "MEOW! MEEEE-YOOOOWLLLL!"

Kat sighed. It was going to be an extremely long trip out to Alpine Grove. She tuned her radio to a heavy metal station and cranked the volume up a bit. Murphee seemed to get into the groove as she yowled along to Metallica. Kat shifted the car into gear and pressed the accelerator. *Rock and roll.*

～

After listening to Murphee yowl for the entire two-hour drive, Kat was delighted to check into the Enchanted Moose motel in Alpine Grove. The lawyer's description had been accurate. It was definitely not the nicest place in town and a better name might have been the Elderly Moose. But the plumbing worked and after being released from her carrier, Murphee was finally quiet.

The next morning, Kat drove out to the property to meet Larry. She had finally gotten a good night's sleep and now she was ready to tackle the changes in her life. Apparently, Murphee had been exhausted by recent events as well. After the trauma of the car trip, she had curled up quietly next to Kat's head and didn't move all night.

As Kat drove down the driveway toward Abigail's house, sunlight streamed through the canopy of evergreens, and Kat was again struck by the peaceful feel of her aunt's little corner of forest. She got out of her car and inhaled the somewhat sweet damp mossy smell that was unique to this place. The aroma outside the house was certainly far better than the one inside.

She turned toward the sound of a truck rumbling down the driveway. Larry's salmon-colored Dodge came into view. The truck shook a bit, sputtered, and spit out a few last coughs as Larry killed the engine.

Today Larry looked quite different than he had the last time Kat had seen him. Instead of his conservative drab brown suit, the lawyer was clad in old jeans and a black-and-red-checked flannel shirt. The geeky outdoors look didn't quite work for him. What did the lawyer do with his weekends, anyway? She hoped he wasn't going hunting, and peered at the back of the truck cab to see if there was a gun rack. It was undoubtedly the season to hunt something in Alpine Grove. Kat was sure she didn't want to have a conversation about the best ways to blow away wildlife and prep it for dinner.

Fortunately, there didn't appear to be any obvious armament in the truck. Maybe flannel was standard weekend wear in Alpine Grove. Kat looked down at the cute, strappy black sandals on her feet. It was possible she might be a bit overdressed for the occasion.

A clattering noise arose from the back of the house, and Linus the gigantic brown dog leaped out from behind the building and raced toward Kat. Although intellectually Kat remembered that Linus was a friendly fellow, that fact didn't seem to register with the rest of her body, which tensed as the great beast approached her at an alarming speed. Kat squeezed her eyes shut, bracing for impact. A whoosh of dust hit her sandaled feet. When she opened her eyes, Linus was sitting in front of her wagging and panting at her. She reached out to pat his large brown head. "Hi. It's nice to see you again, Big Guy."

Larry smiled and said, "It looks like one member of the welcoming committee has arrived. Do you want to walk around and see if we can find the others while we wait for Cindy? She should be here shortly."

Linus stood up and looked up at Kat as if to let her know he was ready to go. Kat said, "Okay, let's look around. I guess there's a barn over there." She headed toward one of the outbuildings with Linus trotting along by her side. As she got closer, the term '*barn* seemed a bit generous in this case. Even *shed* would be a stretch. Upon further inspection, the three-sided derelict structure appeared to be melding with the forest. Some form of vine was growing up the walls covering the dingy grayish wood that looked likely to collapse under the weight of the dense leaves. Kat approached the front opening and peered into the dark area within.

"I don't want to go in there. I think this might be a massive spider habitat," she said. "I'd rather leave them alone to do whatever icky things spiders do."

The lawyer looked at the rickety structure and nodded. "I think you might want to wait until you're wearing more suitable shoes."

"A flak jacket might be good too." Kat was not fond of spiders. Insects and other many-legged creatures freaked her out.

As if to emphasize the point, a disturbingly large, hairy, monster spider skittered out of the building and ran across Kat's sandal. As its tiny arachnoid legs touched her bare skin, Kat half-shrieked, half yelped, "Ewww!" and jumped away. She shuddered and wrapped her arms around herself. "Let's get away from here. I think they're on the move!"

Larry smiled and said, "Spiders are a fact of life in the forest. They're good for the garden, too."

"I've seen the garden and it needs a lot more than spiders, Larry." Kat rubbed her wrists and glanced around her, worried that more insect life could leap out of the forest and attack her. She was overtaken with a serious case of bug paranoia. Every whisper of a breeze on her bare forearms might be a creepy crawly. Kat took a few deep breaths in an effort to calm down. The lawyer probably thought she was a total weenie. How embarrassing.

A loud screeching noise came from the direction of the driveway. Kat and Larry looked back down the graveled path, where a rusty silver hatchback was slowly approaching. The whining noise increased in volume as the car got closer. After the vehicle shuddered to a stop, a man and a woman got out. Kat could tell by their body language that they were not happy with one another.

The woman said rather loudly, "Joel, I don't care what you think; my Hyundai is a great car. Myrtle just needs a little love and then she will be good as new."

"Myrtle is a piece of junk. It was a piece of junk when you bought it five years ago and it's an even worse piece of junk now. Riding around in that thing is like being in a rolling tin can," the tall man proclaimed as he slammed the door shut. The body of the little car swayed from side to side at the impact and a small automotive part clattered to the ground. Kat started to raise her hand to point at the part, but lowered it again. Maybe sharing that information wouldn't be such a good idea right now.

The woman glared at the man and then turned to walk over to Kat and Larry. She held out her hand and said, "Hi, you must be Kat. I'm Cindy Ross. That loudmouth over there is my brother Joel. It's nice to meet you." As Cindy and Joel got closer, Kat could see the family resemblance. They both were tall with short sandy-colored dark-blonde hair and hazel eyes, which currently were squinting at each other in an almost identical fashion. The twin glares made Kat think of the old song, "If Looks Could Kill." She guessed they'd been arguing the entire way out here.

Cindy was obviously dressed to take on some serious dog walking. She wore old jeans and hiking shoes, along with an oversized green windbreaker with big pockets. Kat noticed that Linus had reappeared and was extremely interested in whatever Cindy had in her pockets. Cindy looked down at Linus and said, "Hey, Linus! Keep your hairy self out of my coat. You know the rules. No T-R-E-A-T-S unless I say so. Let's go get everyone else."

As Cindy strode off toward the house, Kat hurried to follow her. She needed more information about the other animals, and Cindy obviously knew what was going on as far as the furry residents were concerned. Kat scuttled after her and the tip of her sandal caught on a rock. Once again, it was obvious that her wardrobe choices were not ideal for Alpine Grove living. She was the only one here who didn't look like she'd just stepped out of an L.L. Bean catalog. The cute sandals on her feet were already looking ratty, and the dainty calico sundress and her fuzzy 3/4-sleeve cardigan would probably just end up covered in dust, dog hair, and who knew what else. It might be a good idea to stop by the Kmart along the highway on the way back to the motel; the Mart might have some appropriately rustic dog-friendly attire.

Cindy marched over to a beat-up looking structure with a chain link enclosure attached to it. This was the outbuilding where Kat had had the brief encounter with the loud, spastic golden retriever the weekend before. Cindy went inside the door and the sound of frantic barking ensued from within. Apparently the dog was extremely happy to see the dog walker. Kat glanced around to see if everything was okay, but Joel and Larry were just standing around chatting; they looked unconcerned.

The golden retriever leaped out of the entryway with Cindy in tow. Cindy was a 5-foot-10, large-boned woman, so she wasn't exactly a delicate frail waif, but the golden had energy to spare. The dog walker looked a little distressed as she tried to hold the dog back and keep it from lunging and leaping all over Kat.

Startled by the sudden canine onslaught, Kat jumped out of range. "Which dog is this?" she asked.

"This is Tessa. We're working on her leash manners."

"She certainly is happy," Kat said in an attempt to look at the positive side of the situation, which seemed to be getting more out of control by the second.

Tessa was spinning around on the end of the leash. Most of her feet seemed to be off the ground most of the time. As a cloud of dust arose around the whirling dog, Kat was reminded of the Tasmanian Devil in Saturday-morning cartoons.

"Okay, let's go, Tessa," Cindy said. Tessa didn't need much encouragement and launched off toward the forest.

Kat hustled to catch up with the pair, who were marching swiftly toward a break in the trees. Cindy whistled and Linus reappeared, followed by Lori, the black-and-white dog that had given Kat the wet willy in the basement. The canines bounded toward Cindy and Kat, ears and tongues flopping in time with their strides.

Now that Kat had (mostly) gotten over her fear of being toppled over by the gigantic dog, she was somewhat relieved to see Linus. He seemed like a nice, calm example for the golden to follow. However, undaunted by the presence of the other dogs, Tessa continued to haul Cindy toward the trees.

"Tessa never gets tired," Cindy said with a note of exasperation in her voice. "Never. I can't believe the stamina of this dog. By the end of the walk, I'm completely wiped out, and Tessa is still like this. She's *always* like this. I'm not sure if she ever sleeps."

Kat looked at Cindy and raised her eyebrows. "What should I do? You look like you're in a lot better shape than I am. Couldn't Tessa just run around like Linus and Lori?"

"Not if you ever want to see her again. This dog has an amazing nose and the attention span of a termite. She'd be gone off in the forest after some scent. With her energy level, she'd end up in the next county."

Kat shook her head. How was she supposed to respond to this information? "Is that why she spends so much time outside in her kennel?"

Cindy waved her hand toward the dog. "Not exactly. You probably didn't notice, but I didn't pet her. If I touch her, she pees."

"Really? So she's not housebroken? Isn't she a little old for that?" No wonder the dog had her own special enclosure outside.

"Yes. Since we're outside, I can show you." Cindy gathered up the leash tighter, reeling in Tessa, who turned and tried to jump on the dog walker.

"Tessa, NO!" she said. Tessa looked chastised for approximately one-tenth of a second and then leaped up again. "NO! Tessa, SIT!"

The dog planted her rear end on the ground for another tenth of a second, then leaped up again. Kat sensed a theme here.

"Tessa, SIT!" Cindy reached out to touch Tessa's head. The dog paused long enough to relieve herself then leaped in the air again.

As Kat witnessed the pee performance, she cringed mentally. Would she be able to walk the dog at all? At 5-foot-3, she was a lot less burly than Cindy, who was an Amazon by comparison. She and Cindy started walking again and Kat looked down at Tessa. The odd thing about the dog was that she never looked at anything. Unlike Linus who stared up at Kat with those big brown soulful eyes, Tessa never seemed to be still long enough to notice people or her surroundings.

They entered the forest and started down the trail. As twigs wedged themselves into her sandals, Kat again wished she had other footwear. After this walk, her toes were going to smell like she'd dipped them in Pine-Sol.

"Where is the other dog?" Kat asked.

"Chelsey is inside. She's kinda weird, so I walk her separately."

"Weird?" Could a dog be more weird than Tessa?

Cindy paused on her march through the forest to haul Tessa to a stop, so she could rearrange the leash in her large hands. "Larry said that you'll be staying here. That would be so great for me. I'd like to take a break from this job. Coming out here messes up my schedule. All my other clients are in town near my house, so I get them all walked pretty fast. When the clients live close together, I can make more money and get back home, so I'm there when my kid gets home from school."

If the dog walker quit permanently, it would be a major problem. Keeping Cindy happy seemed like a good long-range plan. Kat paused and said, "There's a problem with the house, but I'm staying out at the Enchanted Moose, so I can come out and walk everybody tomorrow."

"Great! She whipped a paper out of her coat pocket. Everything you need to do is written down right here."

Kat took the paper, looked down at Linus and sighed. Linus shook his big head, and Kat watched as the shake rippled down his large body, ending with a final flip of his tail. The big dog sat and wagged slowly as if to say, "Lady, you totally walked into that one."

~

After Tessa was reinstalled in her enclosure, Kat and Cindy returned to the front of the house to where the lawyer and Joel had been. Neither man was visible and Kat wondered where they had wandered off to while she was out with the dogs. The hood of the Hyundai slammed. Joel stood in front of the car with his hands on his hips and a scowl on his face. As Cindy walked up toward her brother, he said, "I can't do anything about this thing. I don't know what's wrong. You need to take it to a real mechanic."

"Who are you kidding? You know I can't afford a real mechanic."

"You were making pretty good money here. Didn't that help some?"

Cindy pointed down the driveway at the general direction of town. "I spent it all on Johnny. He needed new shoes. What can I say? The kid keeps growing."

Joel looked down at the ground. "I guess I can give you a loan," he said through clenched teeth.

"That would be great! You're the best brother ever. But we need to go. Kat is going to take care of the dogs here, so

I need to get back and start rustling up some new clients." She smiled slightly at Kat. "Nothing personal. I need clients in town. I'll come out for the walks and feeding tonight, but then I'm done."

Joel frowned and glanced at Kat, who shrugged. Joel looked like he had been roused out of bed before he was quite ready for prime-time viewing. His sandy hair needed to be combed and his facial hair was in that awkward phase beyond "needs to shave" but before "trying to grow a beard." Kat was unimpressed. Who was this guy? Had he just returned from a camping trip or something? When it came to beards, Yoda had it right: "Do or do not; there is no try." Camping was the only excuse for the scruffy, rumpled look this guy had going. His personality seemed equally unkempt, since his idea of sparkling conversation mostly consisted of growling at his sister. On a positive note, he probably wouldn't be back here since Cindy was off Chez Stinky duty now.

Larry walked up to the group and said, "I was just inside. Chelsey is in the basement and she doesn't appear to want to come out."

Cindy looked up and said, "Chelsey. I forgot about Chelsey!" She turned to Kat. "Can you walk her? It's all on the note I gave you. I've really got to run. Come on Joel. Let's go!"

Still looking annoyed, Joel climbed in the passenger seat of the Hyundai, looked up at Kat and mumbled, "It was nice to meet you. Good luck."

Cindy dove into the car and with a sputter, it started and began its squealing journey down the driveway.

Kat glanced at Larry, "It looks like it's just us. Let me look at this note and see what we're supposed to do about Chelsey.

Cindy said she's the weird dog. I'm afraid to find out what weird might mean in this context."

The pair went around the house to the basement door and went inside. Curled up on a large cushion under a table was a petite brown herding-type dog with a white stripe down her nose and a worried expression on her face. Her furrowed brow and the concerned look in her dark-brown eyes made her look like she had been pondering weighty matters deeply and come to no positive conclusions.

"Hi, Chelsey. Do you want to go outside for a walk?" the lawyer asked.

Chelsey glared at the lawyer and didn't move. Apparently, that would be a "no."

The dog did not seem to be particularly pleased to see the two humans in her space. Unlike the other dogs, she didn't seem to be much of a people person. Maybe the dog was shy or maybe she had some type of physical problem. Kat studied the information sheet from Cindy. It said Chelsey could be a "little bit stubborn about things she doesn't want to do." That sounded like dog-walker speak for "willful little furry twerp."

"All right Chelsey, here's the thing. You need to go outside. We know you need to go outside. You know you need to go outside. It's *really* time to go outside." Kat reached down and handed the dog one of the treats Cindy had left behind. Chelsey's eyebrows shot up and she snuffled down the kibble.

"Okay, so you like food. I can give you more food if you go for a walk." Kat held out a treat and waved it around to encourage the dog to stand up and get it.

Chelsey wasn't falling for that that old ploy. She curled her rear paws more tightly under her body and settled deeper into the dog bed.

Kat reached down with the leash and clipped it onto the dog's collar. "Let's go, Chelsey. I mean it." Remembering the British dog trainer she'd seen on TV, Kat added, "Let's go walkies!" in a high-pitched clipped voice while she tugged a bit on the leash.

Unmoved by Kat's faux accent, Chelsey moved farther back on her bed and scrunched her head down between her shoulders. The determined look on her face suggested that the dog had no interest in visiting the great outdoors.

With a sigh, Kat sat down on the floor in front of the dog bed, still holding the leash in her hands. She gazed at Chelsey, considering her next course of action. Food, or more specifically the treats Kat had with her, didn't seem to be enough of an enticement to get Chelsey to move. And she certainly wasn't one of those dogs who yearned to please humans. Kat didn't think the dog was scared, but she couldn't figure out what was going on in that little furry brain.

Kat looked up at Larry, who was still standing, surveying the proceedings. "I'm running out of ideas. I'm not convinced I can ever get her out of there. Any thoughts?"

"I saw her a few times when Abigail was alive. She behaved quite differently then. Maybe something happened?"

"Abigail died, for one thing. Maybe Chelsey wonders where mom went. But it's not like I can explain it to her." Kat sighed again and faced the dog's grumpy stare. "Maybe the poor dog is just really confused."

Kat had read somewhere that exercise was supposed to be good for depression. "Maybe I can make the walk sound like more fun. If she's sad, she should feel better after the walk." Kat scanned the basement for something that might seem fun to an unhappy dog. She spotted an old towel hanging on a rack and reached over to grab it.

"Okay Chelsey, check this out!" she said in an overly happy voice, waving the rag in front of the dog. "It's a big snake. Let's play! Go get it."

Chelsey raised her head, showing mild interest in the odd human behavior. Kat threw a treat down on the ground, which landed next to the bed. Chelsey reached her head over, ate the treat, and then stood up and grabbed the towel.

"Yay, Chelsey! Let's GO!" Kat shouted with glee as she scooped up the leash and skipped toward the door. Apparently deciding that the human was losing her mind, the dog stepped out of her bed completely, dropped the towel, and looked up at Kat expectantly.

Kat tossed the dog another treat, tightened up the leash, and walked out the door with Chelsey trotting along next to her.

Larry, who had been largely motionless while watching Kat leap around the room, said from behind, "That was intriguing. I thought the dog was scared and might bite you."

Kat looked back and said, "I didn't think of that. Maybe this is one situation where the old saying 'ignorance is bliss' comes in handy."

❧

Kat, Larry, and Chelsey walked toward the trail into the forest behind the house and were soon joined by Linus and Lori. Where did the dogs disappear off to? They seemed to be allowed to roam wherever they pleased. That was one of those mysterious canine things she'd have to figure out. Now that Chelsey had been mobilized, she seemed content to walk and relieve herself like any other normal dog. Maybe this was part of the routine Aunt Abigail had gone through with the dog every day. There was no way to know.

Kat's canine ruminations were interrupted by Larry, who said, "This is pretty back in here."

"Yes, I remember walking on this trail with my aunt when I was a kid. She knew all about all the plants that grow around here. I wish I could remember what she said. It all just looks like a bunch of green stuff to me. Speaking of things I don't know, is there a library around here? I need to get some books about dogs and training if I'm going to be able to stay here and deal with Tessa and Chelsey. They seem like serious canine problem children. I need to get a book on canine aberrant psychology."

"Yes, there's a library on the way back to the Enchanted Moose, past the Kmart." Larry cleared his throat. "I was wondering, after you're done here one evening next week, if you'd like to meet me for dinner."

Kat's jaw dropped and she glanced at him quickly. Was he asking her out? Okay, it had been a while since anyone had been interested, but she didn't think she was *that* out of practice and clueless to the signals. But maybe he was just being nice, since she didn't know anyone in town. "If I'm still at the Enchanted Moose, I'll have to feed my cat there after I'm done here, but after I do that, I'm free." Feed her cat? Kat cringed internally. Could she sound like any more of a loser?

"Wonderful. There's a restaurant I think you'd like. It's much better than the one at the Enchanted Moose."

Kat hadn't noticed a restaurant there, but she doubted that anything the Moose would be offering up would count as haute cuisine, since RV parks weren't generally noted for their fine dining establishments. "Sounds good."

"I also was considering the state of affairs regarding the rehabilitation that may be necessary for the roof of the house. I know Mr. Fowler is working on the smell situation, but he may be able to help with the roof issues as well. He has some construction experience, I believe. You might consider giving him a call."

"Did you talk to him? How is he doing with the stink? When we were in the basement with Chelsey, I could smell it, but it wasn't as bad down there as it was in the living room."

"Yes, he has isolated the problem and it is upstairs. I believe he is working on it."

Kat pressed her lips together and then said, "You can spare me the details. I just hope he gets it done soon. I'd like to be able to stay in the house and get a feel for what's it's truly like to live here. I'm not sure I can handle being so far away from everything, but I won't know until I stay."

After returning Chelsey to her nest in the basement and checking cat-food levels, Kat said goodbye to Larry and the dogs and went off to the library and Kmart before returning to the Enchanted Moose. After the exhausting morning, she really wanted to change her clothes and read about how to deal with dogs before heading back out to Chez Stinky for the afternoon animal-care activities. She had checked out a book from the library with the title *Happy Hound*. Since Chelsey was so obviously unhappy, Kat figured it couldn't hurt.

Back in her hotel room, she picked up the phone and dialed Herbert Fowler's number.

"Hiya, this is Bud."

"Mr. Fowler, this is Kat Stevens. I'm the owner of Abigail Goodman's old house. I talked to you the other day."

"Oh yeah, you're the lady with the place with the bad stink. Hey, isn't there some leftie musician with that name? You aren't a Commie are you?"

Kat rolled her eyes, "Yes, that's my house, and no I'm not a Commie. Or a musician. How are you progressing in fixing the problem?"

"Well, I think I have found the varmint in the wall that done died there. I gotta cut out some wood and some drywall and investigate a little more. Then I can get him outta there."

"That would be nice. When can you make that happen? Also, I'd like to talk to you about repairing the roof. Larry said you might have experience with that?"

"Yep, I got lotsa experience doing roofs. I like ladders. It's like being a squirrel up there. You can see everything. So does that mean you want me to do up an estimate then? You know roofs, they're mighty expensive. This is gonna cost ya."

"Yes, I understand. Just please do an estimate. And when exactly will the smell be gone?"

"I can git out there tomorrow. I needed to get some special tools that I got here in my shed."

"Okay, I'll expect you then."

After Kat hung up the phone, she wrapped her arms around her waist. She didn't have a good feeling about Bud's roofing skills. Or any other skills. At least it was only an estimate. Maybe she could find someone else to do the rest of the work after the smell was gone. She picked up Murphee from the floor, placed her on the bed next to her, and curled up to read her new book. "What are we gonna do, Murph?"

The cat responded with a quiet purring sound and snuggled up closer to Kat for her mid-afternoon nap.

Chapter 3

Happy Hound

The next morning, clad in uncomfortably stiff new blue jeans and a markedly non-stylish (but cheap!) teal T-shirt, Kat headed back to Chez Stinky. She had finished the *Happy Hound* book and was now armed with tips for dealing with a wide range of bad canine behaviors, including but not limited to jumping, barking, and "inappropriate urination." Between Tessa and Chelsey, it looked like she'd need to try out pretty much everything she'd read. It was the first time she was going to be dealing with the animals by herself and her stomach was a little jumpy. She straightened a bit in her seat. Why should she be anxious? It was just a bunch of dogs, cats, and falling-down buildings. Yet she couldn't shake the nervous feeling that gripped her as her car bumped down the driveway.

Linus bounded out from behind the house to greet Kat as she got out of her car. "Hi, Big Guy. Let's go find everybody else."

As she walked, she looked up at the tree canopy. The nervous feeling drained from her body as she drank in the calming energy of the forest. The wind whispered through leaves of the aspens, making them quiver and ripple like an ocean of greenery. She smelled the fragrance of Ponderosa pine wafting up from below as her too-white Keds crunched through the bed of pine needles.

Linus was joined by Lori and the pair trotted happily alongside Kat as they went over to the outbuilding that Kat now thought of as the Tessa Hut. Tessa started barking as she heard them approach. Here was the first test: not getting knocked over or dragged on her face by the spastic, nutso dog.

Kat grabbed the leash that was hanging on a nail by the doorway. Tessa was in her indoor enclosure, leaping up and down as if she were on a trampoline. Her head was bobbing up near the top of the six-foot chain-link fence. Kat had to admit the bounce factor was impressive for such a petite golden retriever. Kat stopped in front of the gate, considering how best to extract the rambunctious dog from the enclosure before the animal could vanish off into the forest.

Steeling herself for the onslaught, Kat unlatched the gate, pushed it open, and quickly slammed it closed behind her. Tessa's piercing barks rang in her ears and the dog's claws bounced off Kat as the wild, jumping dervish seemed to surround her. Remembering the technique she had learned in the book, Kat focused on the dog's jumping rhythm and as soon as the dog's front paws hit Kat's body, she reached out and grabbed them. She said, "Tessa NO!" walked a few steps forward so Tessa was going backwards, and then threw the dog's feet to the ground.

Tessa stopped and looked confused by what had just happened. Undaunted, she leaped up on Kat again. Kat repeated the process, grabbed Tessa's paws, and threw the dog's feet to the ground again with a firm "No." The dog started to jump again, but seemed to change her mind and paused for a moment. Kat took advantage of the moment of inactivity and said "Tessa, SIT!" with as much authority as she could muster. The dog placed her rear on the ground for a nanosecond, which was long enough for Kat to quickly clip on the leash. With Tessa secured, Kat gripped the leash tightly and opened the gate.

Glimpsing freedom, Tessa started dragging Kat toward the forest trail. As Kat struggled to hold onto the leash with both hands, keep up with the dog, and not fall on her face, she opted to try another technique from the book. Leaning back, she dug in her heels, turned around, and began walking in the opposite direction. Tessa had no choice but to follow. Every time the dog pulled, Kat zigged and zagged, so she was going the opposite direction. Undaunted by the circuitous progress, Tessa kept pulling and pulling and pulling. The muscles in Kat's arms started to ache and she was rapidly approaching full-body exhaustion. Recalling Cindy's words about Tessa's energy level, she choked back a sob of frustration. She'd never be able to tire this animal out, unless she trained to be a marathon runner. And that was unlikely.

Kat knew her physiology was not built for long-distance running or any other hard-core exercise. Although she was healthy, slender, and in reasonably decent shape, a jockette she definitely was not. About a half-hour into her few jogging or running experiments, she'd be gasping for air and end up collapsing in a heap with a stabbing side cramp. With the exception of these few notable forays into fitness, Kat's body generally returned to its comfortable default state of slight flabbiness.

After Tessa had relieved herself, Kat decided the walk was good enough and turned around. She got Tessa back into the enclosure with relatively little incident, but Kat's muscles were quivering, her ears were ringing, and she had a strong desire for a nap. Preferably in a silent room with no barking dogs located within a 20-mile radius. But Kat couldn't nap yet. The next trick was to cajole Chelsey out of the house.

Kat walked around to the back of the house to the basement entrance and went inside. Just as she had been yesterday, Chelsey was peering out from her bed under the table. Kat flopped down and sat cross-legged on the floor in front of the dog. "Hi, Chelsey. It's me again. And Tessa totally wore me out. How do you feel about just cooperating? I'd appreciate it."

She reached out to pet Chelsey. The dog looked mildly surprised, but didn't move. Chelsey seemed to be some type of Australian shepherd mix and she had mastered the icy glare of a herding dog. It suggested to Kat that perhaps the dog wasn't sure about this human that kept invading her space. However, Kat continued to stroke the soft, brown fur on Chelsey's neck. The dog moved a few inches toward Kat on her bed, so Kat could scratch her back, too. Kat could feel the muscles in Chelsey's back start to relax. Even better, *she* was calmer too. It was relaxing to just sit and pet Chelsey's soft, warm fur. After all the exertion with Tessa, her heart had finally stopped racing.

Once Chelsey was no longer giving her the evil eye, Kat put a kibble treat in her hand. Chelsey furrowed her brow and looked a bit worried, but ultimately decided that anyone who would sit around and give her a back rub was probably okay. She snarfed up the kibble and gazed expectantly at Kat, obviously hoping for another handout. Kat quietly clipped the leash on Chelsey, stood up and said, "Let's go." Chelsey looked dubious for a moment, then stood up and toddled along beside Kat as the pair exited the building.

It was a relaxing walk through the forest; once Chelsey was on the leash and mobile, she was a model canine citizen. When they returned, Chelsey looked somewhat perkier post-walk, but still retreated to her bed under the table. Kat started to turn to leave when an ear-splitting noise came from upstairs. The deafening screech of some type of saw was grinding away on something. Chelsey scuttled farther back in her bed and Kat ran up the stairs to see what was going on.

She reached the top of the stairs and discovered an older man wearing a blaze orange cap in the living room. Wielding a large red machine with a long serrated blade, he turned and raised his eyebrows when he saw Kat. He turned off the saw and waited for it to wind down.

When the saw fell silent, he said, "Lord, you scared the stuffing outta me! Where did you come from, sweetheart?"

Kat said, "I'm not your sweetheart. I own this place. I'm guessing you must be Bud?"

"Yep, that's me and this here is Martha. She's the best goddang jibber-jabber saw you'll ever find." Bud caressed the saw and gazed at it lovingly.

Disturbed by the man's somewhat unnatural attachment to power tools, Kat replied, "Are you using Martha to remove the smell in the house? Because it still seriously stinks up here."

"Yes, ma'am. And I'm getting there! Martha's gonna get that varmint. She's a varmint-huntin' machine, Martha is. Just you wait. She's gonna get 'im."

"Do you think the smell will be gone by tomorrow?" Kat did not want to witness exactly whatever Bud and his cohort Martha had to do to make the varmint and the smell go away. She was going to feed the animals and get the heck out of here.

"I'm gonna git 'er done. That's my whole plan for the day. Nuthin' else. I'll lock up when I leave. And little lady, I give you my word on my blessed grandma's Bible that I'll have that stink outta here no matter how long it takes."

As Kat went back downstairs to feed the dogs, she hoped he was right.

~

Later that evening after Kat had returned to the Enchanted Moose, Bud called to report that he and Martha had in fact been successful in removing "the varmint" from the wall. With the source of the stink removed, Kat decided to check out of the Moose and move into Chez Stinky. It was time to introduce Murphee to the Chez Stinky clan. Kat was anxious about Murphee's reaction to the move, not to mention another battle about the kitty carrier.

Sometime in the middle of the night, Kat woke up and looked around. Murphee was not in her usual spot on the bed next to her. Peering under the bed, she discovered that Murphee was in the exact center of the floor under the box spring. The cat's eyes glowed and she was in a crouch, poised to run if necessary. How did the cat know that tomorrow it would be time for another trip in the Evil Kitty Carrier of Doom? Was she psychic?

Kat rolled onto her back and sighed. She could tell by the determined set of the cat's jaw that the grumpy feline was going to do her utmost to avoid being caught. Fortunately, Kat had the ultimate defense: food. She got up, picked up the kitty food bowl, hid it in the closet, and went back to sleep.

When Kat woke up, she turned on her side and was pleased to note that Murphee was out from under the bed and was wandering around the motel room looking for her food bowl. Plaintive meows filled the room as Murphee loudly explained that there had been a disastrous turn of events and she was likely to starve.

With a phony smile, Kat said, "Gosh, are you hungry, Murph? Your food bowl seems to be missing. That's extremely sad."

The cat mewed in agreement, jumped up on the bed and pressed the top of her head into Kat's arm. Kat said in a purring voice, "Yes, I love you too. And we're going to have sooooo much fun today."

She scooped the cat up into her arms and walked toward the bathroom, where she had put the carrier. With one hand, she grabbed it and quickly placed it on end. Seeing that the dreaded agent of torture was *not* gone from her life, Murphee tensed and began to squirm in Kat's arms. Before the claws started to flail, Kat grabbed the cat's scruff and went for the feet-first approach this time. She lowered the cat's butt down into the doorway of the carrier. Murphee stretched her front legs out across the door opening and tried to clamber up, but it was no use. Gravity took over and the cat thumped into the bottom of the crate. Kat closed the door and did a small victory dance around the bathroom.

Kat returned to Chez Stinky with Murphee in tow. She pulled the carrier out of the passenger seat as Linus watched. The big dog tried to sniff the creature in the carrier and was rewarded with great hissing noises. Having lived with cats for quite some time, the dog was aware that hissing was not a friendly sound. He looked up at Kat and backed away from the carrier.

Looking down at Linus's big head, Kat smiled and said, "I know. She's got a bit of an adjustment to make here. Be nice."

Linus gave her a questioning look as if to say, "I'm always nice, remember? I'm one of the *good* dogs."

Kat laughed and said, "You're a good boy. I'll be back in a few minutes for your walk. We're going to try something different today. It might be fun." She carried the plastic carrier up the stairs and into the house. As she opened the door, she closed off her nostrils, bracing for the olfactory impact. She let out her breath and took a tentative sniff. Much to her relief, the house actually did smell better. Kat put the carrier on the floor and went to open the kitchen window to let in some fresh air. As she walked around the house, memories of staying here with her great aunt returned. The living room had a collection of somewhat tattered-looking rag rugs, where she used to sit and play cards. The rough-hewn wood floors were worn from years of abuse by dog and cat claws. As if to emphasize the point, a big orange cat appeared from the bedroom and sauntered over to greet Kat. He curled his wide body around her right leg and meowed.

"Hi, Louie. How's it going?" She bent down to scratch the cat's head as Murphee hissed and made thumping noises from within her carrier. Murphee was obviously extremely unhappy about all the new smells and animals, but Louie appeared unconcerned. It might be a good idea to put Murphee in a dog- and cat-free area, since she didn't seem impressed with the large, friendly feline or the even larger dog she'd met so far.

Kat got all Murphee's paraphernalia out of the car, including her food bowl. After setting up the cat's new habitat in the bathroom, Kat fed her and went off to find the other cats who supposedly lived here. Because of the smell, she hadn't really explored the house to determine where the feline contingent tended to hang out. They were eating the cat food, but she still hadn't caught a glimpse of Tripod, the three-legged cat, anywhere. Presumably he was still alive and around somewhere.

～

After feeding the cats, Kat faced the prospect of taking Tessa out for her walk. Once again it was daunting, but she'd been thinking about the problem and had an idea for how she might be able to walk Tessa without causing herself undue bodily harm.

The primary issue was simple physics: Kat didn't have enough weight to offset the force of Tessa. More weight could slow down Tessa. In horse races, they put weights on the horses to even the field. If Kat could weigh down Tessa somehow, the dog might actually tire herself out. And a dog that's asleep is usually behaving itself.

On her way back to the motel the day before, Kat had stopped at the local feed store for supplies. At the store, she purchased medium-size and giant dog harnesses, a sturdy leash, two plastic water bottles, and a small nylon saddle-horn bag that was probably supposed to be used for trail rides. That night, using a needle and thread from her travel sewing kit, she had attached the saddle bag to the medium-size harness.

When Kat went out to the Tessa Hut, she was prepared. She had collected Chelsey from the basement without incident and tied her leash to a tree while she dealt with Tessa. Linus and Lori were milling around waiting for the walk to start.

She called Linus over to her and put the giant dog harness on him and attached the loop end of the leash through the ring on the top of the harness. As usual, he was obliging and wagged his tail. "Your job is to be the boat anchor, Big Guy. I hope you're up for this." Linus wagged again, which Kat took as a 'yes.' He followed her to the doorway with the leash dragging behind him.

Tessa started barking furiously as Kat approached her enclosure; she had begun the levitation routine and was bouncing behind the chain link fence. Kat gathered up her supplies and entered the enclosure. Tessa started to lunge at her, but paused briefly as if she remembered that this human didn't like being jumped on. Instead, she jumped up around Kat, getting extremely close to her, but never actually touching her.

Holding the harness out in front of her, Kat waited for the right moment and slipped the harness over Tessa's head. Then she grabbed the dog firmly by the shoulders so she could affix the strap under her stomach. Tessa noticed the extra weight from the water bottles in the pockets of the bag, which slowed her jumping a bit. Kat took advantage of this momentary slowdown to clip a leash on the harness.

She and Tessa went out the door and once again the dog started dragging Kat toward the forest. As she passed Linus, Kat grabbed the top of his harness. The weight of the giant dog combined with her own gave her enough ballast to stop Tessa's forward momentum. Kat picked up the end of the leash that had been dragging from Linus's harness and clipped it to Tessa's. The two dogs were now attached to each other.

Kat then unclipped her leash from Tessa so the two dogs would be free to walk together without her. She knew Linus wasn't going anywhere and he weighed about three or four times as much as Tessa, so she wasn't going anywhere without him. The big dog looked at Kat with a confused expression as Tessa whirled around him in gleeful exuberance.

"It's okay Linus. Your job is just to keep Tessa from running away. Feel free to run around. Tire her out. Please. I'll be right here behind you."

Linus turned back and headed off toward the forest trail with Tessa by his side. The golden retriever was obviously thrilled to be able to go as fast as she wanted, since there was no longer some slowpoke human dragging her down. Kat followed behind with Lori and Chelsey. She laughed as the two harnessed dogs figured out how to work together as a team to deal with obstacles like trees. She was amazed how quickly they caught on, although she did have to untangle them a couple of times after they went on opposite sides of a tree. "Don't do the George-of-the-Jungle thing, you guys," she admonished. "It's embarrassing."

Kat started playing a little game to help give Tessa the idea that coming when called could be fun. She whistled and Linus would stop, perk up his ears and come running back to her. Tessa had no choice but to follow. Then the pair would run ahead again along the trail. Now that she was able to run and was weighted down by the water bottles, Tessa finally was showing signs of fatigue.

With the dogs occupied, Kat was able to relax and simply enjoy the experience of walking through the forest for the first time. She paused to notice the mingling of fragrances wafting through the trees. She recognized pine, wild roses, and the loamy smell of leaves decomposing in the rich, dark soil of the forest floor. Lori and Chelsey trotted along by her side, obviously just content to have a human around to take them on walks.

~

After the walk, Kat was feeling proud of herself. When she had put Tessa back into her enclosure, the dog had curled up on the floor for a nap. It was unprecedented: the spaz dog was tired. The thrill of victory coursed through her body, but stopped at her stomach where it dissolved into a pang of hunger. She was out of most of the "road food" she had been eating at the Enchanted Moose and she was getting tired of subsisting on stale chips and Triscuits, anyway. All this walking through the forest made a girl hungry.

Kat went back into the house and started investigating the kitchen. Although thankfully someone had cleaned out the refrigerator at some point, the cabinets were a different story. Behind the rustic tongue-and-groove cabinet doors lurked some seriously antiquated foodstuffs. Sorting through the contents quickly quelled her appetite. Some of the jars in the back of the cabinets looked like they might contain produce Abigail had canned the last time Kat had been here in the 70s. It also appeared that Abigail wasn't bothered by details like dating her canned goods and the mysterious reddish-brown contents harbored underneath those rusty lids didn't look appetizing.

Death by botulism didn't seem like a good way to go. A trip to the grocery store for food, cleaning supplies, and a giant box of Hefty bags was definitely in order. The thick layer of grayish-brown dust that coated everything would give a health inspector the shakes, and Kat wasn't tempted to cook anything here until she had hosed down the kitchen. Maybe with a massive industrial power sprayer. In the short term, stopping by the deli for a sandwich was probably a good idea.

After getting something to eat and acquiring most of the items on her ever-expanding grocery list in town, Kat returned to Chez Stinky to at least attack the surface filth. She donned a bandanna and put on one of Abigail's old frilly aprons and a pair of rubber gloves. The outfit made her look like a cross between a bag lady and the star of some 50s advertisement for iron supplements. So much for her cute calico sundress and the sparkling clean white tile in her apartment kitchen. Gritting her teeth, she grabbed a scrubby sponge and set to work.

Kat filled two large, black garbage bags with antique food products from the cabinets. It was like an archive of food-packaging history. She knew McCormick spices hadn't had labels like these for decades. The Green Giant looked like he had a terminal disease; the logotype was sporting a decidedly chartreuse look on most of the cans. Figuring that the home canned goods were largely decomposed anyway, Kat took the jars outside. She dug a small hole and tried to close off her nose while she unscrewed the lids, dumped the contents, and covered them with dirt. The vegetables or whatever they were could return to the land. She put the empty jars in a box next to the spider shed, to be hosed out later. Maybe.

Hours later, Kat was lying spread-eagle on the floor, admitting defeat. She'd been cleaning for hours and had barely made an impact on the powerful quantity of dirt and detritus. Looking up at the ceiling, she noticed the cobwebs artfully draped over the lamp fixtures, creating a tapestry of thin fibers that billowed in the breeze.

She turned her head and looked down. Under the refrigerator was not just a warren of dust bunnies, but also a voluminous scary-looking dust dinosaur. That might explain why the motor made an odd woodpecker-like noise and the refrigerator wasn't really particularly cold inside. The windows sported a film of dirt, which gave the sunlight streaming in a somewhat prismatic effect. At least the filtered light made it more difficult to see the blanket of dust all over everything.

Kat sighed. Getting this place clean could take a whole lot longer than one day. Professional intervention might be required. It was worth the money to avoid this extreme level of cleaning activity.

Kat jumped as her reverie was disturbed by a wet tongue slurping her ear. She sat up quickly and found herself face-to-face with Lori, who wagged her tail expectantly. "Hi, Lori. How did you get upstairs? You have a thing about ears, don't you?" Lori looked pleased with herself; her happy panting expression made her seem as if she were smiling almost all the time.

Lori trotted over to one of the big black garbage bags, stuck her head in briefly, and snuffled around. She grabbed something out of the bag and ran down the stairs. Kat leaped up to run after her. Nothing in that bag could be considered fit for anyone's consumption, human or canine.

Lori made a beeline for the doggie door at the back of the hallway. She scampered outside, thoroughly thrilled with her new prize. Kat opened the door to follow her, but nothing was outside. The dog was fast, that was for sure. But from the right, there were incriminating shredding and scraping noises. Kat ran toward the sound and discovered Lori enthusiastically destroying a box of something that might have been crackers. Or pasta. Now it was mostly well-masticated cardboard pieces. The dog was certainly enjoying herself. Hopefully, Lori had a strong stomach.

She picked up the pieces that surrounded the dog and said, "Lori, no. Stealing creepy old food really isn't a good idea." Lori didn't move from her spot. She just wagged and smiled, watching Kat clean up the mess she'd made. She looked down at Lori. If a dog could look smug, this would be the look. Trying to muster up a more stern tone in the hope of sounding more convincing, she said, "Lori NO! This was bad. You were a *bad* girl." Lori wagged again, stood up, and began trotting back toward the house.

Kat ran after her and got to the door first. "No way, little dog. You are *not* going back for seconds. You can just stay outside." Kat went inside and slammed the door behind her.

As she closed the door, a cacophony of unpleasant noises arose from the other side. "RRR, ughghg, hack, BLAP." She opened the door again and found Lori standing in front of a pile of something noxious and stinky. The dog was still smiling and looked even more pleased with herself.

"Well, I guess you feel better now."

As Lori sniffed at her fantastic Technicolor creation, Kat took a moment to catch her breath and noticed Lori was looking increasingly interested in the pile. Too interested. Yuck! The dog might actually be disgusting enough to eat it *again*. Waving her hands to shoo Lori farther back out into the yard, she yelled, "NO! Lori NO!" Grabbing a shovel that was leaning on the house next to the back door, she carefully scooped up the pile and carried it over to a shrub, dug a small hole and buried it underneath the plant. Maybe it would work as fertilizer. Recycled, antique food, plant food, what's the difference to shrubbery?

~

After hours of cleaning, more dog walks and unpacking, later that afternoon Kat was ready for a nice, long, hot shower. She took off her sweat-stained clothes and stood in the bathroom with Murphee circling around her ankles, hoping for an early dinner.

She twisted the knob to turn on the water; a sputtering noise came from the shower head, but no water emerged. After all the cleaning she'd done, Kat knew that the house did have a functioning well and access to water, at least in the kitchen. Having no shower was going to be beyond disappointing. She stood next to the bathtub and gazed up at the spigot, willing it to produce water. Nothing happened. Murphee stopped circling and looked up at her, wondering why she was just standing there.

Kat whacked the shower knob with her fist in annoyance. The knob fell off and clattered into the bottom of the bathtub. Then with a giant whoosh, the shower head blew off the pipe, crashing into the bathtub in front of a massive rush of water. Murphee, who was opposed to water touching her delicate feline self, squalled a guttural "MEEEEYOOOWWWLLL" and leaped up onto the sink, away from the geyser's flow. At the same time, Kat jumped backward, slipped on the tile, and landed with a thud on the hard floor. Soaked and now sporting a large painful bruise on her butt, she scrambled to her feet and fumbled through the rushing water, only to discover that she had no way to turn off the water without a pair of pliers.

Water was gushing everywhere. Kat opened the door and ran down the stairs to the closet that had water-related devices in it. Standing naked and dripping water everywhere, she paused and pondered the various knobs and levers that worked the well, pressure tank, and hot water heater. Something must turn the water off, but she wasn't sure what. Noticing a switch with a yellowed piece of paper labeled 'well,' she flipped the lever. The sound of rushing water upstairs subsided and Kat looked down to see Lori, Linus, and Chelsey standing in a circle around her. Chelsey had her head tilted to one side, as if to ask, "Why are you dripping all over my basement?"

Kat started to shiver as she stood naked in front of the curious canine audience. She shook her head. *How dumb is it to feel embarrassed about being naked in front of a dog? They're DOGS.* Lori helped out by slurping some water off her thigh. "Thanks, Lori. Maybe I'll go upstairs now. Don't tell anyone about this, okay?"

Being careful to close the gate to the basement behind her, Kat returned to the bathroom and picked up the shower head and the knob. In her haste to deal with the water, Kat hadn't closed the bathroom door, and Murphee had disappeared. That probably wasn't good, given all the other animals around that Murphee didn't know and probably wouldn't like. Ignoring that issue for the moment, Kat examined the knob. Some tiny but vitally important plastic part had broken off and the knob clearly wasn't going to work again. She dropped it in the sink and turned the shower head around in her hands. She discovered that the ring that was supposed to hold it to the pipe was cracked and the inside of the nozzle was coated with what could only be described as crud. No wonder it didn't work. She toweled herself off and put on some clean clothes so she could focus on the problem, rather than the cold and her nudity. In the kitchen, she found a butter knife and began chipping away corrosion and other drek from the shower nozzle.

A feline shriek came from the bedroom. The noise evolved into sonic layers of hissing, squalling, and screeching that made it sound like at least one of the cats might be dying. Jumping up, Kat ran to the bedroom and found Murphee and another cat (maybe Dolly Mae?) rolling on the floor, making gruesome noises that seemed impossible for such small animals to generate.

Running back to the bathroom, she grabbed one of the soaked towels and threw it on the swirling pile of felines. The two cats separated and Dolly Mae scurried away from Kat. Murphee went to hide under the bed. Grabbing Murphee, Kat took the unhappy feline and the shower head back to the bathroom and slammed the door.

Most of the crud was out of the nozzle, so Kat attempted to screw it back onto the pipe. It promptly fell off and clattered into the bathtub again. Clearly, she was going to have to find some tools somewhere to turn the water back off in the shower, much less turn *on* the water to the house. Fixing the shower needed to happen sooner rather than later. A spider scampered across the floor. Kat reached over, picked up one of her Keds, and whomped the frisky arachnid. *Don't mess with me.*

A phone rang and Kat followed the sound to the kitchen and picked up the handset on the harvest-gold rotary-dial wall phone. "Hello."

"Kat? Is that you? You sound odd. This is Larry Lowell."

"Hi, Larry. I've had a long day, and I'm tired. Plus, I think this phone was manufactured before I was born. Possibly by Alexander Graham Bell himself. And if it's like most things here, it probably doesn't work right."

"Have you been having difficulties? I'm sorry to hear that. I tried calling you at the Enchanted Moose, but they said you had checked out. So I tried this number."

"Yes. I'm staying here now, but it's more complicated than I thought it would be. You probably don't want to know the details."

Larry cleared his throat slightly. "I'm calling to see if you've considered the idea of having dinner. Would tomorrow evening work for you?"

The idea of not cooking food on the scary stove at Chez Stinky, even for one night, held a lot of appeal for Kat. "Yes, I'd like that, but I need to get the shower fixed. Also, Bud seems to have left a large hole in the wall here. Do you know if he's coming back to repair it?"

"I'm sorry, but I have not heard from Mr. Fowler. I'll make reservations and give you a call tomorrow."

"Okay, I guess I have to call Bud. Talk to you tomorrow."

Kat hung up the phone and considered the possibility that maybe Larry was asking her on a real date. She wasn't sure how she felt about that, but she did know it was going to be exceedingly difficult to make herself look pretty without running water.

～

After the shower debacle, Kat was somewhat afraid to make dinner. It was one thing to get soaked, it was another to potentially set herself on fire. A cold sandwich sounded safer than facing the propane stove which, given the blackened areas on the stove top and around the oven door, clearly had an inflammatory history.

As Kat sat down at the kitchen table with a sandwich, she looked over at the hole in the wall that Bud and his trusty saw Martha had created. A slight scrabbling noise arose from down deep within the cavern behind the drywall. Visions of rodents of every possible size ambled through her mind. Squirrels, possums, rats, mice, shrews. Oh my. The possibilities were many and none of them were appealing. Kat continued to chew her sandwich. *Were bats technically rodents? What about marmots? What the heck is a marmot anyway?* Questions to be asked.

The noise seemed to be getting louder. She didn't want to act like the totally clichéd image of a woman standing on a chair screaming about a tiny mouse. She may be gutless, but she wasn't *that* gutless. Time to suck it up and see what lurked in the wall.

She grabbed a flashlight and a chair and brought them over to the wall. After getting up on the chair, she shined the light down into the gap between the drywall and the wood framing of the wall. Peering down, she was greeted by two eyes glowing up at her from below. Kat straightened and shook her head as her mind tried to assimilate what she'd just seen. *What was that?*

Kat looked again, moving the light around to see if she could determine a shape. Judging by the ears on the head, it looked like it might be a cat. *Uh oh.*

Stepping down from the chair, Kat sat down to ponder her options. Clearly, the cat couldn't get back up to the hole. Maybe it was Tripod. Given that he had only three legs, it might be more difficult for him to extricate himself. And it wasn't like she could throw down a rope for him.

She'd been putting it off, but it was obviously time to call Bud and ask about the hole. Maybe in the process of repairing it, he could remove the cat. She picked up the phone and dialed his number.

"Hi! You've reached Bud. I've gone huntin' and I'll call you back once I got something in my freezer. Leave me a message!"

Kat sighed. "Hi, Bud, this is Kat Stevens. I was wondering when you'd be able to come back to my house and fix the hole in my wall. Thanks."

That failed. Now what?

Maybe the lawyer had cat-extracting tools. It was a long shot, but why not? She called Larry and had a nice chat with his answering machine. It must be a hot night in Alpine Grove. Maybe he had another date. That might be a fun topic of conversation for tomorrow night.

The only other local number she had was Cindy's. Kat felt a little funny about calling her, since the dog walker had so obviously wanted to leave Chez Stinky and never return. But the poor kitty in the wall couldn't stay there forever.

"Cindy? Hello, this is Kat Stevens over at Abigail Goodman's house."

Cindy paused for a moment before saying, "Oh, hi. How are you? Are the dogs okay?"

"Yes, they're fine. Thanks for asking. But I do have a little problem with a cat."

"I'm a dog person. I don't know much about cats."

Kat rolled her eyes. She was becoming less and less fond of this woman. "Yes, I know you walk dogs, but I was hoping you might have some tools. One of the cats here seems to be in a wall."

Cindy somewhat unsuccessfully suppressed a snicker. "Are you serious? In a wall? How did it get there?"

"I don't know how he got in there. The handyman guy—Bud—cut a hole in the wall to remove the thing…animal…varmint…whatever it was, out of the wall, so it wouldn't smell anymore. But he didn't patch the hole back up. I think a cat got curious and fell down there. It might be Tripod, since I haven't seen him anywhere. The poor little guy might be hungry by now. He's been scratching on the drywall, but he can't seem to get up and out of there. It's a long way up from where he is."

"Well, Tripod is missing a back leg, so I guess that would be tough. But the thing is, I can't leave right now. I'm here with my kid, and I can't leave him alone. And I can't fix stuff anyway. I break stuff. Ask my brother Joel. He's always saying I'm mechanically declined since I can't even get my can opener to work half the time. I call him when I break things. Hey, I can call him! He can help you."

Kat wasn't sure how she felt about having Cindy's grumpy brother dragged into this, but she didn't have many other options. "Okay, if you think he won't mind. That would be great."

"I'll call him and send him over!"

Kat hung up the phone and leaned back in the chair. This evening was likely to be supremely awkward: dealing with a mildly stupid and definitely embarrassing situation, and making small talk with a surly guy she hardly knew.

A few minutes later Joel called Kat to make sure his sister wasn't pulling some type of stunt or playing a trick on him.

"So you *really* have a cat in the wall of your house?" he asked.

"Yes. I really do. It would be great if you have a saw or something, so you can help me get him out."

"I don't know what to say."

"If you happen to have pliers and any plumbing fixtures handy, that would be great too."

"You also have a plumbing problem?"

Kat had to admit that although her first impression of him hadn't been that great, Joel certainly had a marvelous phone voice. Deep and resonant, his voice sounded like he should be on talk radio. She could listen to this guy talk all day. Or all night. "Yes. I had to turn off the water to the house because the shower self-destructed today. The knob broke off and the shower head exploded. It hasn't been a great day."

Joel agreed and promised to bring lots of tools and supplies. Kat ran upstairs to the bathroom, looked at herself in the mirror, gasped, and rummaged around frantically for her brush. The term 'bad hair day' didn't begin to describe the catastrophe on her head. As Kat attempted to wrestle her unruly locks into a somewhat more respectable French braid, she had to admit that the day had been just as hard on her emotions as it had been on her hair.

∿

A knock came from the door and Kat ran to answer it. She had done what she could with her hair, but as the mirror had suggested, she was still looking bedraggled after the events of the day. As she opened the door, she found Joel standing on the blue-carpeted stair landing holding a large red toolbox. He looked far different than he had the other day.

Wow, he certainly cleaned up nicely. Like almost every male Kat had seen in Alpine Grove, Joel was wearing a flannel shirt and jeans. But instead of looking like he'd just rolled off the wrong side of an uncomfortable camp bunk, today he looked like he'd walked out of an ad for Stetson cologne.

Kat gawked at him for a moment too long before saying, "Hi, Joel, thanks for coming over so quickly. I appreciate it. Please come in."

Joel smiled and walked by her. "Okay, so where's the cat? I've gotta see this."

Kat felt a blush rise to her cheeks. Joel had shaved and had an amused twinkle in his eye. When he smiled, he was downright cute. *Yowza.* "Um, the hole in the wall is over here. The cat is down at the bottom of the wall. I think it's the three-legged cat, Tripod, so he probably can't climb up to get out. I'm not sure a four-footed cat could, either."

Kat climbed up on the chair and shined the light down behind the drywall so Joel could take a look. At 6-foot-1, Joel was tall enough that he could peer down into the hole and see without the aid of the chair. As they looked down the hole, they brushed shoulders, and Kat flinched slightly at the contact. It had been a long time since she had behaved like a dorky teenager mooning over a cute guy. Hopefully, he didn't realize how attractive she thought he was. She really needed to get out more. Too much time alone here in the woods and she'd turn into some kind of bizarre hermit.

Blinking in the light, the cat scratched the drywall more forcefully to emphasize that he'd like to leave his hidey hole in the wall. "Hi, kitty. Is that you, Tripod?" Kat asked. She jumped down from the chair, sat on it, and crossed her arms. "So what's the best way to get him out of there?"

Joel paused for a moment and said, "I could cut a small hole at the bottom of the wall, so he can just walk out. That's probably the easiest thing to do. I think he has enough room down there where he's settled so that I wouldn't hit him with the saw. Plus, I can use a small hand saw and cut slowly and carefully."

Kat looked into his eyes. They were a forest-green color, not hazel as she'd originally thought. The irises were deep green with flecks of hazel and rimmed with a darker green. "Yes, that sounds like a good idea. Is there anything I can do to help?"

"If you could watch from the top to make sure the cat is okay while I'm sawing, that would be great. Maybe you could talk to him too, if it seems like he's scared."

Kat got back up on the chair with her flashlight. She looked down at Joel, who was crouched at the bottom of the wall. As he gathered the various implements of destruction to begin the process of cutting yet *another* hole in her wall, Kat watched his shoulders move under his flannel shirt. They were rather nice shoulders, in fact: broad, muscular, and proportioned just right.

In general, when evaluating the male form, Kat was a 'shoulder person.' Unlike some women who focused on butts or legs, she found shoulders riveting. After careful deliberation from her perch on the chair above him, she had determined that Joel had mighty fine-looking shoulders. As he began sawing, she attempted to return her focus to the task at hand: the cat in the wall. "Are you okay down there, Tripod? We're trying to get you out."

The cat, who had been oddly quiet except for scratching the drywall, mewed in response. Fortunately, he had backed away from the wall when Joel started sawing.

Joel looked up at Kat. "Is the cat okay?"

"He's moved back a bit, so I think he'll be fine. He seems to know that saws should be avoided."

"Good plan, kitty." Joel chuckled as he continued to saw the drywall.

~

Kat continued her vigil, peering down the hole in the wall until at last Joel was able to pull out the square of drywall.

As soon as the escape hatch was opened, a silver ball of fur zipped by, leaping gracefully over Joel's leg. Tripod could seriously move out when he was sufficiently motivated. The gray-and-white tabby crouched under the kitchen table, assessing his rescuers.

"You're welcome," Joel said.

Kat raised her eyebrows. "I think he's happy to be liberated. Should we do something about the hole? I'd like to keep the critters out of the walls, if possible. Bud is out hunting and didn't say when he'd return."

"Bud could be gone for a while. His eyesight isn't particularly good, and if the rumors are true, he tends to miss a lot. Everyone in town knows that it's not a great idea to go hunting with him."

"Do you hunt?" Kat inquired.

"No. I went hunting once when I was in high school and I didn't enjoy it. My friends convinced me to go, and they killed a rabbit. The hike was fun, but I didn't enjoy the experience of killing something. I guess that's not a particularly macho thing to say is it?"

"I suppose not. But I'm okay with that. I'm a vegetarian, which makes hunting pointless, unless you like to stalk carrots."

Joel laughed, unfurled his long legs from the pretzel-like position he'd had them in, and stood up. "Yes, those rascally carrots. You need to watch out for them. I'll go see if I can find some wood outside to cover up the holes in the short term. Make sure no one decides to hibernate in there while I'm gone."

Kat nodded her head and leaned the square of drywall next to the hole Joel had cut. She couldn't figure out why Tripod would have been interested in the wall, but attempting to understand the workings of the feline mind was usually futile. Murphee had taught her that long ago.

Joel left the house and Kat replayed the conversation in her mind. He didn't like to hunt? That was interesting. Although she hadn't said it, Kat was glad he didn't like hunting. Maybe it was a wimpy girly thing, but all that blood and killing a beautiful wild animal just sounded awful.

But what did Joel do for a living? The guy had to make money somehow. He wasn't hunting, so how did he afford to eat? Most people in Alpine Grove had small service businesses like Cindy's or worked in the woods doing logging or construction-type work. Joel seemed to be in good shape, but he didn't strike her as the logger type. Would it be too nosy to ask? Was he just being polite by laughing at her dopey carrot joke or did he think it was actually funny? It was hard to tell what he was thinking.

Joel opened the door, interrupting her reverie. He was carrying two grayish pieces of what looked like an old pallet. "I found this. It's not very good wood, but this fix is temporary, so it should work for now."

"Thank you. I really appreciate you helping me out. There probably are tools somewhere, but I haven't found them yet. Mostly, I've been cleaning and breaking things."

Joel held the board up to the wall and said, "It's okay. My sister is the Queen of Destruction, so she calls me all the time asking for help. It drives me crazy, but I can't say no. I guess it's an older brother thing. I've been fixing her messes for so long, it's a habit now." He hit the nail with the hammer, driving it into the wood.

"She mentioned that she breaks stuff. I don't usually have this type of problem. At my apartment, most things just work. If something falls apart, I just call the apartment manager. It's easy. Until today, I didn't appreciate how easy."

Kat paused for a moment while Joel whacked the nail with the hammer a few more times. Unable to resist, she asked, "So when you're not helping damsels in distress, what do you do?"

Joel plucked out the nail he'd been holding in his mouth and replied, "Not much at the moment. I worked for an aerospace company in the city as an engineer. I did a lot with computers and was working on a huge government project. Then the project was canceled, and I was riffed."

"Riffed?"

The look in Joel's eyes turned hard and cold. "Yes. Reduction in force. That's the government's way of telling you you're fired. Your job has been eliminated. You've been made redundant."

Apparently, he was still annoyed at the memory. Now Kat was really curious. "So why are you here in Alpine Grove? I can't imagine many engineering jobs are located here."

Joel looked over at her, "You ask a lot of questions, don't you?"

Kat shrugged her shoulders, "I'm just curious. My sisters call me nosy. It's okay if you don't want to answer. I just didn't think you'd be an engineer. I'm a technical writer, and I guess most of the engineers I've met aren't like you."

"Oh?"

Kat certainly wasn't going to say "most of them aren't cute like you are" and paused for a moment, trying to figure out how to respond without sounding like a moonstruck idiot. "Um, most of them are more difficult to talk to than you are." *Nice save.*

"That's funny. Cindy always calls me Mr. Spock because she thinks I'm inscrutable. Not that she'd use the word inscrutable, but I think you know what I mean."

Kat giggled, "Yeah, I get it. All through high school, I was the weird girl with glasses who never said anything. Talk about inscrutable. Everyone thought I was a priss, but really I was just too shy to talk to anyone. I know; I was such a loser. I can't believe I'm even telling you this."

Joel gave the nail a final whack and looked over at her. "A priss? I haven't heard that term in a while."

"What can I say? It was the 80s. High school was stupid for a lot of reasons."

Joel grinned, "You're making me glad I wasn't in high school then. Anyway, I think we're done here. All holes are sealed, and as far as I know, nothing alive is back there."

"I don't suppose you brought something to fix the shower, did you?"

"Yes, I had an old fixture left over from some work I did on my cabin. I can see if it fits."

Kat led Joel up the stairs to the bathroom. She opened the door and shooed Murphee back with her foot. "No Murph, you need to stay in here. We don't want a repeat of your fight with Dolly Mae."

The bathroom wasn't very large and Kat picked up Murphee and wedged herself next to the sink so Joel would have some room to examine the shower-fixture issues. "The water is all still off," she volunteered.

"Good. That was my next question."

"So will it work? I really want a shower. You have no idea."

Joel glanced at her appraisingly, "It looks like you've had a long day."

Kat cringed inwardly. She probably did look scary. After wandering around the forest with dogs, spelunking through ancient foodstuffs, dealing with a cat fight and cleaning dog barf, she probably didn't smell good, either. How mortifying. "Yeah, I don't always look like this. I promise."

Joel smiled faintly, "You look okay. Better than I did the other day when Cindy dragged me out here to deal with her stupid car. Because she's given the car a name, she can't seem to part with it. She always says that she and Myrtle have been through a lot together and she owes it to her. It doesn't make sense. It's a *car*, for God's sake."

"I guess you and your sister don't get along?" Yes, she was being nosy again, but she didn't care. As Joel reached up to screw the new shower head onto the pipe, Kat noticed the way his back muscles flexed as he twisted the nozzle. *Nice.*

"She drives me nuts," he said. "But she's my baby sister. When she was little, she was this adorable little girl with blonde curls. No one could resist her bubbly enthusiasm, and she's always gotten what she wanted. That led to some problems when she got older, though."

Joel turned around from the shower to look at Kat. "Well, it looks like the shower head I brought fits, so it should work. I don't have a knob that is compatible with this style of single-lever handle, but I can leave you a pair of pliers so you can turn the valve that way."

"Could we turn on the water to make sure? This shower and I have a bad relationship. I have a big bruise from falling on the floor after it committed suicide."

Joel raised his eyebrows, "I don't see a bruise. Let me turn the valve off first."

"Good idea." Kat certainly wasn't going to volunteer that the bruise was on her butt. The last time she looked, it had been turning a glorious shade of purple.

The pair walked downstairs, and Joel flipped the well pump switch back on. Kat listened for the sounds of rushing water and was relieved to hear nothing. They went back upstairs, tested the water, and everything seemed fine.

Joel said, "It looks like everything works. I should be going now."

Kat was surprised to discover that she didn't want him to leave. "Are you sure? I should make you dinner as a thank you."

"That's okay. I had something to eat before I got here."

Maybe he somehow knew about her fear of the stove. Given her bad experience with water, he probably didn't want her near fire. She walked with him to the door. "Thank you again. I know I said that, but I really appreciate you coming all the way out here."

"You're welcome. I'll probably see you around town sometime. Have a good night."

As Joel picked up his things and walked out the door, Kat wished she'd had more time to talk to him. Even with all her nosy questions, she still never discovered why he was here in Alpine Grove. But she'd find a way to talk to him again and get the rest of his story.

Chapter 4

Tizzy State

After walking the dogs and making another sandwich for dinner, Kat checked the bedroom to see if there was a cat under the bed. Although she did not see any eyes in the darkness, she found another collection of dust dinosaurs and what appeared to be a pile of desiccated cat turds under there. Apparently, Dolly Mae or Louie spent more time under the bed than she thought.

She found some sheets that looked at least moderately clean, made the bed, and went to get Murphee and her paraphernalia from the bathroom. She set up Murphee's food and litter box and then crawled into bed. It had been a long, complicated day. She closed her eyes and enjoyed the warm rhythm of Murphee quietly purring next to her.

The next morning, Murphee stepped on Kat's head to indicate that it was time for breakfast. As she opened her eyes, Kat had a disorienting moment when she had no idea where she was. All she could hear was the twittering of birds outside. There were no cars, no people, nothing. She rolled over on her side and stroked Murphee's shiny black fur, contemplating the quiet. For most of her life she had lived in cities with their continuous hum of people going about their business. Even at the motel, the road noise and the people staying at the RV park generated a certain amount of racket.

This was the first time Kat could remember lying in bed hearing nothing except the sounds of nature.

The peaceful silence was interrupted by the sound of the phone ringing in the kitchen. Kat dislodged Murphee and jumped out of bed to answer it. She picked up the harvest-gold receiver from the wall and mumbled a greeting.

"Hello, this is Louise Johnson. We met the other day."

"Yes, I hope your allergies are better," Kat replied.

"I've been hearing that you are not taking good care of the animals, and I'm worried. Abigail, rest her soul, was extremely concerned that all of her babies get proper care after she was gone."

Kat raised her eyebrows. Apparently news moved fast in Alpine Grove. "What did you hear from whom? I had a problem with a cat in the wall last night, but everything is okay now."

Louise sniffed with disdain. "Well, word gets out, you know. I know people. And people talk. I heard that cats were fighting and dogs were running around all willy nilly. What in heaven's name is going on there?"

"I don't know what you heard, but everything is fine. There was a hole in the wall and a cat was curious and slipped down behind the wallboard. I couldn't get in touch with Bud, who made the hole in the first place. So I called Cindy, who asked her brother Joel to come out to help me get the cat out because I couldn't find any tools here. Tripod is completely unharmed and doing well."

"I think I need to come by and see for myself. Abigail entrusted me to ensure her babies get proper care. She wants them all to be living in the house in harmony."

"Well, one dog, Tessa, was staying outside when I got here. She has her own enclosure. The dog walker said it's because of her behavior issues."

Louise gasped daintily, "Oh my dear, that's completely unacceptable! Abigail's dogs are all house dogs. She wanted everyone to be a family."

Sure. A dysfunctional family, maybe. "Cindy didn't tell me Tessa was supposed to be inside. The dogs and cats are all getting to know me. Yesterday I had some cleaning to do, but we're all fine."

"No, no. This isn't good. Oh dear, I'm in a bit of a tizzy now. I must see for myself what is really going on there! I'll be out later after I have my hair done."

Kat envisioned Louise waving her hands frantically in her tizzy-state. As she hung up the phone, she had a bad feeling that Louise probably wasn't going to be impressed with what she found here. However, now that Kat had moderately functional plumbing, if nothing else, she was finally going to take a shower.

~

Later that morning, Kat went to take the dogs out for their morning excursion into the forest. She decided to get Chelsey from her basement first, so they could all go for a walk as a 'family.' Apparently, this level of bonding was important to Louise, so if Kat wanted to get on the woman's good side, she'd better start working on critter togetherness. As far as she could tell, the dogs seemed to like each other. Maybe pack harmony would reign supreme.

Again, Kat used her makeshift pack/harness arrangement and attached Tessa to Linus. The pair scampered off happily toward the forest trail with the slow human trailing behind with Chelsey. Because she spent so much time sitting on the floor with Chelsey convincing her the world was not the scary awful place she thought it was, Kat was starting to like the weird little dog. Chelsey was definitely a worrier, but once she was out on her walk, she seemed to relax a bit and start enjoying life. Kat could relate. At the moment, she had a few things to worry about, too.

Lori joined the group, trotting alongside Kat and Chelsey as they walked through the trees. Sunlight dappled the trail in front of them, and the wind whispered through the aspen leaves above. A whole lot of changes had taken place in just the last week. Kat's apartment was going condo and her job was unsatisfying, to put it mildly. Although she liked writing, she didn't actually get to do much writing at work. She'd always been a writer. It had been part of her identity for so long, it was difficult to imagine doing anything else.

On the other hand, listening to the sounds of the woods was peaceful. The setting here was one of the most beautiful patches of forest Kat had ever seen. The idea of never seeing a cubicle again gave her a little chill up her spine. What if she didn't just take a vacation? What if she never went back? What would that feel like? Never seeing Chris or Mark again? Kat closed her eyes for a moment and imagined simply staying here in Alpine Grove. It was possible if she could get all the animals to get along. She'd have enough money to live for a while (well, assuming the place didn't disintegrate any more than it already had). She also was starting to hate the idea of finding the dogs new homes. Even Tessa's exuberance was starting to seem cute instead of obnoxious. Although she was still the out-of-control spaz dog, it was hard not to smile at the outpouring of pure joy that burst from Tessa's furry golden body at the slightest provocation.

As Kat, Chelsey, and Lori looped back around toward the end of the forest trail, their tranquil walk was disturbed by a mighty "WOOF!" from Linus up ahead. He and Tessa had seen something and were heading toward the driveway at maximum speed.

Uh oh.

Kat chased after the galloping canines with Chelsey in tow. Chelsey obviously thought all the excitement and running was great fun and bounded alongside Kat with a level of glee that Kat hadn't seen before.

Kat exited the copse of trees, dashing toward the house surrounded by dogs. Louise was standing in the driveway rummaging through her large handbag. Linus and Tessa were ahead of Kat, speeding toward Louise with the leash spread out between them. Kat wasn't a big sports fan, but she'd seen enough football games to know what the term 'clotheslined' meant.

"Louise, get out of the way!" she yelled as loudly as she could.

Louise looked up from her purse and assessed the situation with surprising haste. She scampered toward a nearby tree and hugged it for security. Linus stopped in front of her, dragging Tessa to a halt with a whoosh of dust. Tessa started leaping on Louise, who had released her hold on the Douglas fir she'd been hugging and had her arms up in front of her face to ward off the canine onslaught.

"Linus! Come here!" Kat shouted.

Linus turned his head and started ambling back toward Kat, dragging Tessa off Louise in the process. Louise stepped away from her savior fir tree and began brushing the dust off her skirt. Kat could tell by the jerking strokes of her hands against the fabric that the older woman was not happy. Her body language oozed fury.

"Hi, Louise. I'm sorry about that," she called as she grabbed hold of the leash between Linus and Tessa. "I'm going to put Tessa back into her enclosure now."

Louise nodded her head in acknowledgment and returned to her ministrations. Kat walked Linus and Tessa slowly toward the outbuilding, dreading the upcoming conversation with Louise. Tessa was panting and jumping with delight and straining to get back to her outbuilding so she could get a drink of water. As they entered the Tessa Hut, Kat chastened the dog, "Tessa, don't look so happy. You do realize we're in trouble now, right?" Tessa wagged her tail and panted enthusiastically. Kat looked at Linus, "Try to look serious when we go back out there, okay Big Guy?"

Linus wagged his tail and gazed at Kat with a lighthearted glint in his eye. Kat giggled and bent down to give him a hug around his hairy ruff. "Oh my God, it was hilarious when she was hugging that tree, wasn't it?" She started to laugh harder and turned her face into his fur in an attempt to muffle the sound. She kept telling herself no, it was *not* funny. Louise could have been seriously hurt. *Really!* It was *not* funny! But the vision of Louise clutching the tree overrode any sense of propriety.

Behind the chain-link fence of her enclosure, Tessa sprang around, happy to join in any silliness that might transpire. Kat tried pinching her own arm in an effort to try to control her hilarity. Her eyes were watering and a terminal case of the giggles returned every time she looked at one of the dogs. "Come on you guys, stop making me laugh!" Both dogs wagged and panted cheerfully.

Kat wiped her eyes and attempted to get herself under control before going back outside to face Louise. "Okay Linus, remember: we're serious now. This is *serious*." Linus closed his mouth, pausing his panting for a moment. Apparently, this was his serious look.

After clearing her throat several times and smoothing her rumpled hair, Kat strode out of the kennel, trying to look composed and not like she'd just collapsed into a laughing fit. With Chelsey by her side and Linus and Lori trailing behind, Kat walked over to the driveway where Louise was standing.

"Louise, it's nice to see you again."

Louise's face was somewhat flushed and her lips were pursed together, giving her a pinched expression like an angry yellow raisin. "Hello, Kat. As you know, I am here to evaluate how you are doing. It's just as I feared. Dogs running everywhere. And the whole town is talking about the cat in the wall incident. I'm too ashamed to tell anyone that I'm supposed to be evaluating your fitness to take care of Abigail's lovely home. She's probably rolling over in her grave right now."

Kat paused for a moment to consider her response. *Lovely home? She had to be kidding. Maybe 30 years ago, but now?* "Louise, I know I haven't seen my aunt in a long time, but she had a good sense of humor. She's probably laughing her ass off right now."

Louise gasped. "Don't you dare use that type of language with me, young lady!"

"You told me that I have to walk the dogs together. I did. Even Chelsey here. Look how happy she is!" Kat patted the dog's head, and Chelsey wagged in agreement. "She wouldn't come out of the basement a few days ago. Cindy told me that and I saw it first-hand."

"Well, yes, but the dogs are running around everywhere!"

"They have a doggie door. Obviously my aunt let them run around. I know Linus and Lori don't go anywhere. Tessa is too strong for anyone except Linus to walk, so I've given him that responsibility. He's being a very good boy, too. Aren't you, Linus?" Kat patted his huge head for emphasis. Linus looked up at her and wagged his tail in response.

Louise brought her brows together. "Well, they do seem to like you, anyway. I'm just worried."

"I've only been here a couple of days. It has been challenging because the house may not be in as good shape as you remember. I had some…ah…cleaning to do." (That was putting it nicely.)

"All right. I must see the cats, though. Where are Butch and Sundance?"

Kat eyes widened. "There are more cats?"

"There are supposed to be five cats here. Have you lost some? That's not good."

"I have met Dolly Mae, Louie and Tripod, who was the one in the wall. I haven't seen Butch and Sundance in the house anywhere."

"No, they are barn cats. They were dumped here a few years ago and were a bit wild. Abigail trapped them and got them fixed, but they don't like the indoors at all."

"Okay. Where is their food?"

"Cindy knows. I can't believe she didn't tell you! Oh, she is just so forgetful. But she's such a darling girl. Everybody loves her."

Kat considered what Joel had said about his sister and her own reactions. 'Everyone' might be a bit of a stretch, but it seemed like Cindy had a vocal fan club here in Alpine Grove. "I can give her a call and ask. She didn't mention outdoor cats on the information she wrote up for me. But I think she was in a hurry."

"All right. Well, I have to go. Mitzi rescheduled my hair appointment." Louise patted her cap of blue curls tenderly. "I must get back to town now. I'll check in again when I have more time."

"See you then."

Louise climbed into her yellow Buick station wagon and slowly picked her way down the driveway, attempting to avoid the most treacherous pot holes.

Relieved that Louise's anger level seemed to have dropped somewhat since the near death-by-clotheslining episode, Kat stood and stroked Linus's head as he leaned against her thigh and waved his tail back and forth companionably. "What do you think, Big Guy? Is she going to throw me out?" Linus gazed up at her face with a questioning look in his eyes. "Yeah, I don't know either. But I'm pretty sure everyone at Mitzy's salon is going to hear about how you and Tessa almost killed her."

∼

Kat devoted most of the rest of the day to more cleaning. It was slow going. The more she cleaned, the more she found to clean. It was like an archaeological dig, unearthing new layers of dirt and trash. Clearly, she was going to have to take a trip to the local dump. Her date with Larry was tonight and she considered the idea of asking if she could borrow his ugly truck. *How romantic.*

After taking the dogs out for another walk, Kat focused on trying to make herself look like a girl again in preparation for her evening out. Getting dressed up seemed like a distant memory, even though she'd been here in Alpine Grove for only a few days. But she was starting to understand why most people tended to wear the clothes they did. Between all the dog walking, cleaning, and associated filth, even Kat's recently acquired Kmart-based wardrobe was taking a beating.

She stood in front of the closet where she had hung up her clothes, pondering her options. Kat loved bright colors and fabric, but she had zero fashion savvy. Looking through her clothes was an exercise in frustration. She was clueless when shopping, which led to a mismatched collection of partial outfits that mostly didn't work together. When she was a kid there had been a clothing line that made it easy for kids to select outfits by matching little animal tags. If you matched a giraffe shirt with giraffe pants, you knew the outfit worked. Why had no one come up with the same thing for adults?

When she was in high school, one of the worst and most absurd teenage angst-laden fights she'd had with her mother was what she now thought of as the dress-for-success argument. Kat had been getting ready to go to work at her summer job, and Mom had gone on a long tirade about how it was important for her to wear a suit. And if she didn't adhere to this rigid rule of workplace fashion, she'd never make anything of herself. Kat had argued that perhaps competence and skill might have some impact on employment success along with the suit, but Mom wasn't having any of it. To this day, Kat had yet to ever wear a suit to work, just on general principle.

Part of the problem with deciding what to wear this evening was that she wasn't sure where Larry was taking her and what dress codes were like in Alpine Grove. Presumably, people didn't wear flannel everywhere. In the end, she decided on the safe approach: her favorite blue dress, which matched her eyes. Every other woman in the world had a little black dress; Kat had the little blue dress instead. And given that it was getting late, it would have to do.

At 7:00 p.m. there was a knock on the door. Freshly pressed and primped, Kat answered it and found Larry standing on the blue-carpeted landing with an uncertain smile. She was relieved to see that he was dressed as he had been at his office, in a conservative jacket and slacks, as opposed to his L.L. Bean look. That implied they might be going somewhere more upscale than an RV park, so her little blue dress wouldn't seem too out of place.

"Hello, Kat. You look very pretty tonight."

Kat looked down at her dress, blushing slightly. "Thanks, Larry. Do you want to come in?"

"I made reservations for 7:30, so just for a minute."

Larry walked through the door into the hallway and looked around. "It certainly smells better here. And it looks like you've done some cleaning."

Kat laughed, "You have no idea. I don't miss the stink either. I haven't been able to get in touch with Bud to get the hole in the wall fixed. Do you know if he's still out hunting?"

"I'm not sure. Did you ask him about repairing the roof?"

Kat shrugged. "Yes, but I haven't heard about that, either. I hope it doesn't rain."

"Where are all the animals?"

"The dogs are downstairs. My cat Murphee is in the bedroom, and the other cats are wandering around. Louise told me there are two more cats outside, but I've never seen them."

Kat had a feeling that Larry might be checking up on her for Louise, but she wasn't sure. Maybe he was just being polite and asking about the critters. It was hard to tell. Although she wasn't sure exactly why, he was difficult to talk to. He was always respectful and courteous, but it always seemed like he was evaluating her and she came up short in his estimation.

Larry turned toward the door. "We should probably go now."

As they exited the house, Kat was relieved to see that Larry had come up with a newer, cleaner vehicle to transport her to the restaurant. Instead of the grungy, salmon pickup truck, a generic, dark-gray sedan was parked in the driveway. As she climbed in, Kat's brain was racing to try to think of something to say. Since they'd covered most of the small talk related to the repairs and animals of Chez Stinky, the conversation had ground to a halt. Driving to the restaurant in silence was going to be uncomfortable.

"So, how long have you lived in Alpine Grove?"

Larry looked over at her and then back at the road. "I grew up here. My parents own the hardware store in town."

"Really? I need to get a new knob thingie for the shower. Mine broke." She wasn't sure if she wanted to get into *that* whole story. If he was a spy for Louise, breaking the plumbing wouldn't exactly improve the old woman's impression of her caretaking abilities.

"I'm sure they could help you with that."

Kat mentally groaned and tried to resuscitate the conversation. "Did you go to college around here?"

"I went to the UCLA School of Law."

"You went off to the big city?"

"Yes, but I didn't enjoy it. I missed Alpine Grove. So as soon I passed the bar, I came back here."

Clearly, Larry wasn't a big storyteller. Kat tried to think of something else she could ask that wouldn't result in a yes, no, or three-word answer. She hoped the restaurant was close by. It could be a long car ride.

"So, what are your hobbies?"

"I don't really have hobbies. I work and then go home and relax."

Kat gave up, and they rode the rest of the way to the restaurant in silence. When they got to the restaurant, their table wasn't ready, so they were escorted to the lounge to wait. The restaurant served Italian food and the air was heavy with the aroma of freshly made spicy tomato sauce, garlic, olive oil and artisan bread. The lighting was cozy and romantic. Quite a few Alpine Grove marriages might begin here with a proposal at the tables that surrounded the huge stone fireplace.

Kat pulled up a stool to the long mahogany bar, and Larry pulled another barstool over next to her, so he was sitting uncomfortably close to her. Kat knew that she probably had an overdeveloped sense of personal space, but his proximity made her anxious. In her family, they weren't huggers. She leaned away from him, trying to increase the distance. It would be better if she could just have a conversation with him.

Kat cleared her throat and decided to go with a situational question, since asking about Larry's life had been a flop. "So, what do you like to eat here?"

"I love Italian food" he said enthusiastically. "My favorite dish is the gnocchi con salsiccia. It has homemade sausage and gnocchi in a basil tomato sauce topped with plenty of mozzarella cheese. I also enjoy the scallops, which come in a light cream sauce with fettuccini noodles. The scallops are perfectly cooked, so they just melt in your mouth. The house salad and dressing is also good. It has olives, chickpeas, and carrots. I like to have dinner with a medium-priced, yet bold Chianti."

Kat raised her eyebrows. Larry certainly knew his food. "I usually prefer vegetarian options. Do you have any suggestions?"

"You might enjoy the Rigatoni al Gorgonzola. It has gorgonzola cheese in a creamy vodka sauce with walnuts on top. It's just wonderful."

Larry continued to expound on the various menu options. Kat came to the conclusion that given his encyclopedic knowledge of the menu, he must eat here a lot. Like maybe every night. She was getting hungry and her stomach growled loudly. How embarrassing.

"I guess I'm getting hungry."

"Yes. I am, too. I'll check on our table." Larry lurched off his bar stool, colliding with Kat and pushing her off her stool onto the floor. She landed unceremoniously on her rump, painfully reminding her that she still had the big bruise on her butt from falling on the bathroom floor. Alpine Grove seemed to be hazardous to her health.

With a horrified look on his face, Larry reached down to help Kat up off the floor.

"I'm so sorry! Are you okay?"

With as much dignity as she could muster, Kat collected her legs under her and stood up. She moved the bar stool farther from Larry.

"Yes, I'm fine. Could you see about our table?"

"I'll be right back." Larry hustled off to the hostess desk and conferred with a tall blonde woman he seemed to know well. Kat could hear them laughing and hoped they weren't laughing about how she had ended up splatted on the floor. The grin on his face became more subdued as he turned back toward her.

"They're getting a table ready now."

The blonde woman, who it turned out was named Traci (with an i), led them to a table near the fireplace. Kat was relieved to be sitting across the table from Larry, instead of next to him.

The rest of the meal passed relatively uneventfully, if quietly. Once they had their food, the menu topic was off the table (so to speak) and Kat had run out of ideas for small talk. She'd unsuccessfully covered family, work, and home in the car.

Larry paused in his meal and asked, "So do you think you'll stay in Alpine Grove?"

"I'm thinking about it, but I'm not sure. I asked my boss about telecommuting, and he wasn't particularly encouraging about the idea."

"You could quit your job."

"I'm not sure I want to do that. I have friends there, and I'm not sure what I'd do instead."

Kat didn't elaborate and Larry resumed his enthusiastic eating. She wasn't sure she wanted to share her decision-making process, since whatever she said to Larry might get back to Louise.

Larry raised his fork and pointed it at her. "Well, if you don't stay, you need to think about finding homes for the dogs and cats."

Kat's heart clenched a bit at the idea of finding a new home for Linus, Lori, and Chelsey. Even Tessa. It had been only a short time, but she was becoming attached to them. She gave herself a mental shake. *I don't have to figure that out now.*

After finishing the meal and experiencing another quiet, uncomfortable drive back to Chez Stinky, Kat was more than ready to say goodbye to Larry and end the long awkward evening. They stood on the blue-carpeted stairs as Kat leaned over to unlock the door.

Larry reached out to put his arm around her. "I had a great time tonight. Can we do this again?"

Had he been on the same date she had? She deftly maneuvered herself out of his embrace and opened the door. "Um, we'll see. I should get in. The dogs need their walk now. Thank you very much. The food was just as good as you said. Really great. I have to go. 'Bye."

As Kat scuttled into the house and closed the door behind her, she leaned back on it, relieved to have avoided what could have been the most awkward good night kiss of her life. Or maybe the history of the world.

She went down the stairs to see how the dogs were doing. With some trepidation, she had boldly put Tessa inside with everyone else, and everything seemed okay. "Hi guys."

The dogs jumped up from the various beds they'd been sleeping on, and with tails wagging, the pack ran over to greet her. She used both hands and reached out to scratch the fuzzy ears crowding around her. "You all look fine. Were you good? I missed having someone I can talk to!"

～

The next morning, Kat sat at the kitchen table eating a piece of toast, reflecting on the prior evening's conversation, or lack thereof. Although the date with Larry had been arduous, he had asked a good question about the roof. Kat knew she had been avoiding dealing with Bud on construction-related matters. But eventually rain or another weather event could cause the roof to fail in its primary mission of remaining over her head. So she couldn't ignore it forever.

As she picked up the phone receiver, she considered what she could say to Bud. Because she was still annoyed about the hole in the wall, she was afraid she'd blurt out something like, "So Bud, are you done hunting yet? Are you ever going to fix the wall?" But that probably wasn't a good approach.

This time when she called, Kat didn't get the answering machine. After five rings, Bud picked up the phone. "Hiya, this is Bud."

"Bud, this is Kat Stevens. I left a message the other day about the hole in my wall."

"Yep. I was out huntin' in the mountains. I got some food now. It took some time to prep, but there's going to be good eats at my house. It feels good to have a full freezer!"

"So does that mean you can come out here and fix the hole in the wall? I'd also really like an estimate on how much work needs to be done to fix the roof and an idea of the cost."

"Yeah, I've been working on thinking about fixing that roof. It could be complicated. I gotta talk to the guys at the lumberyard and get out my calculator."

Kat tried not to think about what lurked in Bud's freezer. Or about his calculating abilities. Maybe she didn't want this estimate after all. Never seeing or talking to Bud again was having some appeal. She had an idea. "I was thinking that I'd like to talk to some of your prior clients. Do you have references I can talk to about the quality of your work?"

"Well, I'll have to get back to you about that. Everyone in Alpine Grove knows me."

Kat wasn't sure if those who knew Bud would vouch for his work, but she figured she'd see if she could extract a few salient details. "Who have you worked for recently?"

"Well, I added a porch on my house."

"Can I take a look at it? I'd like to see an example of your work."

"I'm not quite done. It just needs a few finishing details. I can call you when I got it all straightened out. I have some car repairs that I'm working on right now, too. I got a race car in my yard that I'm fixing up. The wife says that if I don't get it running, she's going to have it towed to the scrap yard, along with the rest of my other cars I'm restoring. So that's been taking my priority right now. And I can only work a few hours before my back starts to hurt and then I need to rest."

"It sounds like you're busy. I plan to get a number of estimates before I make a decision. Thank you for your time."

As she hung up the phone, Kat decided she was done with Bud. There had to be other contractors in Alpine Grove. Or somewhere nearby. All she needed was someone with tools who knew about building. Of course, Joel had tools. Maybe she should call him again. Her mind drifted. He'd had such a cute half-smile when she was babbling at him while he was removing the cat from the wall. But he probably thought she was a complete nutcase. Or even worse, just another woman who breaks things like his sister.

～

After making the command decision that Bud and Martha were never going to touch Chez Stinky again, Kat was ready to attack the house again. The next step in her marathon cleaning program would be to deal with the living room. After walking the dogs and settling them back in their hallway downstairs, she donned her grubby clothes, ready to wage another battle with the dust dinosaurs.

The process of cleaning was by turns bittersweet and disgusting. She swept the rough-hewn floors and discovered old pennies, thousands of dead bugs, and even a desiccated gold fish that had been lurking in a corner behind a shelf. As she went around the living room and carefully dusted the knick-knacks sitting on the various cabinets, dressers, and shelves, she was hit with a bout of nostalgia. She remembered playing with them when she was a little girl. Her favorite had been a little ceramic woman wearing a hoop skirt, which actually was a bell.

Ever the literal one, Kat had named the little musical figurine Belle. As she rubbed the damp cloth over the web pattern of cracks in the ceramic, a tear ran down her cheek. In all the confusion of dealing with the inheritance and the house, Kat hadn't had much time to think about the fact that she wouldn't see her Aunt Abigail again.

Abigail had always been the weird, fun aunt who liked to get out and do things. Whether it was hiking in the forest or deciding that it was time to jump in the car and go get an ice cream cone, she was often in motion. And unlike a lot of grown-ups at that time in Kat's life, Abigail talked to her like an intelligent (if small) person. The sum total of her conversation didn't consist of "Oh, look how much you've grown!"

Abigail had always seemed interested in Kat's little-girl life. She wanted to know about Kat's friends, school, and what she liked to do. Knowing Kat liked creating crafty things, Abigail always had some type of embroidery or craft kit for her to work on whenever she visited. In fact, Kat had discovered a worn woven-loop potholder with crispy edges that she was pretty sure she had created years ago with a loom kit.

After she dusted the surface of an old credenza, she pulled out the drawers and discovered a cache of CDs. Kat hadn't seen a CD player anywhere, so she opened up the double doors on the front of the battered piece of furniture to discover a remarkably modern-looking stereo system. Bose speakers? Now that was a surprise. She riffled through the CD cases and learned that apparently Abigail had a fondness for rock and roll, with the occasional foray into heavy metal. Who knew?

Although Kat had been enjoying the quiet of her little corner of forest, the idea of blasting a few tunes to help her regain cleaning momentum was appealing. She opened up the door of the CD player and put in an old album from Electric Light Orchestra. As the sound of "Tightrope" filled the house, rustling sounds of dogs waking up came from downstairs. Canine nap time was over.

She went down the stairs and opened the gate to let the dogs upstairs. The four-pack, as she'd come to think of them, launched up the stairway and wandered around the kitchen and living room, sniffing to find out what had transpired since they'd last been there. Tessa raced around the living room and kitchen area twice and then screeched to a halt and stared at Kat expectantly.

"Hi, you guys. You all be good. I still have a lot of cleaning to do."

Kat grabbed her damp dusting cloth from the sink with a flourish in time to the music. Spotting the movement, Lori perked up her ears, wagged her tail, and ran over to Kat and Tessa to join in the fun.

"So do you like ELO?"

Tessa leaped around joyfully, and Lori jumped backward a few times in front of Kat to indicate her musical enthusiasm. Linus came over to the kitchen and the three dogs followed Kat around as she danced around the living room and kitchen, dusting various surfaces as she went. By the end of the song, even Chelsey had joined in the parade. All four dogs were panting happily as the next song began. As she sang along to the music loudly and way off-key, Kat was glad that even though dogs have great hearing, they aren't music critics.

By the time the album was over, Kat and the dogs were exhausted. Kat collapsed on the sofa, and Lori leaped up and curled up next to her. Tessa and Linus settled down on the floor in front of her feet, and Chelsey crawled under the sofa, settling in for a snooze. Kat rested her hand on Lori's back and leaned back on the sofa. Closing her eyes, she listened to the quiet snuffly sounds of dogs snoring around her.

~

For Kat, the next few days consisted of more cleaning, memories, reflections, and dog walks. She settled into a comfortable routine and most of the time was able to handle Tessa, Chelsey, and the rest of the canine crew with relatively few problems. No parts of Chez Stinky fell off or disintegrated during her cleaning and no cats ended up trapped anywhere, which she regarded as a great step in the right direction.

Although she had caught only a few glimpses of the outdoor cats Butch and Sundance, those fleeting moments of flying fur, along with the food consumption, assured Kat that the pair were okay and enjoying barn-cat life. Kat also found a number of rodent body parts that indicated the felines were taking their jobs as Chief Mouse Officers seriously.

Even Murphee was slowly starting to adjust to life at Chez Stinky. One afternoon after she had patrolled the upstairs area for other cats and secured the dogs downstairs in their hallway, Kat let Murph out of the bedroom to explore. Murphee wandered around the living room and kitchen, sniffing and rubbing against furniture. Eventually, she curled up with Kat on the sofa and enjoyed some quality lap time while Kat read a novel.

Kat was still worried about the roof, but the weather had been gloriously sunny and it was easy to ignore the problem for the time being and just enjoy what was left of her vacation. Next week, she'd have to return to her cubicle and the rest of her real life. But for the time being, she wanted to relax and enjoy herself.

Now that the house was somewhat more habitable, maybe she could invite Maria up for the weekend. She could get the dirt from her friend on what was going on at the office before she had to face the world of technical writing again. She'd been completely alone for the last couple days, and it would be nice to see another human being.

Kat picked up the phone and dialed Maria's number at the office.

"Hello. This is Maria."

"Wow, you sound so official!" Kat said with a smile.

"Hey, girlfriend! I thought maybe you'd been chewed up by a rabid chipmunk out there in the forest. How's it going? Have you found the man of your dreams lurking behind some big pine tree yet?

"No. Mostly I've been dealing with a guy named Bud who is very attached to a power saw he named Martha. I didn't want to horn in on their relationship."

"Sounds sexy. Things are kinda different out there in the woods."

"Definitely. Do you want to come see for yourself? I was thinking we could do a Wine and Whine up here so you can fill me in all the fun stuff at work before I have to go back there."

"Well, that won't take long. Fun has not been the word of the day around here. I think Mark might be insane. What is wrong with that dude?"

"I couldn't tell you. I don't think he likes me much right now, either. We can talk about that when you're here."

"I'll have to cancel that date I have with Brad Pitt. But for you, anything. I think I might just take a four-day weekend, too. I need to get out of this place for a while."

"I definitely know that feeling. Before I went on vacation, I wanted to commit serious bodily harm to Mark. I think I was getting wound a bit too tight. Oh, one other thing about coming up here. You might want to bring casual clothes. And comfortable shoes. It's a little more rustic than you might be used to. Also, you know about the dogs and cats here. They have fur. It falls off. They shed *a lot*. Just keep that in mind."

"What do you mean 'rustic'? You aren't saying I can't wear my heels, are you? You know I like my heels. I feel naked without my heels. And way too short. I hate that."

"I'm just saying you might want to leave the stilettos at home. But it's your choice."

Kat gave Maria directions and suggested she drive slowly up the driveway if she valued the suspension on her car.

Chapter 5

The Hot Spot

All four dogs started barking uproariously from the basement and Kat looked out the window to discover Maria's little red Mazda Miata picking its way around the holes in the driveway. The poor little sports car was designed for pavement, not rocks and potholes.

Maria looked up at the trees as she removed the scarf from her hair. Kat sighed as she saw the four-inch heels on Maria's sandals as she exited the little car. It was only four days; maybe Maria could make it through the visit without breaking her ankle or any other valuable body part.

Kat opened the front door and ran down the stairs to greet her friend. Linus appeared from behind the house and launched down the driveway when he saw the interloper. Maria looked up from her purse; a look of first confusion and then horror crossed her face when she saw the great hairy animal. She ran behind her car and shrieked, "What is that?"

Linus skidded to a stop and sat in front of Maria. Kat was impressed that in all the times she'd seen him meet people, he never managed to actually knock anyone over. He had amazing stopping skills, like a well-trained rodeo horse.

Kat smiled and said, "That's Linus. He's a dog."

"Are you sure he's really a dog? I didn't think they made them that big."

"Yes, I'm sure. How was your drive up here?"

Maria shrugged her shoulders. "What's with the people here? I'm driving through town and there's all these people waving at me. I didn't know what to do, so I waved back. I felt like I was in a parade. Now, I'm okay with that because you know I've always wanted to be the princess on the homecoming parade float. That's not going to happen at this late date. But I did get to do my best Princess Di wave. Maybe I can be elected Miss Alpine Grove. I need to get a homecoming king, though."

"You never know. It could happen. We can work on finding Prince Charming while you're here. But people are friendly here. And maybe they haven't seen a Miata in a while. There are a lot more pickup trucks here."

"I noticed that. Greta was intimidated by them. She's a sensitive automobile, you know."

"Well, we can give her a break while you're here. Put the top up and park her under that tree, so she can rest up for the drive back. We can take my car. It's already thrashed."

Maria moved her car off to the side of the driveway and she and Kat grabbed the matching purple luggage set from the trunk. As they walked up the stairs, Maria looked down. "What's with the shag carpet on the stairs?"

"I'm not sure," Kat said as she hoisted a large purple suitcase up the stairs. "Someone told me it might be there to make the stairs less slippery. The turquoise blue adds a certain focal point to the front entry I think. *Better Homes and Gardens* would be impressed."

Maria nodded. "Yeah, that's some serious curb appeal you have going on here."

As the pair walked in the door, Maria took a cautious sniff. "Hey, it doesn't stink! It even smells like you cleaned. Wow, you go, girl! Can you come to my apartment next?"

Kat giggled. "No way. I'm exhausted. I've never cleaned so hard in my life. I loved my aunt, but she was no housekeeper, that's for sure. I thought I was bad, but she wins the Golden Dust Bunny Award."

"You're a smart, independent, hot woman and you shouldn't have to clean toilets yourself. I want Rosie the Robot from the Jetsons. When are they going to come up with that?"

Kat shrugged. "I always wondered how Rosie cleaned bathrooms, actually. She's large and unwieldy. Cleaning bathrooms is a job that requires some flexibility. How would she get down into the bathtub?"

"Damn, I never thought of that. Good question. Maybe she had the tub and toilet attachment? So where do you want me to put my stuff?"

Kat nodded toward the living area. "The master bedroom is off to the left. You can have that. I'm going to sleep in one of the bedrooms downstairs. They still aren't really cleaned out and the dogs are down there, which I figured you wouldn't appreciate. I haven't had time to clear out those rooms yet. Have I mentioned that my aunt had a lot of stuff?"

"I like the log walls. It's like being in Davey Crockett's house. He was the King of the Wild Frontier, you know. It's like pioneer days!" Maria dragged one of her suitcases across the floor singing the TV show theme song as she moved toward the bedroom.

Kat followed her and reached around to open the door to the bedroom. "By the way, Murphee has been staying in here, so you have a roommate."

"Murph! How's my gender-identity-challenged cat?"

Murphee looked up from her spot precisely in the middle of the bed, where she was curled up in a tight ball. She stood up and stretched, reaching out her right front paw in greeting.

Maria sat down on the bed, and Murphee crawled into her lap, ready to resume her nap in a warmer spot.

"I'll let you get settled. I just need to grab a few things. The bathroom is right across the hall."

Maria looked up from petting Murphee. "So what's next? I want to go see this town with all the friendly people. I saw a lot of tractors. Maybe I can meet a sexy farmer."

"I've only been to one restaurant, but we can see if there is any place to meet people. I haven't really explored much."

"If there's a hot spot in this town, we'll find it."

Kat closed the door. Finding a hot spot in Alpine Grove might be a bit more challenging than Maria expected.

❦

Kat carried her clothes down the stairs and was greeted by the four-pack of dogs who had been reclining in the hallway. She opened the gate and navigated through the hairy group. Linus, Lori, and Chelsey milled around her, stretching and yawning. Even Tessa, who rarely seemed to sleep, stretched deeply before she began bouncing around. Clearly, the canines were enjoying another tough day.

Kat opened the door to one of the downstairs bedrooms and sighed. The walls had been painted a sickly light purple color and the floor had more of the ugly turquoise shag carpet that graced the front stairs. The room was filled with boxes and a twin bed covered with a purplish floral comforter. The color scheme and thick layer of dust gave the room a grisly, grayish cast. Kat was not looking forward to sleeping in here.

She closed the door, walked across the hall, opened another door, and considered the merits of the other bedroom. Although the walls weren't purplish, they were an equally revolting light baby blue. The room also sported more of the ugly blue shag on the floor. Abigail must have gotten that carpet remnant on fire sale. Like the other bedroom, this room contained vast amounts of stuff, but because it was a bit larger, it could accommodate a double bed, which made it less possible to cram as many boxes into the room. Kat decided this room was a marginally less creepy option than the first one and put her clothes down on the blue chenille bedspread.

The dogs followed her into the room and began giving it the olfactory once-over. Tessa seemed to be almost hyperventilating on all the fascinating smells. What stories was the dog learning about Aunt Abigail from all the clutter that littered the room? After sucking up too much dust into her nostrils, Lori sneezed loudly and shook her head, flapping her ears.

"Sorry, Lori. I probably should have tried to dust a little before you all came in here."

Lori wagged her tail and resumed her sniffing, undeterred from her quest to learn more about the room.

Maria called from the top of the stairs "What are you doing down there?"

"Sniffing mostly."

At the sound of Maria's footsteps on the stairs, the dogs bounded out of the bedroom to greet her.

"Hey, it's the giant hairy thing again! Why is the redhead dog leaping around like that? Does it have a problem?"

Kat walked out of the bedroom. "The redhead is Tessa. Be glad she's just jumping *near* you and not jumping *on* you. Believe me, it's an improvement. The hairy thing is Linus. He's a very sweet boy." Linus wagged his tail slowly as if to emphasize the point.

Maria pulled her hands up toward her chest to get them away from the many wet canine noses that surrounded her. "I didn't think you even liked dogs."

Kat shrugged. "I never really had the opportunity to find out. My mom is the biggest neatnik you'll ever meet. She makes Felix Unger look like a pig. Never in her worst nightmares would she allow something with fur into her pristine house."

Maria walked into the bedroom and looked around. "What's in all these boxes?"

"I have no idea. I've been cleaning upstairs and haven't been down here much, except to feed the dogs. The bedrooms have been closed off to keep the dogs from getting into all the stuff in here."

Bending over a large box, Maria exclaimed, "Hey, this one says photos! We have to check it out. I love looking at pictures of people I don't know."

"I might know some people, I suppose. At least my aunt."

Maria grabbed a photo album out of the box and sat down on the end of the bed. Kat sat down next to her and watched as Maria opened the quilted orange-polka-dot cover. The first page had a note that said, "To Abigail with love from Kelly." Kat squinted at the text. Who was Kelly and why had she made the album for Abigail?

Maria burst out laughing at a photograph of an older woman standing next to a well-built, tanned, and darkly handsome shirtless young man. She pointed at the flower lei around the older woman's neck. "Hey, look! This old lady got leid! Do you know who this is?"

Kat bent over the photo to get a closer look. "I think that's my grandmother. She was Abigail's sister. It's hard to imagine her cutting loose with a sexy guy in Hawaii. My mom may be uptight, but my grandmother makes my mother seem like a wild, free spirit. We've never really gotten along that well. Every time I've visited her, she makes sure to let me know how much of a disappointment I am."

"Have I mentioned lately that your family really needs to lighten up?"

"Yeah, I know. What can I say? I've always been the weird one."

Maria turned the page on the photo album. "Hey, check this out. Somebody has been chopped out of these photos."

"That's probably the Lumberjack. My aunt was married to him and the story is that it ended badly. He ran off. No one knows where he went. He could be dead for all I know."

"Look at this one! Instead of using scissors, she used Wite-Out to remove him from the convertible. That's pretty creative. And sorta creepy. It looks like Casper the Ghost threw up all over that fine '65 Mustang."

Kat giggled. "Like I said, from what I heard, the thing with the Lumberjack didn't end well. You know what they say about a woman scorned. The impression I got was that the demise of that marriage wasn't pretty."

Flipping to the next page, Maria said, "Who is this person?"

Kat looked at the photo, which showed two women and a girl standing in front of a garden holding hands. On the left, a much younger version of the Abigail Kat remembered stood next to a little girl who appeared to be about seven or eight years old. Another woman about Abigail's age stood to the right of the little girl. The year 1960 was imprinted along the rippled edge of the photo.

"I think that's my aunt. I'm not sure who the girl or the other woman is. She looks kind of familiar, though. I wonder if I met her when she was older."

"Well, it looks like they were friends."

Kat squinted at the creased black and white photo. "Oh my God, I think that's Louise. She sure looked different."

"Those bouffant hairdos made everyone look like Doris Day. You can't even tell women apart in those old movies."

Kat looked up and smiled at Maria. "You'll be happy to hear that Louise has changed her hair. It's blue now. And she worries about it a lot too. When I saw her, she was fretting about her hair appointment. I'm guessing the Alpine Grove beauty salon is where you can get all the dirt in this town. Louise certainly seems to, anyway."

"Well, I don't want blue old-lady hair, so I'm not going to that place, no matter how good the rumor mill action is." Maria closed the album with a thump. "We should get ready to hit the town. I'm not here for very long and there could be hot men out there that need to get a glimpse of me. I need to go upstairs and get changed. I have to figure out which one of my outfits would be the best one to wow a farmer."

Kat was less optimistic about Maria's chances for romantic encounters during her visit. Given the men she'd observed so far in Alpine Grove, Maria would be doing well if she found a guy who still had all his teeth.

~

After taking the dogs out for their afternoon walk, Kat changed into the sundress and strappy sandals that she hadn't worn since her first visit to Chez Stinky. It was nice to dress up again after so many days of wearing her grubby cleaning garb.

Maria emerged from the bedroom wearing a skin-tight red v-neck dress that left no curve unattended on her well-rounded form. The little red handbag she clutched in her left hand matched the color of the nail polish on her fingernails and toenails, which peeked out through the front of her four-inch heels.

Kat raised her eyebrows. "Wow. You're ready for action. I feel like Mary Ann to your Ginger. I think Gilligan is going to throw me off the island."

Maria ran her hand across the front of her red dress, trying to smooth out some puckers in the stretchy fabric. "I just hope I don't need to pee. I'm wearing a foundation garment and it's complicated. It takes a lot of work to look this good."

"You mean a girdle?"

Maria gasped. "No! Girdles are for old ladies. A foundation garment is what gives me this fine, smooth look."

"Isn't that what a girdle does?"

"Maybe. The lady at Victoria's Secret says this is different. It's got miracle fabrics. Old lady girdles don't have miracle fabrics."

"I suppose that could be true. Are you ready to go?"

"You know it. I was born ready. And I brought music to put us in the right mood."

After they got into Kat's Toyota, Maria pulled out a CD case and put the CD into the player with a flourish. As the car bumped down the driveway, the music informed them that the two women needed to pull out their umbrellas because it was raining men.

Kat looked over at Maria. "Really? The Weather Girls? Way to have an '80s flashback."

"It's all about your attitude."

The CD skipped and got stuck on the chorus. Hearing that it was raining men on droning repeat seemed a little ghoulish so Kat popped out the CD. "Let's wait until we get on the pavement."

"Yeah, there's a fine line between rain and a flood. Maybe I'll bring another CD next time."

As they approached the main street in Alpine Grove, Kat considered their options. Nightlife and Alpine Grove were words that were not often used in tandem. She'd noticed a bar called the 311. That seemed like a decent place to start.

Maria got out of the car and yanked on the hem of her dress to pull it back down where it was supposed to be. "We need to go someplace where I can stand or lean on something. I need to pose gracefully. Sitting causes issues with my dress."

"There's a bar down here. I've never been to it, so I don't know what the seating situation is there."

"Lead on."

The two women entered the 311 through a heavy wooden door. Kat peered into the dark smoky room. The 311 had all the hallmarks of the quintessential dive bar, complete with dirty wooden floors and paneling. Country music wailed from the jukebox and a few people were sitting at the dark smoke-infused wooden tables, nursing bottles of beer. Kat and Maria walked up to the bar, and Maria hoisted herself up to partially sit and partially lean on one of the Naugahyde bar stools. Her dress mostly stayed down, although the rest of the bar did get a good look at one of Maria's ample thighs.

The smell of smoke permeated the place and Kat coughed, which helped to get the bartender's attention. He walked over to them.

"What can I get you ladies?"

Maria said, "I'll have a sex on the beach."

"Excuse me?"

Maria yelled a bit louder, "Sex on the beach!"

"Are you saying you want sex? Or a drink?"

The music from the jukebox stopped and Maria said forcefully, "I want a sex on the beach!"

Most of the patrons of the 311 looked over at the bar. Someone in the crowd whistled and shouted out, "Me too!" Maria looked over her shoulder. "It's a drink, people! What is wrong with you? Get your mind out of the gutter."

The bartender looked slightly flustered and said, "I usually just pour beer. I'm not sure how to make that. What's in it?"

Maria gave him a stern look. "What kind of bartender are you? It's got cranberry juice, pineapple juice, peach schnapps and vodka."

"Um, I think we have orange juice. What's a schnapps?"

"Fine. I'll have a screwdriver then." The bartender looked blankly at her. "It's orange juice and vodka."

"Okay. Coming right up." He looked at Kat. "Anything for you?"

"No thanks. I'm the designated driver." She pointed her thumb at Maria. "She's the designated drinker."

"I'll be right back."

Maria readjusted her skirt, which was again trying to crawl up her leg. She gave up on the idea of leaning and pulled herself up so she was sitting completely on the barstool with her legs crossed at the ankles. "Why do they make these things for people who are seven feet tall?"

Kat looked over toward Maria. Behind her, Larry Lowell was heading toward them through the smoky haze. His eyes were locked on Maria, and he was obviously quite impressed with the red dress and Maria's shapely form. Kat waved slightly at him. The poor guy was almost drooling.

Larry stood next to Kat's bar stool, and Kat waved toward Maria. "Larry, this is my friend Maria. She works with me and is visiting for the weekend. Maria, this is Larry Lowell. He's the lawyer that's handling my aunt's estate."

Larry stood in silence for a moment, staring at Maria. He suddenly jerked out his hand and blurted out, "Hi, I'm Larry."

Maria smiled demurely, took his hand and shook it gently. "So I heard. Why don't you sit down?" Larry nodded and pulled up a barstool next to Maria.

The bartender stopped by with Maria's drink. She picked it up and looked over the glass at Larry. "Do you know if there are any places around here where you can get a drink that has something other than orange juice in it?"

Larry looked dumbfounded by the question for a moment, then said, "There's another bar down the street. I can show you. We can walk."

Kat rolled her eyes and listened as Larry made small talk about the weather with Maria. This was going to be one long evening. So much for sexy farmers. One boring lawyer seemed to be the best they could do.

After Maria finished her drink, true to his word, Larry led them down the street to another bar, which had a sign above it with old wooden letters that read "Mystic Moon Soloan." Although both bars were on the main street, few people were out and the one traffic light in town had been turned off for the evening. The flashing red light gave the street a sort of eerie glow. All the little storefronts were dark and the only people out were a small group of high-school students clustered around a No Parking sign, enjoying a clandestine cigarette break.

Maria, Larry, and Kat stood outside the bar, each silently evaluating whether or not to enter the establishment. Kat looked over at Larry. "Mystic Moon Soloan? Okay, I give. What's a soloan?"

Larry shrugged. "It's supposed to be saloon. The story goes that the guys who made the sign had a few too many beers and mixed up the letters. No one ever got around to fixing it. If you walk around to the other side, it's spelled correctly there."

Kat and Maria walked down the street past the door to look at the other side of the sign. Sure enough, Larry was right. Spelling obviously wasn't a big priority in Alpine Grove.

The trio walked into the bar. Like the 311, it was dark, but the Mystic Moon seemed smaller, older, and shabbier, which was quite an accomplishment given the ambiance of the 311. The dark walls had an impressive collection of mirrored beer signs. An antique neon Schlitz sign flickered over the mirrored bar.

Several grizzled-looking older men sat at the bar, hunched over their beer glasses. In the back of the room, a burly man in a leather vest leaned over a pool table, preparing to take a shot. There was no music; just a general mumbling hum of conversation interspersed with the occasional clacking sound of pool balls crashing into each other.

Larry looked over at Kat. "This place has a group of regulars who spend a lot of time here. I don't come here often."

Kat glanced at Maria, who had a frown on her face. "I'm not sure about this place. I'm happy to leave if you are."

Maria nodded. "There is not one sexy farmer here. Those guys might have farms, but there's no way I'd get on one of their tractors."

The trio turned around and went back outside. Standing below the Soloan sign, they looked up the street.

"Okay Larry, you're the local. Do you have any other ideas?" Kat asked.

Larry shook his head. "I should go home. I have an early appointment tomorrow. Maria, it was a pleasure meeting you. I hope I see you again before you return to the city." He reached out to shake her hand, but brought it up to his lips instead.

When he released her, Maria flipped her dark curls back with her hand. "It was nice meeting you, too."

Larry walked around the building and disappeared into the night, leaving the two women alone again on the empty street. Kat looked at Maria. "I think he liked you."

"What's not to like? I'm totally hot in this dress. And I didn't see many women in either of those bars. What's the deal? Don't they have females here?"

"I haven't been out much at night. Maybe there's some place that's not so filthy. Larry took me to an Italian restaurant that is nice. I don't think you'd be able to pick up a sexy farmer there, but we could get something to eat."

"Italian? I love Italian! It's my heritage. Let's hit it, girlfriend. I'll work on the sexy farmer program tomorrow."

~

While she was lying in bed the next morning, something poked Kat in the back. She rolled over and found herself face-to-face with Linus's large black nose. Perhaps it was time for breakfast. Sleeping upstairs in the dog-free area had advantages beyond the reduced dust level. Kat sneezed, which startled the big dog, who sat down with a thump next to one of the boxes.

Kat pushed the blue bedspread down and sat up. "Good morning to you too, Linus." The dog wagged his tail slowly and then sank to the floor with a sigh. He gave Kat a forlorn look and put his head between his paws. Clearly, the human was not making motions toward getting out of bed and providing food.

Kat reached down and picked up the photo album she and Maria had been looking at the day before. After they got home from dinner, Kat had gone through the other photos, which were a chronology of the little girl's childhood through adolescence. Kat leafed through the photographs again, wondering if the girl was Louise's daughter. Clearly, they were good friends with Abigail and had spent a lot of time together over the years.

One photo that had obviously been taken after an Alpine Grove Frontier Days parade particularly amused Kat. It was another posed photo with Abigail, Louise, and the little girl, but for some reason they were wearing grotesquely ugly matching turquoise pantsuits that had been adorned with glittery silver studs. The image was emblematic of the worst of 1960s fashion and the little girl was obviously unhappy to be seen looking like a rhinestone cowgirl.

The dejected expression on the girl's face reminded Kat of herself in family photos of her with her sisters. It was like the Sesame Street song that proclaimed "one of these things is not like the other." She was always the weird one. But that feeling was probably because she didn't get along with her mother particularly well. Maybe she could call her mother and find out if she knew who the little girl in the photo was. Or not. It might be better to just feed the dogs and forget about it. Listening to her mother's disapproving voice this early in the morning didn't have much appeal. Besides, her mother was probably working on her morning vacuuming project and wouldn't hear the phone anyway.

Kat got out of bed and Linus leaped up with glee, shaking his head, flapping his ears, and cavorting around the room. "Yes, Big Guy, I'm really going to feed you now. Thanks for being patient." Linus scampered out of the room, presumably to share the good news with the other canines in the pack.

After a joy-filled breakfast, the dogs settled down for their post-feeding nap. Kat sat at the kitchen table holding her coffee mug in her hands. She knew that Maria liked to sleep late, so she had some time to call her mother now. Her curiosity about the little girl in the photographs trumped her dread of talking to her mother. Kat picked up the phone and dialed the familiar number. She recognized her sister Kim's voice greeting her.

"Hi Kim. It's Kat. How are you? I didn't know you were at the house."

"Yes, I have an audition early in the morning, so I decided to spend the weekend here. And Rick and I had a fight, so I left." Kat could imagine Kim sticking out her lower lip in a pout. Kim's on-again, off-again relationship with Rick generally moved to the off-again setting after she rediscovered his unauthorized activities with other women.

"Another fight?"

"Yes. I'm leaving him for good this time. I just need to get this commercial and then I'll have enough money to move out."

Kat doubted that would happen, but her sister's optimism (or delusion) would probably help for her audition. As far as Kat knew, Kim had never gotten a paid acting job in her life. "How is the job at the cafe going?"

"Well, you know it's temporary. And yesterday I saw a director there. You know all the studio guys hang out at the cafe. Well, maybe the guy I saw was actually an assistant director. Or maybe he said he was the guy who loads the film in the camera. I'm not sure. I'm sure he's important."

Kat rolled her eyes. Kim thought everyone was important with a capital I. "Is mother around? I need to ask her something."

"She's vacuuming. Hold on."

The sound of the phone thunking on the counter came through the receiver. Kat heard her sister yelling at her mother over the noise of a vacuum cleaner. A few moments later, her mother's voice came on the line.

"Katherine? Is something wrong?"

"No. Everything is fine. Can't I just call when everything is fine?"

"I'm just checking, dear. What is it? I'm vacuuming."

Interrupting vacuuming was invariably a major issue for her mother, but Kat pressed on. "I am in Alpine Grove, and I have a question."

"Alpine Grove? Why on earth would you be there, dear?

"You know I inherited Great-Aunt Abigail's house, right?"

"Good heavens. No one told me. Abigail is dead? That's too bad."

Given the tone in her voice, her mother didn't seem terribly broken up about Abigail's demise. "Yes, I've been here for the last week or so, cleaning up the house."

"You cleaned? Will wonders never cease!"

"Yes, it has been known to happen, although I'm sure it's not up to your antiseptic standards. I need to do a few repairs to the house, as well. But that's not why I'm calling. I found some photographs. Do you know Louise Johnson? She was a friend of Aunt Abigail's."

The long silence on the line was oddly awkward. Finally her mother said, "Yes, I met Louise a long time ago."

"Do you know if she had a daughter? I found a lot of photographs of a little girl and I was wondering who she is."

Kat's mother paused again before answering. "Louise might have had a daughter. I wouldn't bother worrying about it, though. I think the little girl may have died, and Louise might not want to talk about it."

Kat raised her eyebrows. "Really?"

"Why don't you just forget about all this? Alpine Grove isn't where you should be, anyway. You are a city girl with a nice apartment. What about your job? What is it you do again? Something with computers?"

"Yes, mother. I'm a technical writer. As I have been for a number of years now. But I like Alpine Grove. And Abigail wanted me to take care of her pets. I found out that I like dogs."

"That's nice, dear. But they must shed so much fur! How could you ever keep the place clean? That reminds me. I really should get back to my vacuuming now. The Carrharts are coming over, and I still have some dusting to do as well."

As Kat hung up the phone, she could envision the pinched look on her mother's face as she contemplated the diabolical nature of dust.

Conversations with her mother were not usually a lot of fun, but her mother had acted weird about Kat's visit to Alpine Grove. The question was why. Maybe her mother had a bad experience here. Or maybe she and Abigail had a fight. Or maybe her mother had a torrid affair. That seemed unlikely and definitely not something she wanted to think about. Yuck. Kat gave herself a mental head shake and as usual, tried to avoid dwelling on the fact that her mother seemed to like spending time with her vacuum cleaner more than with her daughter.

~

Having discovered first-hand that the nightlife in Alpine Grove was limited, Kat convinced Maria that staying in that evening might be a better option. But they needed provisions. At the local Save-a-Lot, Kat pushed the grocery cart as Maria scanned the shelves for the evening's Wine and Whine session.

Maria rummaged through the depths of the dairy case. "Do you have cheese at home? I want some cheese." Successful in her quest, Maria held a wedge of Parmesan in front of Kat. "I love cheese, but yeesh this grocery store is cold. I'm getting chills."

Kat raised her eyebrows. "Are they multiplying?"

Maria swayed her hips and said in a sing-song voice, "I'm looosing control."

"I think the power you're supplying...it's rather electrifying."

Overcome with a nostalgic high-school musical moment, Maria grabbed a single Twinkie from the Hostess display and waved it around like a microphone. "Ooh, ooh, ooh. I neeed a man!"

Kat giggled and looked beyond Maria down the cereal aisle where Joel was standing, holding a box of corn flakes and smiling at Maria's impromptu snack-cake performance.

Kat raised her hand and with a somewhat sheepish smile waved at him. With an amused twinkle in his eye, Joel started walking toward her. A little twinge of excitement went down her spine as he strolled down the aisle past the Froot Loops display.

Maria concluded her musical performance and said, "I'm hungry. Don't they have samples at this store? I love samples. I could eat all my meals from the sample people. Sometimes they have those great mini-wiener dogs on toothpicks. All this healthy exercise and outdoor activity really works up an appetite. I don't know how you do all this dog-walking every day. You're going to become an athlete if you hang around here."

Earlier in the day, Maria had accompanied Kat on one of the dog walks. The excursion was cut short when one of Maria's heels got caught on a tree root. She tripped and landed on Linus, who had yelped in surprise, but handled having a human sprawled upon him with remarkable dignity.

With her eyes still on Joel, Kat said to Maria, "I'm just glad you're okay."

"Yeah, I like that big dog. He's soft and squishy. But you need to get a better lint brush. Like one of those industrial-strength ones. That little crappy thing you have barely makes a dent in the hair I got all over myself. I think that animal is doing his seasonal shedding thing. I don't know how one dog can hold that much fur."

"I've never seen an industrial-strength lint brush. If you find one, let me know."

"It's better spending time with the dogs outside because the breeze blows the hair off. Except outside there are the bugs, too. I hate bugs. Why are there so many bugs everywhere? I want to live in a place where bugs aren't allowed."

Kat nodded absently, gazing up at Joel, who was now standing quietly behind Maria, looking amused. "If you find that place, be sure to tell me. Any place with no mosquitoes gets my vote."

Catching a glimpse of her reflection in the chrome of the dairy case, Maria grimaced. "Yuck, my hair is really flat. What happened? Is there something in the air here? I need to fluff it up."

Maria doubled over to shake out her brown curls. "I really do have nice feet don't I? They look so cute in these little peek-a-boo pumps." When she stood up and flipped her hair back over her head, she turned around and found a tall man in front of her.

Maria put her hand on her hip. "So who are you and where were you the other night when the only people out on the town were creepy, toothless old dudes?"

Kat said, "Maria, this is Joel. I told you about him. He helped me get the cat out of the wall."

"Oh, yeah; you're the hero!"

Joel gave a half-smile and shrugged his shoulders. "I don't know about that. But I did get the cat out of the wall without hurting him."

"Maria is a friend of mine from work. She's up for the weekend. We're getting some stuff for dinner."

Joel surveyed the contents of the cart, which included a wide selection of items from the Hostess snack-cake rack, several types of cheese, potato chips, a jar of tomato sauce, spaghetti, and three bottles of wine. "It looks like you have quite an evening planned."

Maria said, "We're all about nutrition. Remember— Ronald Reagan said ketchup is a vegetable, so with the pasta sauce, we've got all the food groups covered."

Kat nodded. "Wine is made from grapes, so that's our fruit. And we have a few extras like Twinkies that defy classification. They are in a class by themselves."

Maria picked up her Twinkie again and pointed it at Joel. "And this individually wrapped Twinkie right here is mine because I'm starving."

Joel nodded and smiled politely. "I'll let you get back to it, then. It was nice to see you again, Kat."

Kat blushed. "Actually, I wanted to talk to you about the roof problem if you have time. Can I give you a call?"

"Sure. You have my number."

As Joel walked away toward the produce department, Maria turned to Kat and gave her an appraising look. "You seriously have the hots for him, don't you?"

"I do not! He was just nice about fixing stuff in the house. I told you I went out on a date with Larry, right?"

Maria poked her Twinkie toward Kat. "One date doesn't mean you're *dating* him. There's a difference. And you said it was horrible."

Kat cringed mentally at the memory. "Yes. It was. But Joel isn't my type. I'm pretty sure he thinks I'm weird."

Maria began unwrapping her Twinkie. "You are weird. But in a good way. That's why I like you."

That evening, Maria held her wine glass in front of her face and swirled the burgundy liquid within it. "We should have just gone to the grocery store to meet men in the first place. That's where the hot ones are. That Joel guy is beyond fine. And now we even have food, too. Whatever you're making over there smells fantastic."

"It's just spaghetti. After our dinner at the restaurant last night, I got inspired and even added some Italian spices." Kat stirred the deep red marinara sauce slowly, causing the scent of basil and oregano to waft around the room. She tasted the sauce and said, "So are you ready to go back to work? I know I'm not."

Maria shook her head. "Me neither. I think I need to find a job where my fabulousness is appreciated. I think Mark is off his meds again. He was acting more mental than usual before I left to come up here."

"More mental?"

"He had me set up an appointment with an image consultant. He wants to seem more loveable. I said to him that maybe if he were nicer to people, they'd like him better. I don't think he took the hint."

Kat smiled. "He told me he was taking gingko to get smarter. Maybe he's on a personal-improvement kick."

"I don't know. He's been going around the office complaining about people's shoes and what they are wearing. He told Anna that she needs to buy the expensive makeup from the mall, not the cheap stuff from the drug store that makes her look like a slut."

Kat raised her eyebrows. "A slut? He really said that?"

"I know! Who cares what we look like, anyway?" Maria waved her wine glass to emphasize her point. "No one actually sees us. The guys have to wear ties and suit jackets now and the women have to wear high heels. Now, you know I love my stilettos, but Jane isn't going to wear heels. She has that new hip and her legs aren't even the same length anymore. She's got those special shoes to even her out, so she doesn't tip over."

"Interesting. Did Jane talk to Mark about that?"

"We were chatting in the kitchen and I asked her exactly that the other day. She said she went to his office to explain she has to wear her shoes for medical reasons. He just blew her off. If she won't follow his instructions, she can find a new job. She was *not* happy about that, either. That woman is seriously pissed off. Like the 'I'm gonna get a lawyer' type of pissed off."

"If her shoes are related to her medical treatment, that has to be illegal, right?"

"Who knows? Maybe you can ask your lawyer friend we met…Larry. I hope she sticks it to Mark, though. And if anyone can, Jane can. That woman is such a stud-ette. I bet she didn't even need anesthesia when she got her new hip."

Kat smiled at the mental image of Jane waving away an anesthesiologist wearing medical scrubs "Yeah, there's no love between her and Mark. When I was in Mark's office one time, he referred to her as a fat cow and he never even said thank you for all that overtime she put in a few months ago. And remember when she went on vacation and he moved her office space to that tiny spot in the back? That was rude."

Maria sipped her wine and then tipped the top of the glass, pointing it toward Kat. "It takes some nerve to pack up someone's personal stuff like that. That guy just gets weirder all the time. I think we need an intervention or something."

"That's for people who drink or do drugs. I don't think an intervention fixes being a jerk."

"Maybe we can find a rehab for loser bosses."

Kat smirked and stood up. "Loser rehab would probably be full. This conversation is getting depressing. I need more wine. We both have to go back to that place all too soon."

~

The next morning, Maria pulled her Miata out from its spot under the tree. After lamenting the many pine needles, pitch, and bird droppings marring the car's formerly shiny red exterior, Maria loaded her suitcases into the trunk. Kat looked at the gray clouds above and took a deep breath. She had been blessed with perfect weather for her vacation in Alpine Grove, which had made it easy to ignore the roof problem. After Maria left, she needed to make some phone calls and see if she could find someone to fix it, since Bud was no longer a contender for her roofing business.

Maria stretched out her arms for a hug, "I'll see you at work! Behave yourself until then. Unless you see the cute guy from the grocery store again. Then all bets are off."

Kat grinned and hugged Maria tightly. "I'll try and be good. My only plan today is to find a roofer. It looks like it's going to rain."

"Maybe that will wash all the forest crap off of Greta. She doesn't like being dirty."

Maria crawled into the little red car and pulled it out into the driveway. Kat waved and shouted, "See you soon!" as the car pulled away.

Turning back to the house, she wrapped her arms around her waist and looked up at the roof. *Please remain in one piece and keep the rain out until I can find someone to fix you.*

After walking the dogs, Kat sat at the kitchen table leafing through the thin local Yellow Pages for roofers or building contractors. After leaving messages at Apex Roofing, Crane Brothers, and Ernie's Building Services, she was feeling discouraged. Apparently, the roofing contractors of Alpine Grove must be busy fixing things, because none of them answered the phone.

Kat looked up at the ceiling as the sound of water droplets began to make plinking noises on the metal roof. The pace of the raindrops increased. One of the dogs was marching back and forth downstairs in the basement. The claws clickety-clacked on the hard floor. She got up and looked down the stairs, "Everyone okay down there?"

With a worried expression on his face, Linus looked up the stairs at Kat. He turned around and returned to his pacing. Apparently, the big dog didn't like storms.

Lightning flashed and a huge rumble shook the house. Linus scuttled under Chelsey's table, crowding her over to one side. The smaller dog didn't seem particularly surprised by his behavior and graciously tried to give Linus some space to hide.

Kat wasn't fond of thunderstorms, either. Maybe Linus had the right idea. She began to head down the stairs. Out of the corner of her eye, she saw a water droplet fall from the ceiling. *Uh oh.*

Looking up, she examined the ceiling more closely. It was constructed with tongue-and-groove boards, and the water was dripping from one of the seams. Maybe there was a way to get up into the attic. Larry said that he and Bud had gone up there. But how? Wandering around the house looking up, she found an attic access hole in the front entry area. *How did Larry get up there?*

Kat dragged one of the kitchen chairs into the entryway and climbed up on it. By standing on her tiptoes, she was able to reach up and push aside the piece of wood covering the hole in the ceiling that provided access to the attic. She could barely muster one pull-up in gym class years ago and unless she magically turned into Wonder Woman in the next few minutes, she was not likely to be able to yank herself up through the hole into the attic. She jumped down from the chair and went outside into the rain to find a ladder.

In her quest, Kat was going to have to brave the barn or what she mentally thought of as the Giant Spider Breeding Ground. Standing outside in the downpour, she peered cautiously into the three-sided building, hoping the rain might have caused the spider population to hide or at least get a little sleepy. There didn't appear to be a ladder, but there was something that looked suspiciously like a huge black widow spider on the back wall.

She shuddered and backed away from the building. Then she turned around and went toward the Tessa Hut. She'd been in the outbuilding many times with Tessa and didn't remember seeing a ladder, but it didn't hurt to look again. Tessa had been spending time in the house, but her empty kennel reminded Kat of how much progress the spaz dog had made in the two weeks Kat had been at Chez Stinky. Tiring out Tessa by letting her run with Linus and being careful about touching Tessa only when she was calm had made a huge difference in the dog's behavior.

Looking around the building, no ladder was in evidence, so Kat walked back outside. Pausing for a moment, she walked around to the back of the building, where she discovered a six-foot step ladder that someone had leaned up against the back wall. Kat checked it for any spiders that might be hitching a ride. After determining that it was indeed arachnid-free, she hauled the ladder up the blue carpeted stairs into the house.

She set up the ladder, clambered up into the attic, and assessed the situation. The smell of warm, wet insulation and dust accosted her senses and she sneezed, which caused a small dust uprising. Amid the mouse droppings, pink pieces of fiberglass insulation, and other filth, Kat observed that water was dripping from the roof and forming puddles in various locations around the attic. The pools of water were then dripping through the cracks in the tongue-and-groove boards down into the house.

Kat scrambled back down the ladder and went into the kitchen. She opened the kitchen cabinets, looking for any container that could hold water and began tossing plastic storage containers onto the floor. Grabbing a stack of old ice cream tubs that her aunt had obviously been saving for decades, she charged back up the ladder.

She placed the plastic containers around the attic so that by the time she was done, it looked like a checkerboard of ice cream. Apparently, Abigail had a serious fondness for butter pecan.

Standing and surveying her handiwork, Kat knew that the ice cream containers were only a short-term solution to the much larger roof problem. With a sigh, she descended the ladder again back into the house. The noise of the raindrops falling into the plastic containers echoed above, creating a musical chorus of plinks, plunks, and splashes.

The steady red light on the answering machine indicated that none of the roofers had returned Kat's calls. She picked up the phone to call Cindy and remind her that Kat would need dog-walking help starting Wednesday, when she returned to work. Cindy's answering machine picked up and informed Kat that Cindy wasn't home, but "you know what to do." After clearing her throat Kat said, "This is Kat Stevens at Abigail's house. I'm calling to remind you that I'll be leaving tomorrow, and I'm hoping you'll be able to come out and walk dogs starting on Wednesday. I've had good luck walking Tessa, so if you could give me a call, I can explain what I'm doing."

Kat hung up the phone a little harder than necessary. *Didn't anyone in this town ever answer the phone?* The rainy weather didn't help her mood. The prospect of packing up Murphee and going back to work was dismal. Getting Murph into the cat carrier again would be a battle, and it sounded like Mark was even more nuts that usual. Plus, Chez Stinky might fall apart as soon as she left.

She debated calling Joel. On the one hand, she had warned him that she might call for recommendations about the roof. On the other hand, she only called him when she had a problem. And somehow he only managed to see her at her most embarrassing and unattractive moments. What was she going to say? "Hi Joel, the roof might cave in. But I have set out 400 ice cream containers in the attic to capture the water before it all comes crashing down." The sad truth was that she didn't know many people in Alpine Grove and time was running out before she had to go back to work. Risking the house or its many furry inhabitants was not an option. Time to set aside her mortification, suck it up, and call.

Kat was surprised to find that unlike the rest of the inhabitants of the town, Joel answered his phone. "This is Kat," she stammered. "Remember how I said I was going to ask you about roofers? Well, I really need one."

Joel paused for a second. "I guess you found a leak when it started raining?"

"It's way more than one leak. It's a lot of leaks. I'm not sure what to do. I have to drive back home so I can go back to work. All I know is that I can't leave the house like this, and Bud is not competent to fix anything. Oh, and roofers in Alpine Grove don't answer the phone."

"I heard about Bud when I was working on my place, too. It's a small town."

Kat was relieved that at least Joel sounded sympathetic, anyway. "I know you don't know me very well and I sound like a whiny girl, but what should I do? I'm worried this place is going to disintegrate before I can get it fixed. What if it falls on the dogs or the cats? What if they get hurt? I'd never forgive myself if something happened to them."

Kat was a little worried that Joel would notice the twinge of panic in her voice, but he responded with equanimity. "I guess you like your aunt's pets better now."

"Yes!" Kat blurted out. "I hate leaving them. It has been a great vacation, even with the plumbing problem and the cat in the wall and all the cleaning. I love Linus and the dogs and even the cats I hardly ever see. It's weird; I feel better here than I have anywhere else."

Joel chuckled. "Yeah, Alpine Grove is like that. This place grows on you. Even with some of the downsides of living here, something about the quiet and the trees seeps into your soul."

"You're the first person I've talked to who understands that. My mother thinks there's something wrong with me. That I don't belong here. I guess to be fair, I did too at first. But now I think she's wrong. I've always been the black sheep...well maybe not black, but maybe the dark gray sheep of the family, so it wouldn't be a surprise."

Joel laughed. "The dark gray sheep? I like that. And I've felt that way too, although not with my family, since I don't have much family to worry about."

"Lucky you. I'm so different from my sisters. It's hard to explain. My older sister Karen is Miss Responsible. She's like my mom in a lot of ways, always wanting to take care of things. In fact, when we were little she was always hovering over me and telling me what to do. I had to run away to my room to get away from her. She made up an imaginary friend, so she'd have someone to boss around. And I'd like to point out that sometimes friends should just remain imaginary."

"Oh really?"

Kat shook her head. "You don't want to know. Then there's my little sister Kim. She has always been the Pretty One. On the wall at home, my mom has a photograph of her in a purple spandex baton-twirler outfit. That's Kim in a nutshell right there."

"So where does that leave you?"

"Well, I can tell you I sure wasn't the responsible one. Or the pretty one. I tried doing everything right. I really did! But I still got into trouble a lot. I'd go off and climb a tree somewhere to read a book and then people would freak out when they couldn't find me."

"I don't know you well enough to know if you're responsible, but I think you're underestimating the pretty part."

Kat sat in stunned silence for a moment. "Thank you. But believe me, if I were standing next to Kim, you'd be looking at her. She has…attributes…that men tend to notice."

"I can imagine. Anyway, I can call a couple of my neighbors and see if we can get a tarp up on your roof to keep the rain out until you can get it fixed. I'll give you the name of the guy who worked on my place, too. The rain is supposed to let up this afternoon and that will give me time to make a few calls."

"I don't know how I can ever thank you enough. You've been so nice since I got here." Feeling overwhelmed, Kat tried to keep the sound of the tears of relief out of her voice. "I'll be back up here next weekend. Can I buy you dinner or something? I really owe you."

"We can talk about that when I get there."

After she hung up, Kat sat at the table reflecting on the conversation. Considering she wasn't generally terribly talkative with most people, something about Joel seemed to bring out her inner chatterbox. And guys she thought were cute *never* said she was pretty. She smiled as a little thrill of excitement rippled through her at the thought of seeing him later.

Chapter 6

The Tarping

Later that afternoon the rain had stopped, but it was still gray and dreary outside. Linus barked downstairs and then launched out the doggie door as several old pickup trucks pulled into the driveway. Kat walked down the front stairs to meet the 'tarp guys' Joel had recruited.

Joel was bending over petting Linus, who obviously was delighting in all the attention. Joel looked over and smiled at Kat. The color rose in her cheeks and she said, "Thank you all for coming out here on this lovely afternoon."

Joel pointed at the three men in flannel shirts who were standing in a semi-circle around Linus and Lori, who had joined in the canine celebration of visitors. "These are my neighbors." He pointed, "That's Cliff over there, Ron, and Joe." The three men nodded in acknowledgment.

Cliff said, "Well, we need to get going if we want to get this tarp on there before sunset." The three men then turned back to their trucks to gather materials.

Kat turned to Joel, "Should I just get out of the way? They look like they are on a mission."

Joel smiled, "That's probably wise. If you have a six-pack to give them when we're done, that wouldn't be a bad idea."

"No worries. I'm prepared. When Maria and I went to the grocery store, she picked up beer along with the wine. I don't like beer, but she wanted some just in case she got in a 'beer mood.' I'm not sure what a beer mood is, but she didn't get one, so I have a lot of extra beer now."

Kat went inside and curled up on the sofa with a novel, trying not to think about the various ominous thumping noises on the roof and the male voices shouting from outside. Later, an old truck engine coughed and sputtered as it started up. Jumping up from the couch, she grabbed the beer from the fridge and went back outside.

She scampered down the stairs and saw Joel talking to Cliff. She ran over to them, holding out the beer. "Can I offer you some beer as thanks for helping me?"

Cliff smiled through his gray beard and said, "That's nice of you. The guys and I are going to head over to my house to watch the game." He took the six-pack from Kat. "It was good to meet you. The game is gonna start soon and Ron and Joe are headed out; I'll give them your regards."

"Thanks again. I'm grateful to all of you."

Cliff tucked the six-pack under his arm and walked over to his truck. Joel turned toward Kat. "I should get going, too."

Kat bowed her head and studied her hands. "Do you have to? You didn't take me up on dinner last time when you got Tripod out of the wall." She looked up into his green eyes. "I really owe you dinner now, and I'm not a terrible cook. I promise! It's the least I can do after dragging you and half your neighborhood out here."

Joel smiled. "I believe you. I'm all muddy now, though. And I have to feed my dog or she'll be upset."

"I know how that goes. Does your dog like playing with other dogs? You can bring him…or her…with you."

"Lady loves everybody. Sure, I'll feed her, load her up, and we'll be back in a few minutes."

As Joel left, Kat went back inside and stood in front of the open refrigerator. The empty shelves didn't offer much inspiration. She still had a lot of Twinkies left over from Maria's visit, but they probably weren't a good option for dinner.

By the time Joel's truck rumbled back into the driveway later, Kat had sauce simmering on the stove. Fortunately, Maria tended to buy in volume and there was still a lot of pasta in the house. Joel didn't know (or need to know) that she'd been eating Italian food for days.

Linus and Lori woofed from downstairs and ran outside to confront the interloper. As Kat went down the front stairs, she found herself studying Joel as he greeted the dogs. Next to the driveway, Linus and Lori were wagging and sniffing a pretty brown and black dog who seemed to be a mix of collie and German shepherd. "I guess this must be Lady?" she said as she reached out her hand so the dog could sniff her.

Joel glanced up from the swirling group of canines and looked at Kat. He pointed at Lady. "Lady, sit and say hello." Lady sat in front of Kat and proffered her right paw. Kat bent down to shake it. "Aren't you a sweet girl?"

She looked up from Lady to Joel. "What a well-behaved dog. I'm impressed. Would you like to go for a walk with the dogs before dinner? The weather has cleared off for the moment."

Joel nodded and they walked around to the back of the house to collect the other two dogs. Kat said, "I have an unusual arrangement for walking Tessa. Linus actually does all the work. The main thing to remember is to always keep the dogs in front of you and pay attention to where the leash is in relation to your legs. You don't want to get clotheslined."

"Clotheslined?"

"You'll see."

Kat harnessed the dogs and explained to Joel that weighing down the hyperactive dog and giving her lots of exercise had made Tessa much easier to live with. "She's actually a good dog now."

They walked outside and Kat let go of the leash between Linus and Tessa. The pair took off toward the forest trail as Kat and Joel walked behind them with Chelsey quietly strolling next to Kat. Lady and Lori scampered around them, romping and playing. It looked like they were forming the beginnings of a great canine friendship.

"Those two certainly seem to like each other," Kat observed.

"Lady doesn't get to play with other dogs much anymore. She used to get to play more often before we moved up here. I'm sure she misses romping with playmates."

The scent of crushed pine needles rose up from the forest floor as Kat's sneakers crunched along the trail. So why did Joel live in Alpine Grove, anyway? "Having friends to hang out with is always a good thing. Did she have lots of doggie friends where you used to live?"

"My girlfriend had a dog who was Lady's best buddy. I know Lady misses her." Joel looked up at the trees along the trail. "It's certainly beautiful here. Your aunt found a pretty patch of forest. There's a lot of diversity in the tree species, which is unusual for this area."

Kat mentally filed the "girlfriend" reference. Joel had a remarkable knack for changing the subject, but he wasn't going to get away with it forever. For the time being, she replied. "I don't know about the species of trees, but I love going for dog walks here. The dogs are so happy. Look at them run through the forest. It's just pure joy. It's going to be hard to go back to work. There is no joy in cubicles."

Joel laughed, "That's for sure. I think the cubicles and flickering fluorescent lights suck the joy out of most offices."

"So is that why you're here? To get away from Cubicle America? Or does it have to do with your girlfriend? I'm guessing she's not up here if Lady misses her…or her dog?"

"It's a long story, but suffice it to say, it didn't work out. Then I lost my job and moved up here."

Kat looked over at him. "But why Alpine Grove?"

"Well, I had a little cabin here that I bought as a weekend getaway place after my sister moved here. The house is basically one room and a bathroom. It's the type of place the real estate listings call a hunting cabin and that most other people would call a shack. But it's got a roof and it's paid for. Plus after things got weird with Allison, I wanted to get away and clear my head. I gave up my apartment, sold most of my stuff, and here we are. Lady loves it up here. As you can see."

Kat looked in the direction Joel had pointed. Lady and Lori were panting and wagging as they chased each other around a particularly large Ponderosa pine. She said, "I love how they are able to play with Tessa and Linus without getting tangled up in the leash. Dogs are smarter than we give them credit for, I think."

Kat didn't have the nerve to ask about the mysterious Allison yet, so she settled for a more innocuous work-related question, "Do you miss your job?"

"I did at first. I've been working since I was 15. It felt weird to not go to work every day. After a while, I relaxed and spent some time fixing up my place, which did need work. Now that's done and I'm starting to get a little bored. But I'm not sure I want to go back to a full-time engineering job again. I don't miss commuting, and I like the quiet. I've been thinking of doing some type of computer-related work from here, but I'm not sure what yet. I suppose that doesn't sound particularly impressive."

Kat smiled. "I can tell you my mother wouldn't be impressed. She's all about the Puritan Work Ethic. And a steady paycheck. You're a little young to have a mid-life crisis, but I understand. I was going along with my life on autopilot. Then everything changed the day I got the call from the lawyer about Chez Stinky."

Joel chuckled and gave her a sidelong glance. "Chez Stinky?"

"When I first got here, the place smelled incredibly bad because of the varmint Bud removed from the wall. When I was talking to Maria, the name just slipped out of my subconscious, I guess. Then it kind of stuck."

"You have an unusual sense of humor."

"I know. I can't help it. Most people don't get it and think I'm strange. But I did have a point. What I meant was that I understand how you feel. I have to go back to work, and I'm not sure I want to. It's weird."

Joel smiled. "You're a little young for a mid-life crisis, too."

"I guess we're just a pair of slackers with no direction. I can feel my mother frowning disapprovingly at me out there somewhere. But right now, I'm a hungry slacker. Let's go back and eat." Kat turned around with Chelsey and called the dogs. "Come on guys, it's dinner time!" Linus spun around and dragged Tessa back with him.

Kat said, "Watch out!" and smiled as Joel deftly dodged the canine onslaught racing toward the house.

⁓

After feeding the dogs, Kat cooked the pasta, and she and Joel finally sat down to dinner.

Joel looked up from his plate. "This is good. I saw all the pasta in your cart at the store. You must like it a lot."

"Maria is what you might call a power shopper. When you go to the grocery store with her, she has a tendency to throw things into the cart when you're not paying attention. When we checked out, I discovered I had six boxes of pasta. I think it was the most expensive trip to the grocery store I've made in five years. We also have Twinkies for dessert, if you're interested."

"I think I'll pass."

"Apparently, they last for centuries. Just let me know if you ever want one. They'll be here unless Maria visits again."

A loud crash and yowling noise came from downstairs. Kat and Joel jumped up from the table simultaneously and ran to the top of the stairs. Dolly Mae scrambled up and over the gate below and shot up the staircase. The orange blur whizzed between Kat and Joel, who both turned and watched as the cat dashed around the perimeter of the living room once, then disappeared under the sofa.

Kat crouched down and peeked underneath the couch. Dolly Mae's yellow eyes glared back at her accusingly. Kat sat back on her heels and looked up at Joel. "Do you have any idea what happened?"

Joel shrugged his shoulders. "I'm not sure, but Lady likes to chase cats. I didn't know there was a cat downstairs."

Kat frowned. "I wonder where Tripod is. And what that crashing noise was."

Dolly Mae obviously wasn't coming out of her hiding place any time soon, so Kat and Joel went downstairs to investigate the damage.

Tessa was galloping around the basement hallway, reveling in the noise and excitement. Chelsey was hiding under her table, and Linus had a worried look on his face. The two "good dogs," Lori and Lady, looked suspiciously pleased with themselves. Kat gave Lori a stern look. "Did you do something bad?" The dog averted her eyes, dropped her head, and looked guilty.

Joel said to Lady, "Did you find a cat?" Lady wagged and sat down. He sighed. "I guess you did." He looked over at Kat. "I hope you didn't like that pitcher on the dresser in the bedroom over there. It's now in about 2,000 pieces."

"I guess I forgot to close the door to the bedroom. Oh well. I'll go get a broom."

Joel wandered around the bedroom picking up some of the larger pieces of the pitcher as Kat swept up the many shards of porcelain. "I guess Lady hasn't been around cats before?"

"No, except to chase them. I think she considers them fat squirrels."

"My cat Murphee isn't fond of Dolly Mae, either. That poor cat always seems to be in the wrong place at the wrong time. Larry tripped over her the first time I came out here.

Louie just kind of hangs out, but Dolly Mae is a bit of a problem child."

"You have a cat, too?"

"Yes, I know it's a cliché to be the single cat lady, but I am. I found my cat Murphee next to a Dumpster near my apartment. She's a wonderful cat, although she's still adjusting to living here with the other felines."

"I'll take your word for it. I'm not really a cat person. I'm allergic to them."

"Allergic? You're not going to turn purple or explode, are you? You were pretty close to Tripod when you removed him from the wall."

"It's usually not a problem, as long as I don't touch my eyes after petting a cat. No exploding."

The couple went upstairs in silence. Kat was digesting the information Joel had shared. He and his dog both had issues with cats. She wasn't kidding when she said she was a cat lady. Who didn't like cats? That was just wrong.

As they sat down at the table to finish their food, Kat moved back into nosy mode. "So I guess your girlfriend doesn't have a cat. Just a dog?"

"No, no cats. She really is allergic. She doesn't quite turn purple, but she sneezes a lot as soon as she walks into a house with cats. She doesn't like cats at all."

"Which means that every cat she meets sits on her lap."

Joel smiled, "Yes, usually."

Kat took a deep breath and decided to confront the large pachyderm in the room. "So where is your girlfriend? Is she still in the city?"

"Yes, Allison is still there." Joel looked uncomfortable at the turn the conversation had taken, but Kat continued to gaze at him intently, mentally willing him to elaborate.

He seemed to have clammed up again, so she persevered. "So when you moved here, she didn't?"

"Yes. It was complicated. And for the record, I'm not sure if she's my girlfriend or ex-girlfriend."

Kat raised her eyebrows. "If you don't know, who does?"

"I guess she might."

"Seriously? How can you *not* know if you're together?"

"We had a fight. I thought we broke up. But I'm not sure she thinks we broke up. I got a letter from her like we never had that conversation. And when I talk to her on the phone, she makes it sound like I am just on a little trip to the country. Like I said, it's complicated." Joel squirmed in his chair and looked down at his plate. "I should really go."

Kat figured she had pushed the nosy factor as far as she could for one night. Clearly, she wasn't going to extract any more pertinent information about the mysterious Allison. "Are you sure you don't want a Twinkie? I have about 700 left."

"That's okay. I'm sorry Lady broke the pitcher downstairs. I hope it wasn't valuable."

"I doubt it. According to Larry, my aunt was a bit of a cheapskate. Looking at the other knick-knacks around here, I think she spent a lot of time at yard sales."

Joel smiled. "That's a relief. I'd feel bad if Lady destroyed a cherished family heirloom. I need to teach her that she shouldn't chase cats. It's never really been a problem, since there aren't any cats around my place." He stood up and carried his plate to the sink. "Thank you for dinner."

Kat stood next to him and touched his bare forearm. "Thanks for tarping my house." He turned his gaze down at her and their eyes met for a long moment. Kat's stomach fluttered and her heart seemed to be beating extremely loudly in her chest.

They walked together toward the door and went outside around the back of the house to collect Lady. The dog scampered around them in circles as they slowly walked beside each other toward Joel's truck.

Joel gestured at the large green Ford. "Lady loves riding in the truck. She sits up and looks straight ahead. I've sometimes wondered if she might think she's driving."

"It's good to keep your eyes on the road. Someone has to do it."

Joel chuckled, "Yes, she's quite a responsible dog, when she's not breaking things."

Kat leaned on the truck, which was probably completely coated with mud. Oh well, so much for clean clothes. She looked up at him. "I'm heading back home tomorrow, but I'll be back next weekend."

Joel reached down toward the truck handle and gazed into Kat's eyes. "I know this sounds like a line, but your eyes are an amazing color of blue. They're exactly the color of the Cornflower crayon."

Kat blushed but didn't move, anticipating what might happen next. "I've never been compared to a Crayola before."

Joel smiled, bowed his head and wrapped his arm around her waist, pulling her closer to him. As his lips touched hers, Kat closed her eyes, tilted her head back, and put her arms around his neck. An electric warmth coursed through her and the nervous feeling that had made her stomach feel funny all night finally disappeared. As she relaxed into the kiss, Joel enveloped her with both arms, wrapping her in his warm embrace.

Lady barked sharply, startling them out of the moment. Kat put her hand on Joel's chest to separate them and looked up into his eyes.

He looked down at her. "Wow."

"You really are a man of few words, aren't you?"

Joel grinned and raised his eyebrows in a mock leer. "Sometimes it's better to just shut up and enjoy the moment. I think Lady is ready to go home now. I'll give you a call next weekend after you get back."

As she watched Joel's truck roll out of the driveway, the beating of Kat's heart finally slowed down to a reasonable rate. 'Wow' was an understatement. She grinned up at the trees and squealed like a giddy third-grader as she ran back up the stairs into the house to pack.

～

After convincing Cindy to take on pet-sitting duty for the rest of the week and explaining her new dog-walking protocol, Kat packed up the car and drove back to her apartment. Since it was only for a couple days, she had opted to forgo fighting with Murphee about the cat carrier and left her in Alpine Grove. The cat probably wouldn't be excited about being cooped up the bedroom, but Cindy had promised to check in on her. Cindy also had made it clear that this was her last pet-sitting stint out at Chez Stinky. Apparently her new marketing efforts had worked well and she was booked up with in-town dog-walking work for the foreseeable future.

Kat spent most of the two-hour drive back home mooning over Joel and his phenomenal kissing skills. Like a horny teenager, every time she recalled the kiss, a little thrill went through her body as she mentally relived the humming electricity between them.

As she opened the door to her apartment, she was greeted by the musty aroma of warm dust, the hallmark of a place that has been closed up for a while. She went around the apartment and opened the windows, starting to regret her decision to leave Murphee at Chez Stinky. Normally she liked quiet, but the stillness and emptiness of her apartment was lonely and oddly depressing. She curled up on the sofa with a novel in an effort to distract herself from thinking about the prospect of returning to work.

Walking into the office the next morning, Kat noticed a heavy feeling settle over her shoulders. The place still smelled of old electronics, burnt popcorn, and anxiety. Some things never change.

She walked through the maze of cubicles to her desk. As she moved from the entryway down the first cubicle corridor, it became apparent that some things definitely had changed. In fact, everything had changed. None of her fellow employees were located in the same cubicles they had been in when she left. She stopped at her cubicle location, but none of her stuff was there. It obviously wasn't her cube anymore. Where was her desk? As she snaked through the labyrinth of cubicles, she waved to a few colleagues.

Bridget was one of the women she often went on walks with during lunch. "Hi, Bridget. Do you know where my desk is?"

Bridget looked up. "Hi, Kat. We missed you. Let me look at the map. Mark made a chart."

"A chart?"

"Yes, everything was moved last weekend. When we came in on Monday, he handed out maps, so we could find our desks. I'm not sure why, but we're not grouped by department anymore. Writers and editors like you and me are scattered all over the place." She studied the piece of paper on her desk. "Okay, there you are! Go down and to the left."

"Thanks Bridget. Are we walking today?"

"Yes, ma'am. I'll be there."

Kat wandered down the corridor, slowly peeking into cubicle doorways to determine who was where now. At the end of the row, she found a cubicle with a map and a banker's box filled with her stuff sitting on top of the desk. Kat picked up the map and looked at it. A graphic artist had obviously created it for Mark, neatly typing all the names on the grid of offices. She noticed that her name was not printed in a tidy Helvetica font, but appeared to have been scribbled in by hand as an afterthought.

Kat dug through her belongings and settled them into place in her new cubicle. Crammed into a corner at the back of the building, this spot was arguably worse than her prior location, which was saying something. She sighed, sat down in the chair, and looked up. One of the fluorescent lights overhead was out. Great. Casting her gaze on the computer monitor, she craned her neck to see the screen. This chair obviously wasn't the one she'd had before. Getting up out of the chair, she crouched down and examined it more closely. It looked threadbare, stained, and tired. Not to mention uncomfortable. One of the wheels appeared to be gummed up with something disgusting. Maybe actual gum. Gross. Stealing someone's rolling office chair was a new low.

Kat looked at the map again to find out where Chris was located. What had happened with the dreadful proposal in her absence? According to the chart, Chris still had a real office with a door. But now he was located closer to the front of the building, near the entrance. She folded up the map, put it in the pocket of her skirt, and exited her dark little corner.

Chris was seated at his desk with one arm thrown over the back of the chair. When Kat appeared in the doorway, he held up a finger at her. "I'm sure you know how busy I am," he shouted at his phone. The disembodied voice on the other end squawked, "What? I can't hear you. Are you on your speaker phone again? Pick up the phone, you fu…" The next words were cut off as Chris grabbed the handset. "Sorry Rob, I have to go. Like I told you, I'm super busy. Someone important is standing in my doorway right now." He glanced up at Kat. "I really need to take this meeting. We'll connect later." He hung up the phone and waved at Kat. "Come in! I'm glad you stopped by."

"I can see that. I'm back from vacation and was just checking on the proposal. Jill was supposed to put my edits into the draft."

Chris shook his head. "Well, you know, I'm not sure. Can you check with her? I'm really busy."

"Could you tell me what the new deadline is? I know there was an extension. How long is it?"

"You'll need to talk to Mark about that. I need that proposal done, so you should get moving. Right now, I need to call Rob back. He's an important contact."

"I get the impression he had more to say to you."

"He's my buddy. You should see his house. It's gotta be worth a mint. Pool, tennis court, orchards. It's incredible!"

Chris reached for the phone as Kat turned to leave. Mark's office was the only one that was still in the same place, so at least she knew where it was. But she couldn't face talking to him yet. She pulled the map out of her pocket and looked for Maria's new cubicle home. She appeared to be located in the middle of the maze, nowhere near Mark's office, which was odd, since she was his secretary.

"Hey Maria, I'm back."

Maria jumped up, stretched out her arms and gave Kat a big hug. "We missed you, girlfriend. Welcome back to the weirdness."

"It's weirder than it was. I'm trying to adjust to the new arrangement. Somebody stole my chair, too."

"I hate to break it to you, but Mark forgot about you when he made the map. He gave me the printout to make copies for everyone, and I pointed out you weren't anywhere on it. I penciled you in."

"I thought that looked like your handwriting. You're a good friend. It's nice to be remembered."

"See what happens when you go on vacation?"

"I have to go talk to Mark about the proposal. It will be interesting to see if he recognizes me."

Kat walked to Mark's office and found him in his typical posture. He was looking down, surveying his manicure, with his Teva surfer sandals up on the desk facing the doorway.

"Hi, Mark. I'm back."

"Oh yeah. How was Tree Creek?"

"Alpine Grove. It was fine. I'm here to ask about the proposal. You got an extension, but I'd like to know when the specific due date is. Chris doesn't seem to know."

"You need to ask Tammy. I put her on it."

"I thought Jill was putting in my changes, but I haven't seen her yet."

"Well, you won't. She wasn't up to the job." Mark leaned forward and thumped his sandals on the floor as he pointed his fingernail clippers at Kat. "I came back from my run and she asked me all these *questions*. She was asking about the numbers in the proposal. Then she wanted verification for the figures. What's with that? We have to provide verification? That's ridiculous. We're an established, respected company here. We shouldn't need to justify our sales to write a proposal! She needed me to hold her hand and help her on everything. I'm the CEO. I can't be doing that type of thing. I've got stuff to do. Decisions to make. So I let her go. She was completely worthless. And I didn't like how she was dressed. She didn't look professional enough to work here."

Kat stood in stunned silence. Jill had been with the company for years. In addition to being friendly and fun to work with, she was the best editor Kat had ever met. "You fired her? If you didn't have the information, couldn't you have found someone else to answer her questions? Delegate?"

Mark stood up and leaned over his desk. "Are you questioning my decision? I'm telling you, she was a moron!"

"She was an extremely good editor."

Mark sat down and waved his hand at her. "What are you wearing? I can't believe you'd come to work looking like that!"

Kat looked down at her blouse. "What I always wear. A skirt and a shirt. It's pretty standard attire."

"Where is your desk? You aren't near the front are you?"

"Actually no. I'm in the corner in the back of the building."

"Good!"

Kat attempted to return to the point. "So about the deadline? Could you tell me where we are with the proposal?"

"I had Tammy put in your changes and I sent it in. If they don't like it, too bad. We're better than that."

Kat shrugged her shoulders. "I hope you're right. If we don't get that work, the company has got a big problem." She started to turn to leave his office.

Mark "You're such a downer. You need to go home and change your clothes. Don't you have something sexier you can wear?"

"I don't think dressing sexy is generally a job requirement for writers."

"Why do we have so many writers anyway?"

Kat narrowed her eyes. "It takes quite a few of us to explain how to use the products. Write proposals. Produce documentation. User guides. Manuals. Remember those? And all those times you called me to nag me over the weekend about emergencies? Remember all that?"

"Writers don't sell stuff and make me money. They're overhead. I took a one-day business course last week. Times are rough. Businesses need to cut overhead to survive. So I'm thinking of making some changes around here. We need to reduce the documentation. No one reads it, anyway. It's not worth it."

Kat glared at Mark. "So what you're saying is that what I've been doing for more than a year is useless?"

"Yeah. I know I don't read that crap. Why would anybody else?"

Kat's body tensed and she dug her nails into her palms in an effort to manage her rising anger. She wanted to hit something. Preferably Mark.

Pressing her lips together, she said in a determined, level voice, "For the record, many of our customers have complimented us on our documentation, including the pieces I've written. Reviewers have said our easy-to-read user guides are one of the best things about our products."

Pausing to try to calm her fury, she glared at Mark's narrowed eyes. Why was she wasting her life here? "Since you seem to think what I do is useless, I don't think I need to be here anymore."

Mark raised his eyebrows and began to wave his clippers at her again. Kat interrupted him before he could say anything. "I quit. Feel free to give the ancient gum-filled chair in my dark hole of an office to someone else. Give my last check to Maria. She'll get it to me."

Kat spun around and left his office without another word. She stopped by her cubicle and slammed her personal belongings back into the beat-up banker's box. Picking up the box, she left the building for the last time.

～

At her apartment, the red light on Kat's answering machine was flashing frantically. Given the speed of the office grapevine, she figured Maria would have called by now. Kat pressed the button and her friend's voice burst forth from the machine.

"Kat! Where are you? What happened? There's a rumor going around you slapped Mark. I hope you did. Call me!"

Kat smiled. She had wanted to slap him. Too bad. Another missed opportunity. The next message was from Cindy Ross.

"Kat, this is Cindy. I don't understand how you leash up the dogs. I'm confused. Call me back."

Uh-oh. What had Cindy done? Whatever she did, it was undoubtedly too late now. Cindy knew Kat was at work. Maybe she had left a message there, too. Oh well. She definitely wasn't getting that message.

The next message played. "Hi, Kat, it's Joel. I had to untangle Cindy from the dogs. Could you call me when you get a chance? Thanks."

Kat sighed. Part of her lamented the loss of her job. The other part missed Murphee and the dogs. Not to mention Joel. Looking around her lonely apartment, she decided to pack up and go back to Alpine Grove. It was only two hours away and driving might distract her from her newly unemployed status.

She called Cindy back and left a message that she would be there to do the afternoon walk. Then she called Maria at work.

Maria picked up and asked about Kat's whereabouts again. "Some people are saying you kicked Mark in the nuts. Did you?"

"No I didn't do that or slap him, either. Sorry. But I did quit."

"I was hoping he'd been kicked. The idea of him bent over clutching the family jewels just made my day."

"Well, I wanted to, if that makes you feel better. I think I do know why he rearranged the office though."

"Why? No one can figure it out."

"When I was driving back to my apartment, I thought about what he said to me before I quit. First, he told me I wasn't pretty enough to work there and I needed to go home and change my outfit. Then he asked where my cubicle was. I told him it was in the back and he said that was good. I think he's arranged people so the people he thinks are pretty are in the front of the office and the people he thinks are ugly are in the back."

Maria didn't say anything for a moment, apparently digesting this information. "I'm looking at the map. I don't think you're right. I'm in the middle, and I'm fabulous. And you were at the back because he forgot you. I'm sorry, but you're not ugly. Mark may be stupid, but he isn't blind."

"Well, you told me he forgot I existed at all, so that doesn't count. Look at the rest of the people. Think about it. Rebecca could be a runway model. She's right up front. And Chris, the former actor, is pretty, too. He has the first office on the left. Oliver has a weight problem; he's in the back."

"Hmm. I don't know about that. But I'm going out for the walk with the ladies at lunch. I'll see what they think. Maybe we can plot a revolution. I feel a rebellion coming on!"

"Good luck with the insurrection. I'm going back to Alpine Grove. Cindy is having some problem with the dogs, and I hate being here without Murph, anyway. I miss her. My apartment is too quiet and depressing. I don't have a job now, so there's no reason to stay."

After Kat hung up the phone, she began packing. She slowly placed her things into her suitcase. What if she moved permanently to Chez Stinky? The idea was not as far-fetched as it had been a few weeks ago. She had to leave her apartment eventually and now she had no job, as well. The real question was what could she do in Alpine Grove to make money? There didn't seem to be much call for tech writers. She needed to do something or she'd starve. Unemployment had some unpleasant implications. Plus, she might go stir crazy in such a tiny town. Being on vacation was one thing, but living there permanently was another. Maybe she could find some other type of job. That was another dreary thought. Being a writer had been her dream for as long as she could remember. She didn't want to do something else.

Kat shook her head, wishing she could cast out all the confusing thoughts clattering through her mind. Maybe walking through the trees and feeling the calmness of the forest would help her think more clearly so she could figure out what to do with the rest of her life.

Chapter 7

Ideas

During the two-hour drive, Kat slowly relaxed. It was a relief to be leaving her job and the city behind again. By the time she got to Chez Stinky, she was even happy to see the pot holes in the driveway and the huge ugly gray tarp on the roof.

Linus and Lori came shooting out from behind the house. Kat jumped out of the Toyota and crouched down to greet them. She hugged Linus around the neck, digging her fingers into his great fluffy mane. "I missed you guys!" Lori wagged so hard her whole body moved back and forth. Kat stroked the smooth fur on the dog's head and rubbed her soft tulip ears.

"Okay, let's all go for a walk. I heard the last one didn't go too well." Kat went around to the back and found Tessa bouncing up and down in the basement. Chelsey emerged from under her table and wagged happily when she saw Kat. After hooking up Linus and Tessa, the group went out to the forest trail.

As the other three dogs ran ahead, Kat and Chelsey strolled through the trees. The birds in the tree canopy above were whistling and trilling, having a complex conversation about the state of the arboreal universe. Swallows twittered and swooped through the branches. Kat stopped for a moment and closed her eyes, letting the sounds and fragrances of the forest wash over her as the tension left her body. Chelsey stood next to her, wagging her tail. She tilted her head back to look up at Kat, causing her ears to flop backward.

Kat gazed down at the dog. "It's good to be back, little girl. I missed you and this place more than you can imagine. Definitely more than I thought I would. Now I need to find a way to stay here. First, I have to talk to Larry and Louise and find out exactly what I need to do to keep this place." She reached down to pet the dog. "What do you think, Chelsey? Would that work for you?"

The typical worried expression Chelsey often had on her face had disappeared. She looked happy and hopped backwards a couple of times to demonstrate her enthusiasm.

Kat nodded. "Good girl. We'll figure it out."

After the walk, Kat called Joel. "What happened with Cindy?"

"She had a problem with Tessa's leash arrangement. I definitely know what you mean by clotheslined now. You may need to find someone else to walk the dogs."

"That's okay. I'm back at the house again. I drove up this afternoon and walked the dogs. Cindy's off the hook. I don't suppose there's another dog walker in Alpine Grove, is there?"

"No, Cindy is the only one. Having a monopoly works for her. I thought you had to work?"

"Not anymore. It's a long and stupid story. Suffice it to say, you're not the only one who is unemployed anymore. I'm joining you in embracing my inner slacker."

Joel chuckled. "You're making me feel better about my slacker-hood. I'm sorry about your job, though."

"It's okay. To be honest, for a long time my job was fine. Not great, but not horrible, either. Mostly I was afraid of losing it because then I wouldn't be able to pay my rent. I do love writing, but by the time I got back up here, all I felt was a big sense of relief that I never have to go back to that office. Also, I think my boss may be losing his mind. He was always a little odd, but he went off the deep end when I asked him about a deadline. When he called my work useless, something in me snapped."

"Useless? It sounds like you're better off."

Kat shrugged. "Maybe. Being unemployed does have some financial downsides, though. I need to figure out how to qualify to receive Abigail's inheritance, so I can stay here and afford to fix up the place. And of course, figure out what to do with the rest of my life."

"I can relate to that problem. I'm still working on it."

"I guess we need to figure out what we want to be when we grow up. So far I've learned I can write well and walk dogs even better than a professional dog walker. It's a unique skill set."

"People pay Cindy. Maybe this town needs another dog walker."

"I don't want to go into town for the same reason she doesn't want to come out here. It's too far to go back and forth every day. I bet I'm not the only one who has this problem. People go on trips and they can't get anyone to take care of their dogs because they live too far out of town. What if people brought their dogs to me? Is there a dog boarding kennel around here?"

"Not that I know of. It would be easy to find out."

A little tingle ran up the back of Kat's neck as an idea started to take shape. "I've got to walk my dogs anyway, so I can walk other people's dogs at the same time. I could still write, too. Maybe I could be a freelance magazine writer. They don't care where you live or when you write. Even if I wrote in the middle of the night, they wouldn't care."

"Maybe. I think you need to work on the getting-money idea first. Where would you put the dogs you're going to be boarding?"

"I could build a kennel. The building could be back in the clearing." Kat's mind began racing as she considered the possibilities. "The driveway for the kennel could go off to the left, away from the house, with a circular driveway. I could gate off this section of the driveway to the house, so people don't end up on my doorstep. But the dogs would still be close enough for me to take care of them. I could take them out for walks, feed them, and then write articles in between. Maybe I could set up some fenced-in areas for doggie play yards too." Kat paused in her stream–of-consciousness brainstorming. "The other night, I forgot to ask you about the roofer. What's his name?"

"John Wolf. He's in the phone book under Contractors. He helped me fix the roof on this place."

"Thanks! I need to make some calls." Kat paused for a second. Was she overwhelming Joel with all this entrepreneurial inspiration? "So are you going to be around? I was hoping I could see you again. Soon."

Joel paused before saying, "I'm not sure. It looks like I may have someone visiting this weekend. I'll give you a call, okay?"

Kat hung up the phone and rested her hand on the receiver. Was Joel regretting the kiss the other night? If the visitor was the mysterious Allison, he might be trying to distance himself. Dwelling on that idea was way too depressing. Best to think about new opportunities instead. Kat got out a legal pad and started making notes about her new business idea.

~

Before she could move forward with her boarding-kennel idea, Kat needed to get a better understanding of the terms of Abigail's will. She picked up the phone to call Larry.

He answered on the second ring. Perhaps things were slow at the law offices today. "Larry, I was hoping I could see a copy of Aunt Abigail's will. I have decided to stay here in Alpine Grove permanently, so I need to understand all the stipulations."

Larry cleared his throat. "Could we meet? I can bring the document with me and explain it to you."

"That would be fine. When can you do that?"

"I have to be in court today. Perhaps we could meet for dinner later?"

Kat had a sinking feeling in her stomach that Larry might be considering the dinner another date. She sighed quietly. On a positive note, at least they'd have something to talk about. "We can do that. Could you also make a copy of the document for me to keep? I need to understand what I need to do to get the inheritance, so I can fix the house. I have other plans for the property, as well."

"That's fine. I'll pick you up at seven."

Kat had a bad feeling about the evening, but to be fair, how could this date (if that's what it was) possibly be worse than the last one?

Moving on to more pleasant ideas, she looked up John Wolf in the phone book and had a nice chat with his answering machine. Maybe there was an agreement among the contractors of Alpine Grove that no one ever take or return phone calls. So far, she was getting exactly nowhere on the Chez Stinky reconstruction project. Maybe she should go to trade school and learn how to do it herself. It might be faster.

Failing in her mission to talk to anyone about the house, Kat went to the library to get books on how to start a business. Running a kennel and freelance writing were actually two businesses, so she needed all the help she could get.

At the library, it was story time, and a group of little kids had gathered in the corner along with a few parents. Cindy Ross had contorted herself into a tiny chair and was looking bored. Kat waved at her across the room, catching her attention. Eager for an excuse to talk about something other than a hungry caterpillar, Cindy launched herself out of the chair toward Kat.

Cindy whispered urgently, "I got your message! I'm so glad I don't have to go back to your place. Joel said he went for a walk with you and the dogs with that leash thing and it was fine. I don't know how you did it. I guess it works for you, but not me. Tessa is such a pain."

Kat was a little taken aback by Cindy's vehemence, but whispered back. "It's okay. All the dogs are fine, and I'm staying here. I plan to fix up the house if I can ever get a contractor to call me back. The roof leaks and it sounds like it needs to be replaced."

"Joel told me he went out there with Cliff and a couple other guys and tarped it."

"Yes. It was nice of him to do that. I was going back to work, so it was a bit of an emergency. But I gave the guys some beer and they seemed happy."

"So how come you're here?"

"I quit my job."

Cindy said much too loudly, "*What?* You quit your *job?* Why?" The librarian at the desk pointed at Cindy and put her finger to her lips.

Cindy continued in an emphatic whisper, "What are you going to do? That's just like Joel. He's been sitting around feeling sorry for himself after he got laid off. He's so lame."

"It's a long story, but I have an idea of what I can do here, so I'm working on that. I need to do some research. I think Joel has plans, too. He didn't seem like he was moping around to me. Or lame."

Cindy raised her eyebrows. "Oh reeeeally? You seem to know more about what he's thinking about than I do. So what's going on there? Did I miss something?"

Kat blushed and stammered, "No. No, he just helped me out the other day and we were talking about work, that's all."

"I wonder what Allison thinks about that. She's coming up this weekend. This could get interesting."

Kat's heart did a painful back-flip in her chest. Allison *was* the visitor. She shook her head and stood up straighter, trying not to look surprised or disturbed. "He told me about her. It's fine. Nothing is going on with us. He just helped me out. As I understand it, he does that for you, too. He's a nice person."

Cindy raised her eyebrows. "Sure he is. Real nice. I know he's my brother, but I'm not blind. He's quite the catch for Alpine Grove."

"I admit that he does have all his teeth, which is a big plus."

Cindy laughed and glanced quickly over at the librarian, who was glaring at her. "I hear you on that. I hope you're not moving here for the hot dating scene. You'll be disappointed."

"My friend Maria and I discovered that the other night. We went out on the town and it was a bit of a bust."

"You didn't go to the saloon, did you?"

"Yes. That was a mistake."

Cindy giggled. "I can imagine." She glanced over at the circle of kids. It looked like story time was ending. "I gotta go grab my kid. Good luck with Joel. I can never figure him out. It sounds like you do better with him than I do. At least you get him to talk. That's better than Allison, too. Here's hoping they don't kill each other this weekend. That shack of his is pretty small."

"I told you, nothing is going on with us. Really. I know he has a girlfriend."

"Yeah, right. Whatever you say. I gotta go. Thanks for letting me out of dog duty! See you around."

Kat waved as Cindy marched off to collect her little boy. It was interesting to discover that other people found Joel difficult to talk to. She had enjoyed her conversations with him. Yes, she thought he was cute (okay, *really* cute), but she wasn't just being polite to Cindy when she said Joel was a nice person. She liked him as a human being, too. The fact that she thought he was attractive and they obviously had some serious chemistry was a bonus. But not if he already had a girlfriend.

Turning back to the shelves of books, Kat considered the impending weekend. What *was* Joel going to be doing this weekend with Allison? Probably nothing she wanted to know about. As she mulled over the implications of the impending girlfriend visitation, her mind delved into increasingly distressing territory. Pulling a business book off the shelf, she attempted to distract herself by immersing herself in the world of entrepreneurship instead.

~

After the library, Kat's next stop was the hardware store. Using pliers to turn the shower on and off was getting tiresome. She stood in the plumbing department studying the wide array of pipes, fixtures, and water-related gadgetry. She knew she needed a shower handle that had one lever as opposed to two. Beyond that, it was hard to tell these things apart. She grabbed a package and turned it over, trying to determine from the tiny, cryptic exploded diagram if it would work for her shower.

She jumped when Joel tapped her on the shoulder. He grinned at the startled expression on her face. "Looking for something?"

Kat blinked a couple of times, feeling unreasonably flustered. She had been thinking about the evening Joel had fixed her shower and about other things related to being close to him, so it was a little spooky to suddenly find him standing right next to her.

"Yes. I was looking." She proffered the package at him. "It's plumbing stuff." She shook her head. "I guess that's obvious."

He smiled. "How's it going?"

"Not too well." Kat shrugged. "I think I need a magnifying glass to read the diagram."

He leaned over her shoulder, looked down at the package, and pointed at the picture of the shower knob. "This one should work. See how it connects to the pipe? That's like your shower."

Kat could feel the warmth of his body and the slight scent of fabric softener from his flannel shirt. She closed her eyes for a long second. *No. Stop it. He has a girlfriend.* "Right. I'll get this one. And I can return your pliers to you. Thanks for leaving them so I can shower." *Ugh, could she sound like any more of a dork?*

"No problem." He smiled again. "I can stop by and help you put it in if you want."

Kat hesitated before replying, "You said you had company. I don't want to take up your time…again."

"That's not until this weekend."

Kat looked up into his eyes, which seemed especially green at the moment. "Well. Okay. Yes. That would be great. I still don't know where Abigail has tools. Maybe they are in the downstairs bedrooms. I haven't really cleaned them out yet. But if you could put on the shower knob that would help. I'm used to the pliers, but Maria didn't appreciate the rustic nature of my shower fixtures."

"I'll bet. It shouldn't take long. I'll stop by later."

Kat watched him walk down the aisle. It was best not to dwell on how good it had felt to have him close to her again. She repeated to herself, "He has a girlfriend. He *has* a girlfriend."

After a quick stop at the grocery store for non-snack-cake items so she'd have something to eat other than Twinkies, Kat went home and walked the dogs. During the walk, she pondered the mess downstairs. Today was the day she would attack the clutter in the downstairs bedrooms and see if tools were in there somewhere. It was embarrassing to admit to Joel that she still hadn't found the stupid toolbox. No one could live at Chez Stinky as long as Abigail had with no tools. They had to be somewhere.

She waded through the maze of boxes to the bedroom closet. When she opened the door, an avalanche of moth-eaten sweaters and dust fell off the shelf and landed on her head. Kat shrieked and leaped backwards, frantically brushing herself off, hoping that nothing with six or eight legs was living within the pile of clothes. Coughing and spitting out dust, she bent down and peered at the floor of the dark closet.

Linus barked sharply, startling Kat. She jerked upright and hit her head on something heavy in the closet. She put her hand on her chest in an effort to still her racing heart.

A knock came from the front door and she ran upstairs to answer it. On the landing, she found Joel petting Linus. Given that Joel and Linus together weighed probably 400 pounds, the rickety-looking plywood landing must be sturdier than she thought. She coughed, causing a flurry of dust to arise around her. "Sorry, I was downstairs."

Joel gazed at her, put down his toolbox, and reached out to touch her hair. "Did you collide with a spider web?" He pulled a bit of cobweb off her, shook it off his hand, and then reached back to tuck a wayward lock of her hair behind her ear.

Kat flushed slightly and warmth spread through her as his fingers grazed her cheek. "I was looking for tools in the closet. Some things fell. Then I hit my head." She reached up to rub the bump that was forming on the crown of her head. Feeling something sticky clinging to her hand, she pulled more cobwebs out of her hair. "Oh gross!" She whirled around. "Is there a spider on me? Yuck!"

Joel leaned in closer, looking for wayward arachnids. "I don't see anything. Can I come in?"

Kat looked up from her frantic cobweb-removal activities. Joel and Linus were still standing outside. "Sorry. Spiders freak me out."

Walking through the door, Joel passed close by Kat, followed by Linus. She was again acutely aware of his nearness to her. She followed him into the kitchen and handed the shower package to him. "Here's the thingie."

"That would be the technical term for it."

"Of course. I am a technical writer, you know. Or I was anyway."

Joel laughed. "True. Let's get this thingie installed."

Kat leaned on the sink in the bathroom and looked down at Joel, who was crouched in the bathtub working to restore her shower to full functioning status. She paused in her quiet admiration of his shoulder muscles moving under his flannel shirt. "I called John Wolf. He hasn't called me back. Nobody calls me back. I think I have cooties."

Joel looked up from his task. "Cooties? I don't think people have cooties after third grade."

"Well, I must. Or every contractor in the county is booked up."

"A lot of them may be working or hunting. It will be worse this fall. Stocking up the freezer is a big deal around here."

"I got that impression from Bud. But how am I ever going to get my roof fixed? I think you are the only male in the area who has tools and doesn't hunt."

Joel stood up in the bathtub. "That may be. I did a lot of the work on my place myself. Before I went to college, I worked construction for a while to save up money for tuition."

Kat's eyebrows shot up. "Really? So you do know what you're doing. I knew it! I've seen men use tools who obviously weren't sure how they worked. You're not like that. You don't even cuss at things or hit them in frustration."

"Not usually. Anyway, I'm done here." He stepped out of the bathtub, crowding Kat closer to the sink in the small bathroom. He smiled. "Happy showering. You might need one after the spider episode."

Kat looked down, "Spider? Eww, is there a spider?" She spun around, scanning herself again for creepy-crawlies.

Joel reached out and grabbed her to stop her spinning. "It's fine. You're fine. In fact, you're better than fine." He tilted his head down to kiss her. At his touch, Kat wound her arms around his waist. All of her nerve endings were on fire. As the kiss deepened, Kat gripped him more tightly, in an effort to erase the Impending Girlfriend Visitation from her mind. It seemed like he had forgotten about the visit for the moment, as well. And then nobody was thinking much at all.

The sink was digging into Kat's back and she paused to come up for air. "Yikes. You're very good at that."

Joel grinned. "Thank you. You're not so bad yourself."

Kat remained wrapped in his arms, but as the beating of her heart slowed down, her brain started to function again. "Would you be willing to help me fix up this place? I can pay you. I have an inheritance, if I can figure out how to get it. But there's some money. You are unemployed, and I really need someone to get the house fixed up before winter comes and the roof caves in. It's what they call a win-win in corporate America."

Joel made a cringing face. "You aren't tempting me with the marketing-speak. But I'll think about it. I did enjoy fixing up my cabin. It was satisfying to build something tangible again instead of programming circuit boards."

The phone rang and Kat disentangled herself from Joel and ran to answer it. "Maybe that's a contractor and you're off the hook!"

Joel packed his tools in his toolbox and then followed her into the kitchen. Linus was lying in the middle of the floor doing his imitation of a bear rug. Joel crouched down to pet him.

Kat said, "Okay, thanks for calling. I'll see you later tonight."

Joel stood up and looked at Kat. "I should go. It sounds like you have plans."

"I'm meeting Larry at the Italian restaurant later. He really likes that place."

"I've been there."

"So will you help me fix my house?" Kat smiled slightly and raised her eyebrows. "It could be fun."

Joel shook his head. "I'm not sure. Maybe we can talk after this weekend. And Larry might have ideas, too."

Kat shrugged. "I don't think so. He's the one who suggested Bud. Bad suggestion." She reached out and touched his arm. "If I have to spend a lot of time fixing up Chez Stinky with someone, I'd rather it be you."

"What does Larry think about that?"

Kat's smile faded. Why was Joel suddenly backing off and acting weird? She raised her eyebrows. "Larry? No. A hundred times no. He's the lawyer in charge of my aunt's estate. We're talking about the will tonight. He can't talk at his office because he's in court all day today."

The tense expression Joel had on his face relaxed. "I see."

Kat was mildly annoyed that he'd be jealous of Larry, given his upcoming house guest. "By the way, I met Cindy at the library and she told me who your visitor is this weekend. It seems that there are few secrets in Alpine Grove. Your girlfriend might not appreciate you spending time here either." Kat smiled overly sweetly. "Not to mention what just happened in my bathroom."

Joel flashed a grin. "Yeah, that was nice."

Kat leaned back on the front door and looked up at him. "Yes, it was. Kindly remember that while you're entertaining your house guest this weekend."

He moved to nudge her away from the door, picking up his toolbox with one hand and wrapping his other arm around her waist. As he bent down to kiss her again, he murmured, "I think I need one more reminder."

∽

After Joel left, Kat walked the dogs and took a shower to ensure that any cobwebs, spiders, or spider parts were no longer lurking anywhere on her person. It also gave her an opportunity to try out the new shower thingie. As she turned on the water and it came on without incident, she smiled at the memory of the impromptu post-repair lip lock. Who would have thought a tiny bathroom could be so romantic?

She spent some time selecting an outfit and working on her hair in an effort to look more like a girl again. Even though meeting Larry wasn't really a date, it felt good to put on nice clothes and go out to a restaurant.

At the restaurant, Larry was standing next to the hostess station talking to Traci, the tall blonde woman who had been there last time. Maybe Larry hit on every available female in Alpine Grove. Or maybe Traci was related to him somehow. It was a small town, after all. Kat knew hardly anyone and yet she had managed to run into those few people she knew whenever she left the house.

Larry looked up from his conversation and waved at her. "Hi, Kat. I've got a table over here."

Kat followed Larry as he led her back to a dark corner with a small two-person table with a votive candle flickering in a carved glass holder. Maybe it was just the nature of the restaurant, but the setting looked suspiciously cozy.

Larry pulled out her chair for her and as she sat down, he leaned down with his face next to her ear. Startled by the feel of his breath on her neck, Kat jumped in her chair. "What was that?" Kat whirled around in her chair and faced Larry. She rubbed her neck. "I've had a lot of spider issues today. That was you, right?"

Larry backed up looking bemused, and walked to his side of the table. "Yes, I'm sorry I alarmed you. I was just going to ask if you wanted to see a menu."

Kat relaxed a bit and settled back into her chair. "Yes, thank you. That would be nice. I'm sorry. It's been a complicated day."

"It seems like you have a lot of those, if you'll pardon my saying so. Is everything okay?"

Kat held up her hand, ticking the day's events off on her fingers. "First, I hit my head and it still hurts. I may have a giant spider colony living in one of the downstairs closets. The roof leaks and may fall in. I also quit my job, so I'm unemployed. And finally, I'm concerned Louise hates me, so I'm not sure I'll be able to qualify for the inheritance, according to her specifications. That's what I wanted to talk to you about today."

Larry looked thoughtful for a moment, apparently digesting the litany of issues. "I see. Well, I brought you a copy of the will as you requested. Perhaps we could have dinner first."

Kat smiled. "Yes, that would be nice."

As Larry droned on about the merits of Italian food again, Kat's mind began to wander. What exactly was Joel going to be doing this weekend with Allison? They'd be shacking up in his shack, no doubt. She'd never even *seen* the shack. But she definitely wanted to. She frowned at the idea of Allison seeing the shack before she did.

Larry interrupted her reverie. "It's okay, you don't have to have the vegetarian lasagna if you don't want it, but it is the special today."

Kat nodded her head. "Yes, the lasagna would be fine. Thanks."

Larry ordered for them and after the food was served Kat decided to preempt another discussion about the merits of Italian food. "Larry, you've read Abigail's will and talked to her for years, so you must know what her wishes were. Can you give me a few more details about what I need to do? I wish I could have talked to Abigail before she died. I can't figure out why I inherited anything. Why me? Obviously, I appreciate it, but I don't get it."

"Yes, I know you must miss her. I'm sorry. I miss her too." Larry stopped eating and pointed his fork at Kat. "I know she had a special place in her heart for you. But also for her animals. So she added a special codicil to her will that Louise is the one to decide whether or not you are fit to take care of the animals. As I mentioned, Abigail's estate includes quite a large sum of money, which could be used to repair the house. But as I told you before, you have to live there permanently and demonstrate that you are an adequate caretaker for Abigail's pets."

"Define adequate. What does that mean? I think that's my main question."

"Unfortunately, that's the difficult part. Louise needs to decide. She then will confer with me on any legal issues for confirmation before the funds may be released. For example, if you were arrested, that would invalidate your inheritance."

Kat raised her eyebrows. "I tend to be fairly law-abiding. Let's face it; I don't get out much."

Larry looked stern, clearly not understanding that she had been trying to make a feeble joke. "Well, I certainly hope that's the case. As I'm sure I mentioned to you earlier, as an incentive, Abigail specified that if you don't live in the house or take adequate care of her pets, the money should be given to charity. She provided a list."

Kat straightened in her chair in an effort to look like a responsible citizen. "I'm not sure if you know, but I have decided to live in the house and make a commitment to the animals. I think I have made progress with them. At this point, it sounds like I need to talk to Louise. The last time I saw her, she wasn't particularly happy with me."

"Yes. I heard about that. I suggest you clarify matters with her. Louise has some issues with your family."

"Issues? What issues?"

"I'm not at liberty to say."

Kat's expression grew more serious. Now she was even more confused. "It sounds like I can't access the inheritance money to fix the roof, can I?"

Larry nodded. "That's correct. The money is inaccessible to you until you prove that you are fulfilling Abigail's wishes to Louise's satisfaction. If you'll excuse me for a moment, I'm going to ask Traci for the dessert menu."

Kat nodded and watched as he went over to the hostess station again. He certainly looked more relaxed talking to her than when he was speaking legalese. She looked down at her hands sitting in her lap. All the cleaning had been hard on her hands. They looked chapped and most of her fingernails were torn and rough-looking. Having no money to fix the roof was going to be a problem, no matter who worked on it. She'd told Joel there was money, but at this point, there wasn't. Maybe he would take a credit card. Probably not.

She placed her elbows on the table and rested her chin on her folded hands, as she contemplated her repair options. Feeling something on her neck, she jolted upright and whipped around in her chair. She found Larry bent over, attempting to kiss her neck and mumbling something unintelligible in her ear. Taking a deep breath, she caught herself before she slapped him and made a scene. Narrowing her eyes, she glared at him and whispered through gritted teeth, "*Please* don't do that Larry."

He looked surprised at her fierce look and pulled his head back away from hers. "I was just saying that I hope we might go somewhere more private after dinner."

"What? I didn't hear what you said. No. Definitely not. You are the lawyer in charge of my aunt's estate. I'd prefer to keep our relationship on a professional level."

Larry seemed taken aback by her vehemence. "I see. I felt we had a connection. It seemed quite powerful."

Had he been in the same room she had? Or the same planet? To say they had zero chemistry would be an understatement, at least from her perspective. "I don't think so. I'm sorry if you got the wrong idea."

Larry sat down and crossed his arms. "I think you've made things quite clear now."

"I hope you're not angry. You're a nice person, but I have too much going on right now. I just finished telling you that I have no job and my house is falling apart. My life is a mess. But I hope we can remain friends, since we'll be talking to each other about the estate."

With a stony expression on his face, Larry picked up the dessert menu stiffly. "I think we should order dessert."

Kat sighed and picked up her menu. Administering chocolate was probably a good idea at this point. Thank goodness she had driven her own car to the restaurant, thus averting a long uncomfortable drive back out to Chez Stinky with an angry lawyer.

Chapter 8

Sirens

Kat spent the next few days attempting to clear out the downstairs bedrooms. Tiring herself out doing menial labor was a good way to avoid thinking about what might be going on over at Joel's place over the weekend. She didn't know what Allison looked like, but in her mind, the woman dressed like a Playboy Bunny and was completely irresistible to all men, particularly Joel.

In the process of hauling and unpacking boxes, she found more photographs and old news clippings. She alternated between bursts of cleaning and pausing to rest and pore over the old photos. She amused herself by inventing stories about the people she didn't know, which was just about everyone, except Louise and Abigail.

On Sunday afternoon, after hauling four big garbage bags full of old clothes out to her Toyota to be taken to Goodwill, Kat was lying on her back spread-eagled on the bed, resting. Tripod appeared and sat down next to her, then settled into feline meatloaf position. She reached out to stroke the fur on his silvery head. "Hi there. Thanks for making an appearance. Be glad you missed out on meeting Lady. Dolly Mae wasn't too impressed."

As she petted the cat, she heard sirens wailing in the distance. There were a whole lot of trees in Alpine Grove and the idea of a fire here in the forest was scary. She silently hoped all was okay out there in the big world, because she was too exhausted to move. Maybe a sexy firefighter could come to rescue her. That would be nice. As the sirens faded away into the distance, Kat fell asleep.

She was jarred from her nap by the sound of the phone ringing. She ran upstairs and grabbed the receiver. Smiling at the sound of Joel's deep voice on the line, she asked, "How was your weekend?"

"I've had better ones."

"How's the girlfriend? Do you know if she's still your girlfriend? Or I guess I should ask, does *she* know?"

"I think it's definitely over now. She threw my computer out a window."

Kat raised her eyebrows. "I'm guessing she wasn't happy."

"No."

"So what was your response?"

"I wasn't happy, either. She also threw a coffee cup at me. And…other things. My place is a mess. Can I bring Lady over there while I clean up?"

"Sure. Anytime. Like I said, I owe you. Are you okay?"

"I don't want to talk about it. I'll be by with Lady in a few minutes."

Kat hung up the phone and stared at it for a few moments. That was interesting. What had happened at the shack? She smiled. No matter what had happened, one thing was clear: Joel was a single guy again. Kat did a small victory dance around the kitchen. *Bye-bye Allison.*

Later, Joel's truck rumbled into the driveway. Kat dashed down the stairs, almost beating Linus and Lori in the race to the truck. The dogs had a disadvantage since they had to run from the back of the house, but they still got to the driveway first. Kat stood with her hands clasped behind her back and watched as Joel and Lady emerged from the old green vehicle.

Lady ran over, sat, and held out her paw for Kat. "Hi, Lady. It's good to see you again. But we need to have a talk about your attitude toward cats." Lady looked serious for a moment, before giving in to Lori's invitation to play. The two dogs scampered off, twirling around each other and yipping happily. Joel stood next to the truck with his hands in his pockets.

Kat looked up at him. "Do you want to come in for a minute? You look kind of…um…tired." That was the polite way of putting it. Joel obviously hadn't shaved and had dark circles under his eyes. It looked like he'd been up for days and his gaze had a weary, deadened look Kat had never seen before.

"No. I need to get back, clean up the house, and see if I can find the various pieces of my computer in the yard. I might be able to put it back together. Maybe. I'd been discussing some consulting work and now I can't even check my email. Thanks for taking Lady. I was afraid she'd eat or step on something. It would have been hard to keep an eye on her."

"No problem." She reached out and took one of his hands in hers. "Is there anything else I can do?"

The expression on his face softened. "No. Thanks for asking. I'll be back later." He turned around, got back into his truck, and left.

Kat turned around and slowly walked back up the stairs into the house. Joel definitely seemed upset and he looked terrible. Maybe her initial elation at the demise of his relationship had been a little mean. Maybe Allison really did look like a Playboy Bunny. Or worse, maybe he really loved her.

Not wanting to go down that mental pathway, Kat returned to her endless menial labor. The bedrooms were getting closer to being habitable and she was thinking of turning one of them into an office. She needed to get a computer if she was going to be a freelance writer. Maybe Joel would have some advice. It sounded like he was in the market for a new computer, too.

～

Later that afternoon, Joel returned to collect Lady. Kat had taken the dogs for an extra-long walk, so Lady and Lori had released all of their pent-up play energy. The two dogs stood outside with Linus, wagging at Joel as he got out of his truck. Although he had shaved and looked less rumpled, his eyes were still shadowed and he looked completely exhausted.

Kat remained curious as to what had happened. She took his hand and attempted to lead him toward the house. "Lady is all nice and tired now. Why don't you to come in and sit down for a minute? I could make you some tea. Or give you a beer. I have lots of beer, remember?"

Joel smiled and didn't resist Kat's insistent tugging on his hand. "All right. The beer convinced me."

They sat down at the kitchen table and Kat handed him a beer. "Want a glass?"

"No." Joel twisted off the cap and took a long drink from the bottle. He smiled wearily at her. "That's not necessary. Thanks."

"Glad I could help."

"It's been a long day."

"I got that impression. Did you find all the parts of your computer?"

"I'm not sure. But it may take divine intervention to get it to run again. At least I had backed up my data. And it didn't get burned."

Kat raised her eyebrows. "Burned? As in fire?"

Joel sighed and slumped down in his chair, holding his beer in between his hands. "Yes. Fire. I think I mentioned my place is small. When Allison started throwing things, I was mostly trying to get out of the way, which is difficult in a small space. I guess she stopped paying attention to what she was cooking. She burned dinner to the point it caught on fire, then she threw the pan too. It burned a hole in the floor before I could put it out by smothering it with a rug. But she called the fire department anyway." He rested his forehead on the table. "Which means everyone in Alpine Grove now knows about it. Cindy will never, *ever* let me live this down."

Kat sat in stunned silence for a moment. "Wow. I don't know what to say."

Joel lifted his head again and looked at her. "The worst part is that I cleaned everything up, but the whole place reeks of smoke and whatever she was making for dinner. It's awful."

"I'm familiar with bad-smelling homes. This is Chez Stinky, remember?"

Joel burst out laughing and looked relaxed for the first time since he'd arrived. "Why yes it is, isn't it?"

"I bet burnt dinner smells better than dead varmint."

"Tough call. Depends on what was for dinner."

"There's always the Enchanted Moose. I stayed there to avoid the smell here. As you know, Bud is not a speed-demon when it comes to repairs. The patch you put on the wall is still there, too. But my shower works!"

"That's good to hear. At least I did something right."

"Are you hungry? Do you want some food? It sounds like you haven't eaten much lately. I promise I won't throw it at you."

Joel grinned. "I do like that about you."

"Yes, we're all about fine dining here at Chez Stinky. We have standards. No food is allowed to go airborne."

"That tends to make dinner more relaxing."

Kat stood up to go ponder what they might eat. She opened the refrigerator and looked over her shoulder. Joel did look a lot more relaxed. He had slumped down in the chair and closed his eyes. "Well, you look like you're taking it easy, anyway."

He opened his eyes. "Sorry. I'm not very good company right now."

Kat walked over to the table and looked down at him. She put her hand on his shoulder. "Are you okay?"

Joel put his hand over hers and looked up into her eyes. "I'm just tired. It's nice to not be fighting or shouting anymore. The peace and quiet feels good."

"The dogs snoring on the floor enhances the peaceful ambiance here at Chez Stinky. Except that Linus snores particularly loudly. I guess it's a guy thing."

Joel reached up and pulled Kat down into his lap. "The other thing that was bad this weekend was that I missed you." He wrapped his arms around her, giving her a hug and nuzzled his face in her hair. "I can't stop thinking about you."

Kat pulled back her head and looked into his eyes. "I have the same problem. Although, to be honest, I spent most of the weekend hauling heavy boxes around, so I wouldn't think about what might be going on at your place."

"Did it work?"

"Not really. I did hear the sirens, though."

Joel smiled. "You and everyone else. That wasn't a high point."

"I fell asleep and dreamed of sexy firefighters." She wrapped her arms around his neck. As she leaned in to kiss him she continued, "One of them looked a little like you."

A few minutes later, Linus marched over and poked Kat in the back with his nose. She unwrapped herself from Joel and looked down at the dog. "Yes? Do you have a problem?"

Linus wagged and perked up his ears looking expectantly at her.

Kat took a deep breath and her racing heart slowed back down to a more reasonable rate. "Oops. I think it's dinner time. Sorry Linus. I got distracted." She looked at Joel. "I was going to feed us, too."

He smiled at her. "I wasn't thinking about food."

"Me neither. I'll be right back."

Kat untangled herself from Joel and the chair, made a half-hearted effort to straighten her clothes, and went downstairs to feed the dogs and the cats.

By the time she got back upstairs, Joel was fast asleep with his head in his arms, his cheek resting on the table. She tapped him on the shoulder. "Do you want to stay here?"

He raised his head, blinked, and looked around. "That's embarrassing. I don't generally fall asleep like that."

Kat rolled her eyes. "Yeah sure, that's what guys always say."

"I guess I'm tired."

"I mean it. You can stay here if you want. I don't know what's going on with Allison or how you feel about that. You can stay in one of the bedrooms downstairs; they are mostly clean now, thanks to many hours of effort on my part. We can talk about…stuff…in the morning. I still want to know what you think about fixing this place. Except there's a problem with that, too."

Joel looked unreasonably distressed at the idea of yet another problem and Kat quickly volunteered, "Don't worry. I'll figure something out. In the meantime, I'll go get some sheets."

Kat went to the linen closet in the bathroom, grabbed some sheets, and handed them to him. "Sweet dreams."

Joel looked at Kat for a moment, then put the sheets on the table and took her into his arms. He gave her one last bone-melting kiss, grinned, and said, "Same to you." Kat slowly sank into a chair and watched silently as he picked up the sheets from the table and went down the stairs. Her sexy firefighter dreams were nothing compared to the real thing.

∼

The next morning, Kat got up and fed the dogs and cats. She was getting ready to go back upstairs to take a shower when Joel emerged from the bedroom looking tousled and bleary-eyed. He also wasn't wearing a shirt. As he stretched, Kat let out a tiny gasp. His shoulders were mighty fine buried under layers of flannel, but it didn't compare to seeing them *au naturale*. She tried to remain casual, as if she had shirtless men wandering around her house all the time. "So did you sleep well?"

Joel stretched out his arms toward Kat and grabbed her in big bear hug. "I feel so much better! It's the best night's sleep I've had in ages."

Kat pressed her ear against his bare chest, listening to the beating of his heart and enjoying the sensation of being in his arms again. "That's good" she mumbled, getting increasingly distracted by the feel of his skin on her cheek. She closed her eyes and stroked his back, which was warm, smooth, and incredibly inviting.

He released her and looked down into her eyes. "I'm hungry."

"You missed out on dinner last night. How do you feel about breakfast?"

"Food would be good, too."

Kat raised her eyebrows. "Yes. Food. I'm going to go take a shower. Feel free to forage in the meantime. There are still a lot of Twinkies."

"I'll see if I can do better than that."

Kat went upstairs and turned on the shower. She adjusted the temperature somewhat colder than usual and leaped in, emitting a small shriek as the chilly water hit her flushed skin. Having a half-naked man in the house was problematic. The feel of his skin was intoxicating. She wasn't sure she could make it through the whole day without jumping him.

After her shower, Kat's sanity had been restored to some degree. She still needed to talk to Joel about the state of the house, and it would be better if her brain had checked back into the station for that conversation.

Kat walked into the kitchen and found him fully dressed again (thank goodness) and standing in front of the stove. She peered around his body into the pan of scrambled eggs. "Do you cook?"

"It beats starving."

"I can't argue with that. It smells great."

Joel looked down at her. "So do you. Nice shampoo."

Kat shook her wet hair at him. "I'm clean! Usually when you see me, I'm sweaty and covered with dust or cobwebs. And let's not even talk about spiders."

"When I fixed your shower, you smelled a little like dog barf."

Kat laughed. "Oh yes. *Eau d'*dog puke. Now *that's* sexy."

While stirring the eggs, Joel reached over with his other arm and caught her around the waist, pulling her toward him. He murmured quietly into her ear, "If I thought you were sexy then, imagine how I feel now."

Kat's heart melted a teeny bit, but she tried to retain composure. "After the fire at your place, you might want to concentrate on the food."

"Good point. The eggs are done, anyway. Sit down and I'll grab the toast and bring it over."

Kat settled into her chair and tried to focus on food. It turned out to be good. A man who was willing to cook. Did it get any better than that?

After gobbling down her food, Kat sat in companionable silence and watched Joel finish his eggs. The phone rang, disturbing her from her quiet contemplation, and she jumped up to answer it.

"Kat, this is Cindy. I don't suppose Joel is there, is he? I've been trying to reach him since last night. There's no answer at his place. I've been calling everyone. He put a tarp on your roof, right? Did he check on it or something? I can't think of anyone else to call. Or where he might be. I'm losing it here. There's a rumor the fire department got called out to his shack. I'm scared something really bad happened and he's dead or in little pieces on the highway."

"No. I'm sure he's not dead. He's here. Do you want to talk to him?"

Cindy exhaled loudly. "Oh my God, that's a relief. I'm glad he's not dead, because I need to kill him. Yes, let me talk to him. Now."

Kat raised her eyebrows as she handed the receiver to Joel. "It's your sister."

With a resigned expression on his face, he took the phone. "Hi, Cindy. No. I'm quite alive. I'm sorry I wasn't there to help you last night. No, my place didn't burn down. It's still there, but it smells like smoke." He looked up at Kat and shrugged his shoulders. "Uh-huh. Yes. Uh-huh. I don't think so. Okay. Goodbye."

Joel leaned back in his chair, looked up at the ceiling, and sighed. "I have to go now. Cindy's car is dead again."

"Well, at least you got a good night's sleep and some food before she found you."

He smiled. "Yes, that will help me deal with the interrogation I'm going to get."

Kat sat back down at the table and folded her hands in her lap to keep from fidgeting. She looked down at her fingers. "Will you come back later? I can keep Lady here if you want." She looked up into his eyes, trying to gauge his response.

Joel met her gaze. "If you want me to. I'm sure my house still smells like smoke, so I'm not eager to go back there. I need to take out all the furniture and get it cleaned or something. I'm not sure what to do about that." He moved to get up.

Kat reached her hand across the table. "Wait. Before you go, I wanted to talk to you about working on the house here. You said you were going to think about it."

Joel pulled his chair back in and rested his elbows on the table. "I have no computer at the moment, so I can't do any consulting work. I need to do a little research and get a new one. But in the meantime, I should be able to work on your roof."

Kat sighed and leaned forward in the chair, putting both of her arms on the table. "There's another problem you need to know about before you say yes. I don't really have much money. I talked to Larry last night. Abigail's inheritance is tied up until I can prove to Louise that I'm a responsible dog-and-cat caretaker and deserve the money. So I can't pay you now. I can pay for materials with my credit card, but I can't pay you for your time. That means you'd have to trust me. Or I guess trust that I can meet the stipulations of the will, so I can give you money later when I'm an heiress."

Joel moved his shoulders in a noncommittal shrug. "Why wouldn't you meet the stipulations? The dogs and cats seem happy to me."

"I think it is better now. But Louise seems to hate me. It didn't help when Linus and Tessa almost clotheslined her. They didn't make a good impression. Larry says she also has issues with my family. I don't know what that's about. But she definitely doesn't seem to like me much. I need to talk to her and find out what she's thinking."

"That sounds like a good idea. Thanks for explaining things to me. I'll come back for Lady after I see what's up with Cindy."

Kat looked up. "Since you're going to be working here, you can stay here too, if you want."

Joel raised his eyebrows, giving her a quizzical look.

"Well, unless you don't want to, of course. You said you slept well. And it doesn't smell like smoke. Or even a dead varmint."

Joel smiled, "Okay. I'll stop by my house and pick up some stuff. Tell Lady to behave herself."

"I'm sure she will. As long as she doesn't find any cats."

Kat walked with Joel to the door. "Cindy is going to ask you a lot of questions about what you were doing here and what's going on. The other day, I told her nothing was going on between us, but I don't think she believed me."

Joel grinned and dipped his head down to kiss her quickly. "I don't believe you, either."

Kat wrapped her arms around his waist and splayed her fingers across his back, remembering how good his bare skin had felt earlier. She looked up at him. "People are going to talk if you stay here."

"It's a small town. That's what they do."

Kat smiled and stood on her tiptoes so she could press her lips to his one last time. "Maybe you should sleep upstairs with me tonight so they really have something to talk about."

~

Kat walked the dogs and resumed the endless cleaning of the downstairs bedrooms and closets. Although most of the boxes were out of the rooms, there was still a lot of stuff to sort through and clean. She picked up a dusty photo of a lake scene that was sitting on the dresser, turning it around in her hands absently. It wasn't every day she invited a guy to jump into her bed. As her mother would say, she just wasn't that kind of girl. Dusting off the frame with a damp rag, she smiled as she envisioned the evening's potential recreational activities.

Yes, she'd had boyfriends and a number of somewhat disastrous relationships over the years, but she'd never felt the level of attraction she felt for Joel. This was new. And scary. All the feelings she had swirling inside her whenever she was near him were bewildering. And who knows what he actually thought about her. He wasn't exactly forthcoming. Hopefully, he didn't think she was a slut by inviting him to stay. Or that sex was how she planned to pay him for fixing the roof. Kat frowned at that idea. She *really* wasn't that kind of girl.

Linus barked and ran outside, disturbing Kat from her myriad tangle of thoughts. It seemed soon for Joel to be returning.

She went out the back door and walked around the house. Louise's car was parked in the driveway and Louise was standing and petting Linus with one hand and holding a handkerchief to her nose with the other.

"Hi, Louise. How are you?"

"I've been better. I talked to Mr. Lowell this morning and he told me that you are trying to extract Abigail's money."

"Extract? Not exactly. I met him last night because I wanted to get a copy of the will, so I could see what the requirements are to inherit the house and the money. I want to stay here."

"You do? I thought you wanted to work at your job in the city and find homes for the dogs and cats. I told a friend of mine about Linus. She wants a big watch dog."

"I spent more time here and changed my mind. And I'm sorry, but your friend can't have Linus. I plan to stay here and take care of the animals like Abigail wanted."

Louise sniffed twice and then sneezed mightily into her handkerchief. "Well, I heard that you have a man living here. And that his last girlfriend just burned down his house. What sort of people are you associating with? Are they drug addicts? I don't want you to be risking Abigail's lovely home by inviting in riff-raff."

"I don't think anyone would consider Joel Ross riff-raff. He's Cindy's brother. You met him that day he was helping her with car trouble. He helped me with the roof. He's an engineer, not a drug addict." Kat pointed up at the house. "He even helped put up that tarp to keep out the rain."

Louise shook her blue curls. "Oh, that fellow? As I recall, he looked rather unwashed. He does shower, doesn't he?"

"As far as I know."

"I don't think he should be here. What if he's an animal killer? Or a child molester? Or an abuser. What do you know about this man?"

Kat shrugged. "Well, I've only known him a few weeks, so not much, I guess. But he's been very nice to me. Even when he didn't have to be."

Louise pursed her lips. "Oh, you'll just end up like Abigail. Or Kelly. Single with no one to take care of you and a child to support. I don't like seeing this type of promiscuity."

Kat started to get annoyed. Who was this woman to dictate her sex life? Particularly when nothing had happened. Yet. "I don't think that's any of your business." Kat raised her eyebrows as something dawned on her. "Wait a minute. Abigail didn't have children."

Louise looked momentarily startled. "No. No, that's not what I meant! Don't be impertinent, young lady. You're just like your mother. Always trying to tell people what to do."

"I'm not trying to tell anyone anything. I'd like to understand what I need to do to meet the requirements, so you will sign off on the inheritance. As I pointed out, the roof leaks and I can't afford to repair it. Plus, I have a few ideas for some other improvements I'd like to have done, so I can stay here and earn a living."

"Why you're just a little gold-digger aren't you? Just thinking about the money so you can shack up with that man and live in sin. You little harlot!"

Kat narrowed her eyes. She might be a lot of things, but she definitely wasn't a harlot. "I don't think that's fair, considering you hardly know me. I think it might be a good idea if you left now. I'll communicate with you through Mr. Lowell's office."

Louise made a harrumph noise, waved her handkerchief in front of her face, and then wiped a tear from her eye. "You haven't heard the last of this young lady! Abigail, rest her soul, was my best friend. And I will not have you dishonoring her memory or risking her property or her animals!"

Kat sat on the bottom step next to Linus and watched as the yellow Buick thumped its way out of the driveway. She stroked his head slowly. "That didn't go well. What are we going to do, Big Guy?"

Linus looked up at her and wagged his tail in sympathy. Then he perked up his ears and ran out toward the driveway, woofing as Joel's truck slowly pulled in. Perhaps Louise had rammed her car into his truck out of spite. But if she had, the old green machine looked unscathed.

Joel got out, saw the expression on Kat's face, and said, "What's wrong? You look like you just lost your best friend."

Kat smiled faintly. "Maria is fine as far as I know. But Louise hates me even more than I thought. She called me a harlot. And said I'm dishonoring my aunt's memory."

"Wow."

"You weren't immune from her wrath either. She thinks you might be a child molester. Or a drug addict. And you don't shower."

Joel grinned. "I do too." He shook his head. "Look! Wet hair. When I stopped by my place to get stuff, I took a shower." He stopped and bent down to look at her face again more closely. "Wait, you're really serious, aren't you?"

"Yes. It was awful. She even wanted to take Linus. I finally told her to just get out."

Joel sat down on the stair next to her and gathered her in his arms. "I'm sorry. Let's go inside. We can talk about it if you want."

Kat looked over at him. "Not really."

"What do you want to do?"

"I think you know."

They stared at each other for a long moment. Joel grinned, grabbed her hand and dragged her up the stairs into the house, and slammed the door behind them. By the time they got to the bedroom, they were breathless. Joel flopped down on the bed and pulled Kat on top of him. Murphee, who had been sleeping on the bed, launched out the door.

Letting Murphee out was probably a bad idea. But that glimmer of rationality passed as Joel's hands touched her skin. She laughed and started clutching and yanking on Joel's shirt. There was way too much clothing in the way.

She worked at unbuttoning his flannel shirt, kissing his chest as she moved downward. Joel groaned, but wasn't exactly idle himself. He ran his large hands along either side of Kat's body and pushed her shirt up over her head.

He threw her shirt off the bed and paused for a moment, gazing at her appraisingly. "I thought so."

"Hey, I was just sitting around cleaning the bedroom. I didn't think Louise would show up. Maybe she thinks I'm a harlot because of my lack of proper undergarments."

Joel pulled her back down to him and started nuzzling her neck. He pulled his head away to look at her and raised one eyebrow. "You don't see me complaining."

Kat laughed. "You can do Spock eyebrow! Maria would swoon."

"I'm not thinking about her right now. I'm thinking that the image I had in my mind of what you might look like naked doesn't even come close to reality. And I have a pretty good imagination."

"Yes, I've noticed you're very creative."

Kat's body was on fire, and it was obvious where this was going. Her one remaining brain cell fired and she stopped, pushing Joel away. "Uh, this is awkward, but do you have… something?" She rolled over and rummaged around in the nightstand beside the bed. "Hmm. I'm not sure about this. It looks like Abigail had more fun than I thought. That's a big box. But I'm not sure how old these are. Is there an expiration date? Do they still work?"

Joel looked confused for a second, then seeing the box in the nightstand, clued into what Kat was talking about. He rolled onto his side, resting his head on his hand and looked into her eyes. "I stopped by the drugstore on the way over here. You implied I might be sleeping upstairs."

Kat giggled. "Yes, I did. I think my harlot status is confirmed now. Way to plan ahead."

"I'm an engineer. We're all about logical conclusions. If [this], then [that]. But then you distracted me and I never grabbed my stuff out of the truck."

"Now I guess all of Alpine Grove knows that you didn't die a fiery death, after all."

He chuckled, kissed her quickly, then rolled over and leaped out of the bed. "Nope. I'm very much alive," he said as he yanked on his jeans. "Be right back."

Kat wrapped herself in the tangle of sheets and looked around the room. Where had Murphee gone? It probably wasn't good that the cat was MIA. That thought disappeared as soon as Joel returned. He collected her back into his arms and kissed her slowly. She was consumed with heat and warmth and any lingering thoughts she had left, evaporated in the fire.

Much later, Kat was dozing, cradled in the crook below Joel's collarbone, her head on his chest. She was listening to his heart beat and idly stroking his arm when Murphee jumped up on the bed. The cat walked over Kat's body, stomping on her hip and settling in by her side. "Hi, Murph."

Joel caressed the leg Kat had thrown over him. With the other hand he reached up and rubbed his eyes. Noticing the movement, Kat mumbled, "Are you okay?"

"I'm way better than okay. But I was wondering. Where does Murphee sleep?"

"Usually next to my head. On the pillow."

"I was afraid of that."

Kat propped herself up on her elbow and looked down at Joel face. His eyes were watering and they looked angry and pink. "You look like a diseased albino rabbit."

"Thanks. It's the cat. It might be good to change the pillowcases before we return here."

"So I guess that means you like sleeping upstairs?"

He grinned. "Yes. Although I don't know how much sleeping we'll do."

Chapter 9

Distractions

Later in the day, after multiple distractions in the shower and miscellaneous diversions in other rooms throughout the house, Kat went out to walk the dogs while Joel went up on the roof to determine the extent of the repairs. After spending most of the day exploring his body, Kat wasn't sure she could stand to witness it crashing down off the roof. It was a long way down.

He had assured her that he had spent a lot of time up on top of houses, but she still couldn't watch. If something horrible happened, she'd be close enough to hear, anyway. As she strolled through the forest with Chelsey trotting alongside her, she opted to think positive and assume Joel would escape bodily harm since she'd seen for herself that he was in extremely good shape. Instead, she considered the various other problems that needed to be addressed. The biggest one was money.

Until she got her inheritance (*if* she got it), the whole boarding kennel idea was out. She needed money for a computer so she could start sending article query letters to magazines for freelance writing work. And she needed money for the roof. Given what Larry had told her about how oddly the roof was constructed, that was looking like an expensive proposition. She sighed and wished her credit card had a higher limit.

When she returned from the walk, she was relieved to find Joel standing in the driveway still in one piece. He had his hands in his pockets and was glaring at the house.

"I'm guessing by the look on your face that there was no happy news up on the roof."

"No."

"Care to elaborate?"

He took a deep breath and sighed. "The roof was not constructed well. Like you said, there's no plywood sheeting and not enough stringers, but there's another problem. The metal needs to be replaced."

"Really? It looks okay from here."

"You probably noticed that the metal roofing has ridges. So there are hills and valleys. Normally you attach the metal using screws in the valleys. For some reason, on this roof, the screws have been put on the hills. Over the years, snow and weather has pulled out a lot of the screws because they are sitting up on the ribs. That's part of the reason the roof leaks. The other reason it's leaking is because of condensation. The plastic under the metal is virtually gone."

"So that means new metal?"

"Yes."

Kat dropped her head and covered her face with her hands. "That's going to be expensive. The roof is huge."

Joel looked up at the house thoughtfully and put his arm around her. "Yes, it is."

Kat opened her eyes and peeked through her fingers down at the ground. "Look, it's a piece of plastic."

"If you look around, you'll see little pieces of black plastic are everywhere. The little screws with red grommets on them are from the roof, too."

"Perfect. Half of my roof is strewn around the yard."

"Pretty much. I took some basic measurements while I was up there. I'm going to start doing some calculations."

"Yuck. That gives me a headache. I hope you're good at math."

Joel smiled. "Engineer. Remember?"

Kat turned around, wrapped her arms around his waist, and smiled up at him. "Oh yeah, I keep forgetting that since I've discovered some of your other skills."

"If you distract me again, you're never going to get a new roof. I'm going to go to the library now and look through some construction magazines. And computer magazines. I need to get a computer and research roof-metal suppliers. I'm not sure how much I'll find, but I know that for electronics, there are a lot of listings of the big catalogs in the back of trade magazines. Maybe the library has a list in the reference section, too."

Kat looked dubious. "I've seen the library. I wouldn't bet on that."

"True. But the lumberyard here has a monopoly. It would be good to know if there are less-expensive options for the metal."

"Thank you for doing all this. I was just thinking that at some point, I'm going to need to go home and pick up my bills, so I can find out how broke I actually am. In my excitement about quitting my job, I forgot to have my mail forwarded here. And I guess I need to get a post office box here, too." She sighed heavily at the prospect.

Joel furrowed his brow. "Are you having second thoughts about moving here?"

Kat looked up into his eyes with a steady gaze. "No. I'm not leaving. After talking to Louise yesterday, I realized how much I want to stay. It feels right. But at this point, everything is kind of complicated."

With a wry smile, Joel bent down to kiss her. "Big life changes usually are," he murmured before their lips met.

~

Leaving Joel contentedly tapping numbers into his ultra nerdy-looking engineering calculator, Kat went off to the Alpine Grove Post Office. Larry had told her that the postmistress was getting on in years and everyone in town knew to allow a lot of time to take care of postal procedures like shipping or picking up packages. Kat was afraid getting a P.O. Box might take most of the day.

When she arrived, the line was out the door and snaking into the area where the mail boxes were located. People were passing the time chatting amongst themselves as the line slowly inched forward. Periodically, someone would burst out laughing. It was quite a social scene, and everyone seemed to know each other. Maybe she should bring Maria to the Post Office to find a date.

Kat dutifully positioned herself at the end of the line and spent some quality time studying the postal rate posters on the wall, since she didn't know anyone. Cindy Ross walked through the door and scuttled over to Kat, securing her place at the end of the line.

"Oooh, I've been hoping I'd run into you!"

Kat smiled politely at her. "Really?"

"I was talking to Joel the other day and he drives me nuts. He's the most tight-lipped guy in the world. Is he living at your house or what? I couldn't get anything out of him. What's going on?"

"His house smells like smoke and I have room, so yes, he's staying at my place. It's a three-bedroom house and I had just cleared out the downstairs bedrooms, so it's much better than the last time you saw it. After the repairs he's done for me, it was the least I could do."

Cindy smirked. "I'll bet. You expect me to believe that he's sleeping in one of those downstairs bedrooms and you're not?" Narrowing her gaze, she eyed Kat circumspectly. "Well, that is, unless he makes you crazy too with his annoying habit of clamming up. I don't know how anyone stands him."

"Actually, he's been nice. He even went up and looked at the roof this morning."

"He did work construction for a while. As I understand it, he was good at it, too. He's good at everything, once he sets his mind to it. The trick is getting him to want to do something. He's incredibly stubborn. I can't get him to do anything."

"Didn't he help you with your car the other day?"

"Well, yeah, but he just drove me around. He didn't fix it. He said he's tired of fixing my car. Then said a lot of other nasty things about Myrtle."

"Myrtle?"

"My car. She's wonderful. But a little temperamental sometimes."

"Can't you take it…or her…to a mechanic?"

"I can't afford that. Joel knows that. He was going to lend me money, but then Allison burned up his house. That seemed to put him in a bad mood."

Kat nodded. "I can see why."

"Did he tell you about the fire?"

"A little."

Cindy leaned in closer as the line inched forward. "Well, the way I hear it, she threw a pan at him that was on fire."

"Good thing she missed. Do you know why she threw it?"

Cindy raised her eyebrows. "Did you ever meet Allison?"

"No."

"She is a model. She goes by Alli professionally."

Kat raised her eyebrows. "Alli? You mean she's *that* Alli?"

"The one and only. She's used to getting her own way. And having people fawn all over her because, of course, she's gorgeous."

"Uh, yeah."

"Apparently Joel wasn't particularly happy to see her. That didn't go over well with Allison."

"I see."

"Joel is a loner. He goes off and reads and spends a lot of time by himself doing who-knows-what weirdo geeky things. He's such a nerd. Allison likes attention. Which she usually gets."

"I can imagine."

"So anyway, I guess he wasn't paying attention to her. He was doing something on his computer. So she threw it out the window. Then things went downhill from there. He wouldn't tell me and I haven't seen the place, but it sounds like it was trashed. Then after torching his house, she left in a huff."

"Wow."

"I know! But Joel is so stupid. He had the perfect relationship for a guy. He had one of the most beautiful women in the world who only wants him for sex every once in a while. That, and she wanted him to take her to parties with models. What a hardship. Talk about no strings. She didn't even care that he was unemployed. I mean jeez, he's cute, but he's not *that* cute."

Kat started to feel sick to her stomach. Joel had dated Alli? How on earth could she ever compare to that? She smiled weakly at Cindy. "I think the line has moved about ten inches since I got here. Is there a better time of day when this place isn't so busy? I need to get a post office box and it looks like it could take forever. Maybe I should try again another time."

"Earlier in the day can be better. Ethel is a little more alert then. I think she might be slowing down by now."

"I think so. I have to do some other errands, so you can have my place in line."

Cindy stepped forward as Kat moved away. "Thanks! Wait, come back! You never told me if you're sleeping with my brother or not!"

Kat just waved and ducked her head, trying to ignore all the people in line staring at her as she scuttled out of the building. Walking back to her Toyota, she refused to cry. After all, nothing had really changed. She crawled into her car, squeezed her eyes shut and leaned her forehead on the steering wheel, trying to block out the vision of Alli's face, which she'd seen on thousands of magazine covers.

~

Kat returned to the house with no post office box, but lots of dog and cat food, since she'd stopped by the store. That would make her popular at home. Joel was apparently still at the library, and she was relieved to have the place to herself for a while.

She took the dogs for an extra-long walk to try to clear her head. Maybe the forest would work its magic to calm her racing thoughts. Now that the glow of last night's incredible love-making had worn off and Joel wasn't nearby melting her brain, she had time to think about what Louise had said. What did she really know about him? The answer was not much. And why was he interested in her? He was dating a super model for God's sake. The guy could certainly do better. He already *had* done better.

It reminded her of growing up with her sister Kim. On one particularly memorable first date, the guy had come to pick her up, then ended up talking to Kim. Her date and her sister decided to stay at the house to hang out. Kat had gone upstairs and hid in her room until he left the house. Kim had dated the guy a few times and then dumped him. The whole experience had been humiliating and demoralizing.

Cindy was right. Joel had the perfect set up. A gorgeous woman who didn't want to tie him down. What could be better?

Where did he even meet a model, anyway? Super models don't hang out at aerospace companies. Maybe he wasn't really even an engineer. Maybe he'd lied about everything. But why would he lie?

Maybe sleeping with her was just convenient. Or maybe he was getting back at Allison. But if that were the case, why would he be willing to work on Chez Stinky? Kat's brain whirled with more questions, stories, and possibilities, leaving her feeling even more confused and sad. So much for clearing her head.

She went in the back door and unhooked Tessa and Linus. Seeming to sense that Kat was upset, Chelsey leaned on her and accepted some affection before returning to her spot under the table. If anyone knew about brooding, it was Chelsey.

Kat slowly went up the stairs. Because of Joel-related distractions, she had never put Murphee back in the bedroom to keep her away from the other cats. Where were Dolly Mae and Louie?

Louie never seemed to have much of a problem with anybody, but as far as she knew Dolly and Murph had not resolved their issues. She looked into the bedroom and found two cats sleeping on her bed. Dolly Mae and Murphee had each claimed a pillow for her own. Murph had even tucked her nose under a front paw and was curled up in a tight ball snoring quietly. It appeared some form of feline detente had developed while Kat was gone.

Kat made herself some tea and was sitting at the kitchen table clutching her mug, when the clattering rumble of Joel's truck came from the driveway. She looked up as he came in through the front door with Linus, Lori and Lady.

"How was the library?"

"I'm guessing better than the post office. You don't look happy."

"I learned that the post office is the social mecca of Alpine Grove. And that I need to go earlier. Ethel was moving extra slowly. I gave up."

"Sorry. Some people drive to Gleasonville to ship packages. It can be faster, even with the extra drive."

Kat looked up at him. "Good to know."

Joel sat down in the chair next to her and gazed into her eyes. "What's wrong?"

Kat shook her head. "While I was in line, Cindy found me and wanted to talk. I probably shouldn't talk to your sister too much."

"You won't get any argument from me."

"She told me who your girlfriend was. Is. I don't know."

"I told you about Allison."

"You didn't tell me she was *Alli*. You were dating a super model? How does an engineer even *meet* a super model, much less sleep with her?"

Joel frowned. "I'm not sure what difference that makes. We broke up. I think if you almost incinerate someone's home, it's over. But why do you care? I'm not with her anymore."

"But why not? Cindy said you had the perfect arrangement. Get hot super-model sex whenever you like and go to parties with other super models. It's like every warm-blooded male's wet dream!"

"We didn't get along. You may recall, she has a temper. She throws things."

"Okay, fine. But she's beautiful. She's on magazine covers! Last night must have been a major step down for you."

Joel looked surprised for a moment, then angry. He pressed his lips together and said quietly, "Is that what this is about? Are you regretting last night?"

"Well I have to figure *you* are. I've looked in a mirror. No one is putting me on magazines, are they?"

"Isn't that for me to decide?"

Kat slumped in her chair, put her elbows on the table, and put her face in her hands. "I just can't imagine what you could possibly see in me when you've had…her."

Joel got up and kneeled next to her chair. He took her hands in his and looked into her eyes. "Kat, what happened to you that makes you so down on yourself? Did you ever think that maybe I *want* to be with you? Sure, Allison is pretty, but she's not a person I could ever spend any real time with."

"Why not?"

Joel smirked. "Well as you probably guessed, we have different…and extremely incompatible…personalities. You haven't thrown anything at me yet, after all."

"I guess I get extra credit points for that." Kat looked down and picked a tuft of dog hair off her pants. "But I'm not beautiful. My sister is. But me? No."

Joel touched a tendril of Kat's brown hair that was hanging in front of her face and smoothed it behind her ear. "I think you're beautiful. But it's more than what you look like. I feel good when I'm around you. Not just last night, which don't get me wrong, was amazing. And I'd very much like to do that again. But just being with you, too. I can be myself around you."

Kat looked up into his eyes. She was slowly starting to believe him. "But I hardly know you. I started to wonder if everything that's happened over the last few days wasn't real. Maybe it's all a lie. Maybe you're not even an engineer."

"Well, not anymore, if you want to get technical about it. Do you want to see my resume? If I ever get my new computer, I'll print it out for you."

Kat smiled as the painful lump in her throat started to dissolve. "I suppose I'm not a technical writer, either. Maybe you can print my resume while you're at it."

Joel stood up and pulled her out of the chair into his embrace. "I think you were right about talking to Cindy. It's not a good idea. If you have questions about me, ask me."

"I'm sorry. It's just everything is so confusing. My life here. Unemployment. You. I have all these feelings and I guess I'm a little scared."

He smiled and locked his hands behind her spine, drawing her closer. As he angled his head down to kiss her, he whispered, "Me too."

∼

Later, Kat was awakened by a thump on the bed. She was lying on her side with Joel curled up around her, one arm hugging her around her waist. When she opened her eyes, she found herself nose-to-nose with Murphee, who was staring at her intently. The cat's yellow eyes glowed in the moonlight. "Hi, Murph."

Kat shifted position, since her neck was twisted in an uncomfortable way. The cat-hair infested pillows had been thrown on the floor and various articles of clothing were strewn around the room. She reached out to stroke Murphee's smooth black fur. "Can I do something for you?" Murphee mewed plaintively and curled up in a ball in front of Kat's stomach.

Kat stared into the darkness. She was a little embarrassed about her meltdown earlier. Joel had asked her why she was afraid, and she had told him about her sister's date-stealing ways, a few embarrassing stories about past relationships, and Mark's new obsession with pretty people. Joel had pointed out that those things shouldn't affect their relationship.

Kat continued to pet Murphee, who had moved into feline power sleep and was snoring surprisingly loudly for such a small animal. Joel was right; she usually let self-doubts cloud her mind. That little voice in her head had an unfortunate habit of sabotaging her confidence. But the effects of feeling like the dark gray sheep of her family ran deep. It would be good if she could keep her rampant insecurity from ruining what was turning out to be a remarkably good thing. She closed her eyes again, and her stomach fluttered as she tried not to dwell on the fact that she was falling in love with Joel.

During their conversation, he had somewhat obliquely given her the answer to the question every woman wonders about but is too scared to ask: was the prior girlfriend better than she was in the sack? Kat smiled as she reflected on their conversation. He said that being beautiful and on magazine covers wasn't always as glamorous and wonderful as people might expect. Allison never knew if people liked her for who she was or if they wanted something else from her. Joel thought that was at the root of a lot of her anger and other issues.

Joel had also volunteered that he didn't like parties. They were exhausting to him, and he and Allison had repeated fights about his preference for solitude. He even answered the question of how a lowly engineer meets a super model. They'd gone to the same junior high school and Allison had recognized him when she attended a ribbon-cutting for a new building at the aerospace company where Joel worked. He also had no love for his former employer. Two months after dedicating the building, they had laid off a bunch of people, including him.

Kat rolled over, dislodging Murphee, who meowed in protest but resettled herself in the small of Kat's back. She looked at Joel's sleeping face, which was bathed in moonlight, and stroked his cheek gently. He opened his eyes and smiled. "Hey, there. I thought you'd be tired."

"A little. Murph woke me up."

He shifted to wrap Kat's body more closely in his arms and pressed his lips to hers. He pulled his head back to look at her. "Suddenly, I'm not so tired anymore."

Kat smiled slowly. "Me neither."

As the covers shifted, Murphee was dislodged from the warm spot she had created. With a mighty "meow!" of disgust, the cat jumped off the bed and sauntered off into the moonlight. She knew that whatever happened next, it obviously wasn't going to involve feeding her breakfast.

～

The next morning, Kat resolved to get to the post office when it opened. She made a valiant effort to keep Joel from distracting her again and left the house with time to spare, so she was only tenth in line. Ethel was operating with blazing speed (for her) and Kat was pleased that at last she was the proud owner of Box 164.

When she came home, Joel was downstairs in one of the bedrooms, which he was slowly transitioning into an office. He had pushed the bed off to one side and found an old folding table that he set up along the opposite wall.

Magazines and papers were starting to multiply in the space. When Kat walked into the room, he looked up from his piles of paper and calculator. "Hi. Did you get a post office box this time?"

Kat waved her shiny new key in the air. "Yes! Ethel was on fire this morning. I can get mail like a real Alpine Grove resident now." She leaned over the table and looked at the papers. "So what are you doing?"

"More math."

"Eww."

"It's a good thing I have a high-end calculator."

"That bad?"

Joel pointed at the number at the bottom of the page. "Yes."

"That's disturbing."

"Construction, or in this case *re*construction, is expensive."

"So it seems. Speaking of money, or the lack of it, I'm going to need to go back to my apartment and get some stuff. Like my bills, which are probably piling up in my mailbox there. Would you be willing to take care of the dogs and cats here?"

"I can do that. Even Murphee is starting to get used to me, I think."

"She's an extremely discriminating feline. If you feed her, that helps a lot, too."

Kat went back upstairs to make a few phone calls. She made an appointment with her apartment manager and left a message with Maria to let her know she'd be back in town for a couple of days.

As Kat was packing, Joel walked into the bedroom and leaned on the doorway. "How long are you going to be gone?"

"It depends. I made an appointment with my apartment manager. The place is going condo, so they are throwing me out in three months anyway, but I need to try to get out of my lease early, since I need that rent money for other things. Like a roof. I'm not sure how that will go. Whether or not they let me move, I need to make a bunch of calls to turn off everything. I don't want to be paying for electricity and phone if I'm not there. I also need to work on getting my stuff moved. Or maybe selling some of it. We'll see. I'm not sure how long all that will take, but I'm guessing I should be back in a couple of days."

"Okay."

"I'll call you when I get to my apartment. Last time I went home without Murphee, I found out that being in my place without her around feels weird. Bad, in fact. I guess I'm really a dyed-in-the-wool cat lady now."

Joel crossed his arms in front of his chest and looked glum. "I'm going to miss you."

Kat looked up from her packing and smiled. "That's good to hear. I'm going to miss you too. Like I said, my little apartment is a pretty lonely place these days." She looked back down at her suitcase.

With three strides of his long legs, Joel was across the room. He took the underwear that Kat was holding in her hand and threw it into the suitcase. He caressed her chin, moved his hand across her neck and wound his fingers into her hair, gently tugging her head back, so he could kiss her thoroughly.

Kat closed her eyes as her body melted into the kiss. She wrapped her arms around him, clasping her hands behind his neck. "Okay, I'd like to restate that. I'm *really* going to miss you. A lot."

Joel smiled. "Just making sure you don't forget about me while you're off in the Big City."

"I think that's extremely unlikely."

Chapter 10

Keys & Ferns

Far from forgetting about Joel, Kat spent most of the drive to her apartment mooning over him. Sometimes she was such a *girl*. But it was a beautiful day and she rolled down the car windows and sang along with even the most egregiously sappy songs on the radio.

She opened the door to the apartment and once again was surprised at how empty it felt. Her little apartment that once was so cozy now just seemed lonely without Murphee. She looked around at her furniture. Giving it up wasn't going to be any great loss. Selling it wasn't going to net her much money, either.

The plan was to meet Maria after she got off work, but first Kat had to deal with Jean Hartland, the manager of her apartment building. Jean was one of those people who was so efficient and businesslike that she often seemed rude. Kat wasn't looking forward to the meeting. She changed her clothes and washed her face, which made her feel a bit better, so she could brave Ms. Hartland's disdainful gaze.

Kat walked across the parking lot, passing by what she thought of as the "Murphee Dumpster." Was Murphee okay back at Chez Stinky? Was Joel? At this point, the tables had flipped. This apartment complex wasn't her home anymore. Chez Stinky was home now. Even walking through the

231

courtyard here felt different and foreign, although she'd done it a hundred times before.

The sounds of a rousing game of Marco Polo came from the pool area. That was something she definitely would not miss. The sound of a leaf blower droned monotonously and the hum of cars on the highway were a continuous background noise. How had she never noticed that before? She missed the peaceful quiet of the forest and the joy of watching dogs romping among the trees.

Arriving at the apartment manager's office, she walked in and found Jean sitting at her desk with a furious expression on her face. Kat paused for a moment before saying, "Hello. I'm Kat Stevens. I have an appointment. Is this a bad time?"

Jean jumped up out of her chair and slammed her palm on the desk. "The owner of Choice Management should be shot!"

Kat backed toward the door. "Maybe I should come back another time?"

Jean smoothed the front of her flowery dress, sat back down and crossed her fingers in front of her, and placed her hands on the desk. "I'm sorry about that. I'm having a bit of a problem with management. Who are you again?"

"My name is Kat Stevens. I live in Apartment 152."

"Oh. Yes, you're right on time."

"I was hoping I could talk to you about my apartment. I got a message from you a couple of weeks ago that it is being converted to a condominium. I'd like to move out now and get my deposits back."

"We are offering tenants advantageous financing to purchase their units."

"Thank you, but I'm not interested. I can be moved before the first of the month."

"I shall need to inspect your unit. Let me get your paperwork." She whirled around in her chair and began rummaging through a lateral file cabinet behind her desk. "What is your unit again?"

Kat looked around at the posters on the wall. Some of the scenic photos looked like they might have been taken in Alpine Grove. "I'm in 152."

Jean pulled a folder out of the cabinet, slapped it on the desk and opened it up. "Hmm. It appears you don't have any pets."

"I have a cat."

Jean looked up. "You never paid the pet deposit."

Kat cringed inwardly. Oops. Volunteering that little bit of information about Murph had been a tactical error. "I found a kitten next to the Dumpster in front of my apartment and I took her in."

"You should have told us that you have an animal in your unit."

"I didn't really think about it at the time."

Jean offered a brittle, insincere smile. "I am definitely going to need to take a look at this unit myself and evaluate. You are liable for any damage. If I find anything, the repair costs will come out of your deposit."

"You won't find any damage. And the cat isn't there anymore. She has already moved out."

"We'll see about that. When can you hand in your keys?"

"I need to move my stuff out. I should be able to do that soon. I need to talk to a friend who has a truck, first."

"Make sure you don't block any of the parking spaces when you move. The new association has strict rules about that!"

Feeling like a fourth-grader who had just been sent to the principal's office and reprimanded for bad behavior, Kat left the office. The odds of her getting her deposit back were low. If Jean found even one dust smudge, she'd cry "damage!" and get the whole place painted. The cost would almost certainly come out of Kat's deposit, so she could kiss that money goodbye.

Kat went back to her apartment, made a few calls to utility companies, and got ready to go out with Maria. Maria wanted to try out a new hot spot and Kat had agreed to meet her there for happy hour.

After fighting traffic for an hour, a hot and annoyed Kat walked into the Fern Oasis. Maria waved from the bar and Kat walked through an archway of ferns.

Grazing a fern frond with her head, Maria jumped up and stretched out her arms for a hug. "Hey, girlfriend! I missed you. Watch out for that pot. That fern isn't a friendly one."

"I'm not sure I've seen this many ferns in one place before."

"They're trying to revive the fern bar concept, but I think they might be overdoing it."

"I don't think it's been long enough. If you're not nostalgic for something, it's not ready to be resuscitated."

Maria grinned. "Do you want a Lemon Drop? They're kinda good and it's happy hour, so they're cheap!"

"That sounds like cough medicine. What's in it?"

"Lemon juice, sugar, and alcohol. You know you want one."

Kat settled onto a bar stool and put her hands on the bar. "All right, lay it on me."

Maria turned and looked at Kat appraisingly. "You look different."

"Nope. Still me."

"No way. Something's different. You look happier. More relaxed. You're getting some aren't you?"

Kat raised her eyebrows and pursed her lips, attempting to look prim. "I have no idea what you're talking about."

Maria poked her in the ribs. "You know you do. I heard that the sexy engineer is living in your house."

"How do you know that? I didn't think the Alpine Grove gossip grapevine reached all the way here."

"I met with Larry for drinks the other night."

"Here?"

"Well, not *here*. We went to an Italian restaurant near my place. That man knows his Italian food."

Kat grinned widely and turned to face her friend. "Oh my God, you went out with *Larry*? What was he doing here in the city?"

"He had some court thing. Or some legal thing. I don't know. But he remembered me and looked me up. I can be pretty memorable, you know."

The bartender came by with the Lemon Drops and placed them on the bar. Kat reached out and took a sip. "That's revolting and good at the same time."

"Wait 'til you've had more than one. They grow on you."

"Like a fungus. How many have you had?"

Maria giggled. "Only one before this one. But I'm pretty sure the bartender thinks I'm cute. I think he put in extra hooch. I feel gooood. So good, so good."

"You knew that you would, now."

Maria raised her drink in a toast, "Whoa! Here's to James Brown!"

Kat clinked her glass with Maria's. "So tell me about your date. Do you like Larry?"

"I do! He's cute! Well, cute in a buttoned-up, lawyer-type way. But after the Italian food, I took him out drinking and dancing and he really loosened up."

"That's amazing. Did he tell you he asked me out? I think I hurt his feelings."

"No, he didn't mention that. He said lots of nice things about me, though. I like that in a man. We didn't talk about you much. Just that the engineer's house got torched. I guess that was big news. Oh yeah—one other thing. He talked to some guy about your Aunt Abigail's will. Larry says the guy could get the house."

Kat almost choked on her drink. She put it down and stared at Maria. "What? I thought I was inheriting it? Who else is there?"

"You'll have to ask Larry. He starts talking legal stuff and I kinda tune out. After he tells me I'm pretty, I tune back in. All that legal talk is kinda relaxing, actually. 'The first party did this, then the second party did that.' He's got a nice voice. It's like listening to talk radio."

"Why didn't he tell me about this?"

"He's doing some legal thing. I'm not sure. But wait, you threw me off and didn't answer my question. Is the sexy engineer sleeping in your bed or not?"

Kat grinned. "Yes."

Maria raised her glass in a toast again. "Well, here's to sex! It's about time you got some action. You were starting to get cranky."

"I was not."

"I'm just saying it's been awhile."

"I can't argue with that. It was worth waiting for. Or I guess more accurately, he was worth waiting for."

Maria smiled and raised her eyebrows. "Oh really? He's *that* good."

"At the risk of sounding like a lovesick teenager, yes."

"Well, let's face it—you deserve it after that last loser."

Kat sighed. "Let's not go there. I need to ask you a favor. Can you sell my furniture for me? I'll give you a commission. I need to get back to Alpine Grove, but I have to move out by the first. There's already plenty of furniture at my aunt's house and my stuff is junk, anyway. It's even more junky than my aunt's junk, which is pretty sad. What if I gave you twenty percent of whatever you sell?"

"Twenty-five."

"Deal. I'll put the ads in the paper and give you the key to my apartment. Sell whatever you can. There's a kind of ugly sofa, tiny table, chairs, bed. The usual."

"I'm on it. Let's talk pricing. What do you think I can get for your crap? I need to know how much money I stand to make. I have my eye on some fine red stilettos. They're calling to me."

By the time they had finished their Lemon Drops, Maria and Kat had discussed the relative merits of the furniture and come up with a list of prices. Kat promised to call the newspaper to run classified ads.

Kat hugged Maria. "I have to go. Thanks for selling off my old life for me."

"It was a good life. But I think you may be working on finding a better one."

"I hope so."

~

After Kat got back to her apartment, she tried to call Joel at Chez Stinky. There was no answer and she left a message. It was odd to talk to herself on her own answering machine.

On her way inside, she had noticed some cardboard boxes next to the Dumpster, so she grabbed them. It would be good to get started on the whole sorting and packing program. She started pulling dishes out of the cabinets and placing them in piles: keep versus unload. The pots and pans she had here were in far better condition than the ones at Chez Stinky. She was looking forward to using younger, less-burnt cookware again.

The phone rang and a little thrill of happiness coursed down Kat's spine when she heard Joel's deep soothing voice on the line. "Hi. How's it going?" she said in a cheerful voice.

"It has been an interesting day. I thought you were going to call when you got there."

"I forgot how awful traffic is. By the time I got to my apartment, I had to run to the meeting with the manager. Then when that was done, I had to go meet Maria. But everything worked out and I'll be out of here soon. I think."

"That's good to hear."

"I do need to ask you one thing. Do you think I could borrow your truck? And your body. I need help moving. Maria's selling my furniture for me, but there's other stuff."

"That's fine. I think you've already had my body."

"True. That doesn't mean I don't want it again, though."

Joel laughed. "Okay, that's *really* good to hear."

"So how's life at Chez Stinky?"

"Fine. I walked the dogs, fed the cats. Watched furry animals sleep. The usual. But I did buy a computer. I researched it and found just what I wanted. I made the call to the catalog company this morning."

"You can spare me the details. If you say megahertz or CPU, I'll just fall asleep."

"I'll control myself. Another thing did happen while you were gone. Lady tried to chase Louie. He just sat there. I don't think she knew what to do. She sniffed and poked at him and then he whapped her on the nose. Lady went and hid under the table with Chelsey."

Kat giggled. "Good for Louie!"

"Yeah, but I decided to take her outside and do some remedial 'leave it' training. She knows the command, but I'm not sure she gets that it applies to *all* things. So I threw a ball and didn't let her chase it until I said so. She's disgusted with me."

"No wonder Lady is so well behaved. I'm impressed."

Joel cleared his throat. "There's one more thing. Tonight something strange happened. I was sitting around reading, and Linus ran out of here barking frantically in a way I've never heard before. He completely lost his mind about something happening outside the house. Then I heard a gunshot. I ran outside and tried to call him in, but I couldn't find him in the dark. For a few minutes he was gone. I'm not sure where he went. But then he came back a little later."

"Is he okay?"

"He seems fine. But he got really angry about something. Maybe someone was outside. I guess he's a good watchdog."

"I wouldn't have guessed. He seems like such a pushover. Having armed people in my forest is a little creepy."

"You do realize that almost everyone is armed here, right? All those hunters have guns."

Kat sighed "I suppose so. I just hope no one hurts Linus. Could you lock the dog door?"

"I already did."

"Tomorrow, I'm just going to make a couple of calls and then drive back. I miss it there. I miss you."

"I miss you too. We'll be here."

Chapter 11

What Happened?

By the time Kat got back to Chez Stinky, it was early afternoon. Traffic had been terrible in the city and she was not feeling love toward her fellow drivers. It was a relief to drive down the largely empty rural roads as she got closer to Alpine Grove. By the time she got to her driveway, she was beyond ready to get out of her car.

As she pulled boxes out of the trunk of the Toyota, Lori ran up to her with a welcoming bark and a steady wag. Kat looked up. "Hi, Lori. Where is your buddy Linus?"

Joel walked up from the back of the house toward the driveway. Kat smiled, but her smile faded when she saw the expression on his face. "What happened?"

Joel hugged her tightly. "I tried to call you, but I guess you'd already left. Something is wrong with Linus. I'm glad you're here. We have an appointment at the vet in half an hour and I need to get him into the truck."

Kat pulled away from him. "Linus! Oh, no." She ran down the hill to the back door and went inside. Linus was lying on the floor with his head between his paws. He did not look happy. She stroked his head. "What happened, Big Guy?"

Linus raised his head and wagged the tip of his tail. Joel walked in the back door. "We need to go." He bent down and cradled the large dog in his arms. "Could you get the door?"

Kat rushed to open the door. Tears were streaming down her face. "What happened to him?"

Joel met her eyes over the large pile of brown fur in his arms. "He was fine this morning. We went for a walk and he hung out outside for a little while afterward like he always does. Then he came inside and took a nap."

"About a half-hour ago, I got up and went outside. But he didn't follow me. When I came back inside, he didn't get up, which is unusual for him. I went over to him and he *wouldn't* get up. That's when I called the vet."

Kat reached over to pet Linus. "Don't you dare get sick, just when I finally have gotten to know you."

Joel loaded the big dog into the cab of the truck and he and Kat sat on either side. Kat stroked the big dog's head and leaned over to whisper that everything was going to be okay. This had to be the longest car ride she'd ever taken, even though the vet clinic was only a few miles away in downtown Alpine Grove.

They walked into the vet clinic and the receptionist exclaimed, "Good heavens, he's huge. Why don't you just carry him in there." She pointed down the hall, directing Joel to bring Linus into an exam room.

Joel carefully placed the big dog on the examination table. Linus was drooling and looking queasy. A tall woman in a white coat walked in and extended her hand to Kat. "Hello, I'm Dr. Cassidy, the veterinarian here."

"Hi. I'm Kat Stevens and this is my dog Linus. I think he's sick. I don't know what's wrong with him, but he doesn't want to get up and he's never like that."

The vet went over to the table and lifted Linus's large jaw with one hand and stroked his head with the other. "What's the trouble here, big fella?"

Linus moved his tail in a half-hearted wag. Then his brown eyes widened, and he looked startled. With a giant heave, he threw up on the veterinarian. Dr. Cassidy leaped back, looked down at herself and said, "I'm guessing you might be feeling better now."

Kat reached out as if to help, but pulled back her hand. Attempting to scrape the goo off the vet's lab coat probably wouldn't be constructive. "I'm so sorry about that. Maybe he ate something?"

Linus stood up on the table and wagged vigorously. Joel reached over and grabbed the dog's collar to keep him from jumping off. "Settle down, Linus. I fed him his kibble this morning and he didn't eat anything odd that I saw. The only time he wasn't right next to me was for a few minutes after we went for a walk."

Kat volunteered, "He's not a trash-eating dog, either. I have one of those, but he's not it."

The vet looked down at her no-longer-white coat. "I'm going to take a sample, just in case."

Kat asked, "In case of what?"

"Poisoning."

Joel and Kat looked at each other. Kat said, "That's horrible. Who would do that?"

Dr. Cassidy said, "From your description, this dog hasn't had hamburger. And this…" she pointed at a spot on her lab coat "…looks like hamburger. Why don't you carry him outside, so he doesn't get into it again? Let me change my coat. I'll get someone to clean up in here and I'll give him a quick look in the other room."

Kat said, "I'm sorry he threw up on you…and the mess. Linus really is a nice dog."

"It's an occupational hazard. This happens a lot more than you might think. Fortunately, I have a lot of lab coats. They're very washable." Dr. Cassidy smiled sympathetically and left the room.

Joel picked up Linus, who was less amenable to being carried around now that he was feeling better. After carrying the squirming dog to the other exam room, Joel placed him on the floor. Linus sat next to Kat, slowly wagging his tail as they all waited in silence for Dr. Cassidy to return.

When the vet walked into the room, they all looked up at her expectantly. She nodded at Joel. "Would you put him on the table for me?"

Joel hoisted Linus up from the floor to the table. Dr. Cassidy looked in the dog's mouth, in his ears, and gently prodded various parts of the dog's body. She looked up from her examination toward Kat. "We did a preliminary look at the food under the microscope. It appears that there was something in there. We're not sure what, but it looks like it may have been a sleeping pill." She stroked Linus's head. "He seems fine now, but we'd like to keep him for observation for a few hours, just as a precaution." She nodded at Joel. "You can put him back on the floor now."

After Joel put Linus down, the dog was obviously thrilled to be going home. He walked around the room wagging his tail enthusiastically, eager to be on his way. Dr. Cassidy clipped a leash on Linus and he stopped wagging when the vet opened the door that led to the back and walked him out of the room.

Kat turned to Joel. "What happened?"

He frowned. "I told you exactly what happened."

"Yes. I know that. I'm not blaming you. Do you think it's the guy who shot at Linus last night? Did we lock the dog door? What if there's more poison out there? We need to get home and check before one of the other dogs finds it."

Joel reached out and pulled her into a hug. "I know. Let's get out of here. Linus is in good hands."

~

Back at the house after a high-speed drive home, Kat and Joel went downstairs and checked on all the animals. All dogs and cats were accounted for and apparently healthy and well-rested, having been awakened from their afternoon naps. They seemed to wonder why the humans were agitated, but willingly participated in being checked over. The barn cats Butch and Sundance were sleeping on shelves near their food bowls in the Tessa Hut. Although they wouldn't be happy about it, Joel quietly secured the door of the outbuilding to keep them safe for the time being.

After the flurry of activity, Kat locked the dog door, walked into the downstairs bedroom Joel was using as an office, and flopped onto the bed. A tear slid down her cheek as she looked up at Joel, who was standing at the foot of the bed. "I'm so sad and mad all at the same time. Who would want to hurt Linus? Or any of these dogs? Or any animal, period. It makes me sick."

Joel crawled onto the bed and stretched his body alongside hers. He propped himself up on an elbow and looked down at her. "I'm sorry. I don't know what to say. I've never heard of this type of thing happening around here. People generally don't even lock their doors."

Kat rolled over to face him. "Thank you. If you hadn't been here paying attention, Linus might have died." She smiled. "It seems like I'm always thanking you for something."

He reached out to caress her cheek. "You just like that I can fix stuff."

"No, that's what your sister likes. I like you for way more reasons than that."

Joel gathered her in his arms and kissed her tenderly. "Good to know."

Kat curled up closer to him and closed her eyes. Before long they were both fast asleep, joining the dogs and cats in an afternoon nap.

∼

Kat was jarred awake by the sound of the phone ringing. She ran up the stairs less than gracefully as her sleepy muscles cramped. It was beyond time to get a phone extension in the downstairs bedrooms. She recognized Dr. Cassidy's voice. "You can pick up Linus now. He seems fine. It's a good thing your husband is so observant and got him here quickly. Throwing up all over me was probably the best thing the dog could have done."

Kat giggled. "Linus is a smart dog. Thank you so much! We'll be back there in a few minutes to get him." Oops. She hadn't corrected the vet about her marital status. Joel wasn't her husband. She'd only known him a few weeks.

Joel and Kat drove back to the vet clinic and collected Linus, who was thrilled to see them both. He wagged and trotted happily around the reception area, panting and smiling while Kat paid the bill. She sighed as she signed her name. As if her credit card needed any more workouts. She looked down at Linus. "Please stay healthy, Big Guy."

Louise came into the clinic lobby where Kat and Joel were standing next to Linus. The older woman sneezed mightily and pointed her handkerchief at Kat. "You! I heard you were here. You poisoned your dog. How could you?" She sneezed again for emphasis.

Kat was too stunned to speak for a moment, but then gathered her wits enough to blurt out, "I did not! I would never poison Linus. Or any dog. But I intend to find out who did."

Ignoring the protestations of innocence, Louise marched up to the receptionist. "I'm here to pick up Dr. Cassidy's donation for the Ladies Auxiliary auction." She started waving her handkerchief in front of her face more frantically. "Oh, oh, there's too much hair in here. I need to go outside! Can somebody bring it to me outside?"

Having paid their bill, Kat, Joel, and Linus followed Louise out to the parking lot and walked toward the green truck. Louise turned around to face them and pointed at Kat. "You are just irresponsible. I knew it. I can't believe Abigail thought you could take care of her animals. You are just like your mother, and you'll never see a cent of Abigail's money! I'll make sure of it!"

Joel looked at Kat and raised his eyebrows. "You weren't kidding. She really doesn't like you at all."

"I know. It's a problem."

~

Kat spent the rest of the day worrying about Linus. Keeping an eye on him was easy, since he liked to be within 18 inches of her anyway. Joel retreated to his office. Kat noticed that he tended to escape into the rationality of numbers and calculations when he was disturbed about something. The day had certainly been disturbing and exhausting, so she couldn't blame him for wanting to think about pretty much anything else.

That afternoon they walked all of the dogs on leashes. Fortunately, Joel was heavy enough and strong enough to deal with Tessa. He attempted to give her a few insights into the "heel" command, with limited success.

After dinner, tired of feeling anxious and helpless to do anything about the mysterious someone who might be lurking outside in the forest waiting to hurt her animals, Kat announced, "I'm going to go read in bed. Come on, Linus." Linus happily trotted into the bedroom after Kat.

Joel stood in the doorway. "Everything okay?"

"No. But I'm going to read for a while and try to forget about today."

"Good idea. I'll be there in a few minutes."

As Joel's footsteps thumped down the stairs, Kat picked up her book and rolled over on her side. She reached down to pet Linus's head every once in a while to make sure he was okay.

Linus growled quietly and stood up next to the bed. Kat looked at his giant muzzle, which was now about three inches from her face. "What's up, Big Guy?" Linus growled more loudly and menacingly. The growl rose in pitch and then he barked sharply, spun around and ran to the window. Kat jolted up into a sitting position and put her hand on her chest. "Linus! You scared the crap out of me."

Linus had his paws up on the windowsill and was barking furiously. Joel ran into the room. "What is going on?" he shouted over the din.

Kat looked at Joel and raised her eyebrows. "I don't know. We were just sitting here. Linus, stop that!"

Linus was running around the room, periodically running back to the window, jumping up on the sill, and barking hysterically. Joel went over to the window and looked out. "There's somebody out there. It looks like an old man."

Kat jumped and ran to the window. "Who is it?"

"I don't know, but I'm going to find out. You stay here."

"I will not."

"Yes, you will."

"Don't get all macho on me. It's my house. If there's some guy in my yard, I want to know who it is."

"He could be the guy who shot at Linus last night. Or who poisoned him. You stay here."

"No way." Kat turned and went toward the front door.

Joel grabbed her arm. "Don't be stupid."

"Let go of me," Kat snarled as she wrestled her arm out of his hands. "Don't *you* be stupid. And don't tell me what to do in my own house. We're just going to have to be stupid together. Deal with it."

Linus was jumping and barking at the front door. Kat looked at Joel and pointed at the dog. "Put a leash on him and bring him with us. He's pretty intimidating when he's like this. I wouldn't want to tangle with an angry 200-pound dog. Maybe he'll chase the guy off. Or at least bite him."

Joel nodded and snapped a leash on Linus's collar. They opened the door and went down the stairs. Joel shouted toward the forest. "Whoever you are. Get off this property."

Kat gripped Joel's hand and they walked closer to the man, who didn't move at all. Kat glanced at Joel. "Is he dead? Why is there an old dead guy in my yard?"

Joel shook his head. "Were you expecting company?"

The man was lying spread-eagled in a patch of weeds. Linus sniffed at him and poked him with his nose. Kat looked up into Joel's eyes. "Who is he?"

Joel shrugged and looked down at the old man. "I don't know him."

After being repeatedly poked, sniffed and growled at by Linus, the man in the grass finally stirred, shaking his mane of long gray hair. He sat up and rubbed his gray beard, wiping off some Linus drool. "Damn! What is that? It's huge! Get that thing away from me."

Joel handed the dog's leash to Kat and grabbed the front of the man's shirt with both hands, pulling him up to a standing position and then lifting him off the ground so he was face-to-face with the old man. "Who the hell are you?"

Kat shuddered. Joel was normally fairly quiet and composed. She'd never seen him really angry before and it was a little scary. "Yes, and why are you on my property?" she squeaked.

The older man squirmed, "Put me down, dude. Jeez man, what's your problem?"

Joel loosened his grip and lowered the man to the ground. "My problem is that you're creeping around here in the dark, and I don't like trespassers."

"I'm not trespassing! This is my house."

Kat was irritated now. She stood up straighter. "It is not! This place was owned by my Aunt Abigail. She left it to me."

"Well, you might get it someday, but it's mine now. I'm her husband. So it's mine. And all the trees, too."

"She wasn't married. She left it to me."

"Yes, she was married. To me. We never got divorced. I helped build this place."

Kat raised her eyebrows. "Wait. You're the Lumberjack?"

Joel looked at Kat. "The Lumberjack?"

"I'm Jack Palmer. And yeah, I did some logging back in the day."

A muscle twitched in Joel's jaw as he leaned toward the man. "You haven't explained why you're here. And why you shot at and tried to poison this dog."

Jack scratched his beard. "I didn't poison any dog. I went out hunting the other night. There was a bunch of barking in the forest. It was echoing in the trees and I couldn't tell where it was coming from. And then I saw a bear. That freaked me out, man! Damn. That thing was huge! I dropped my gun and it went off when I ran away. Now I can't find it. I put some of my Valium into some hamburger, so the bear might take a nap and I could go look for my gun. That's what I'm doing. Like I said, it's my place and I can hunt on it. Well, when I find my gun again."

Kat looked at him more closely. "So you really knew my aunt?"

Jack looked over at Kat and the expression on his weathered face softened. "Yeah, she was really young when I met her. Man, she was so beautiful. Really long, dark wavy hair." He glanced at Kat. "She looked kinda like you, actually. I'd just come back from Korea and I was pretty messed up. I ended up coming through here and she was nice to me. I met her at the cafe. It's not here anymore, but she worked there. Anyway, we got together. Abby was amazing, man. She took me out here to this place and told me how she wanted to build a house. It was good at first. Really good. But she kept inviting her friend's kid out here and that was a drag. And I figured out she wanted to stay here, like, forever. I couldn't handle that. I wasn't ready to deal with that kind of responsibility, man."

Kat nodded. "I think I heard about that part. You left."

Jack shrugged. "There was a guy and he told me that I could score some...uh, well, you don't need to know about that part. But I went to Vegas. And I kept meaning to come back, but I liked the casinos. Then it was the sixties and the seventies. Things were really happening."

Joel looked at Jack. "You do realize it's the nineties now, right?"

"Time sorta got away from me, man. Then an old buddy of mine came through Vegas and I heard Abby died. I didn't even know she was sick. But I knew she never would have sold this place. And look at the trees. They gotta be worth a fortune. Do you know what cedar sells for?"

Kat narrowed her eyes. "Actually, I don't."

Jack looked excited. "If you stripped this place, it would be a lot of money. I mean, *a lot*, man."

Kat glared at him. "I found some of my aunt's papers. She had foresters come out and a few years ago they did a little logging to clear out some dead trees. But she wanted to keep the forest healthy. Not sell off the trees. I read the plan the forester did for her."

Jack shrugged. "She always was an eco-nut. But that's not my problem. When I get this place, I'm clear-cutting it. And selling it. I talked to a developer the other day. He's got ideas."

Now Kat was getting angry. She said through clenched teeth, "That's not going to happen. I read the will. Abigail was very specific in her wishes. She wanted someone to take care of the animals and the forest. I'm going to do that. I'm not going to clear-cut anything."

Joel moved toward Jack. "I think you'd better leave. If I see you here again, I'll call the police." Linus contributed a low, menacing growl to emphasize the point.

Jack raised his hands up, "Hey man, take it easy. I'm going. But I talked to that lawyer guy. Don't get your hopes up about staying here." He started ambling toward the driveway. "And if you find my gun, I want it back. I'm at the Enchanted Moose."

Kat was freezing. Her body started to tremble in a combination of fury and tangled emotions. She looked up at Joel and said through gritted teeth, "That was more than unpleasant. I don't believe this."

"I know. Do you think he really has a case?"

"I have no idea. Maria told me someone had talked to Larry about the will. I guess I know what it was about now."

With Linus by his side, Joel took her hand and they walked slowly back toward the house, which was silhouetted in the moonlight. Kat looked up at the simple log structure she had grown to love. *I'm not going to let him destroy this place.*

~

The next morning, Kat made an appointment to meet with Larry. If she was about to lose the money and the house and all the dogs and cats that lived within it, she wanted to find out sooner rather than later. She was sitting at the table slowly chewing on a piece of toast, pondering her options if the Lumberjack ended up with Chez Stinky. The idea of him razing the forest and tearing down the house made her feel a little sick. The toast tasted like cardboard in her mouth.

Joel walked into the kitchen, bent down, pushed Kat's hair aside, and kissed her on the neck. "Hi."

Kat reached up to take his hand before he walked away. "Long time, no see. Last night, after our little chat with the Lumberjack, you distracted me, and I forgot to ask if you could keep an eye on things while I go talk to Larry this morning."

Joel smiled. "That was an enjoyable distraction. No, I don't have plans to go anywhere. I'm hoping my computer arrives today. I had it shipped here. I hope that's okay."

"Definitely okay. I think after you defend me from weird old men in the yard, you pretty much can have free run of the place. You and Linus are the brave defenders of Chez Stinky."

"Linus did do some serious growling. I was impressed."

"I think we may have underestimated the Big Guy. He's quite the studly dog when he sets his mind to it."

Later, Kat drove over to the Law Office of Lawrence Lowell. She found Larry sitting at his desk, looking almost exactly as he had the first day she arrived in Alpine Grove. A lot had happened in a very short time.

With a big smile, Larry stood up and extended his hand. "Hello Kat. It's good to see you. Please sit down."

Kat shook his hand and was struck again by how different he looked when he smiled. Larry was obviously in a remarkably good mood. "Thanks Larry. You seem happy."

"I am. Your friend Maria is just wonderful. I think I'm in love!"

Kat smiled. Did Maria know about the lawyer's feelings? "That's really sweet. I think Maria is wonderful, too. She's been my friend for a long time now."

"She's coming up to visit this weekend, and I can't wait!"

"That's great, Larry. I hope I get to see her, too. But right now I'd like to talk about Abigail's will. The Lumberjack was passed out in my yard last night. He said my aunt never divorced him, so he should inherit everything. Is that true?"

"Ah yes, the Lumberjack. Jack Palmer. I was hoping to have this resolved, so you wouldn't have to worry about it. I'm sorry, but it hasn't worked out that way."

"So you're saying he has a case?"

"Possibly. I did some research and found the initial divorce paperwork your aunt filed, but no evidence that it was ever finalized. According to law, in the case of abandonment where the spouse is missing, you must attempt to locate the person. You might search through telephone books and contact family members. That type of thing. It was many years ago, but I did find the paperwork that details Abigail's attempts to find him."

"That's good, right?"

"Yes. But the other issue is that the spouse filing the divorce must notify the spouse that he or she is being divorced."

"How could Abigail do that if she didn't know where the Lumberjack was?"

"She would have to provide service by publication. It requires that you publish a notice of the divorce proceedings on a regular basis for a specific period of time in newspapers that circulate in the areas where you suspect the spouse may currently reside."

"I don't know if she knew, but from what he said, it sounds like he was in Las Vegas. He said he lost track of time. I'm not sure he remembers much of the sixties or seventies."

"That's a challenge. Much of this type of archival information is on microfilm and it takes quite a while to search through it."

"Will finding that invalidate his claim?"

"Possibly. I have no evidence of the service by publication, so we have no reason to believe she wanted to go through with the divorce. Maybe she changed her mind. Or maybe she just didn't do it. There is no final paperwork. But it may have been lost in the fire of 1958. If we find evidence that the service by publication happened, that would signify that the divorce went through, even though the documentation has been lost."

Kat sighed. "There was a fire?"

"Yes, many Alpine Grove records were lost. Those destroyed records have caused a lot of problems. The courts around here have been liberal about accepting service by publication as evidence when nobody can find an actual divorce decree."

"Great. That figures. But I still don't understand. She had a will."

"Mr. Palmer's argument is that because she was sick, Abigail was not in her right mind when she created the will. He will argue that the decedent did not have the proper mental capacity to create the will and trust documents. If the court decides that is the case, the documents could be declared invalid. As a spouse, he would have more inheritance rights. Her familial connection to you is less direct than a spousal connection. As a spouse, he would own half of the property and would gain the other half upon her demise."

"So you're saying if Abigail never divorced him, it's his."

"It's possible. I suggest you retain an attorney. Because I was your aunt's lawyer, it could be construed as a conflict of interest if you hire me. But I can give you a few names of people to call."

Kat bent her head and covered her face with her hands. "I can't afford that. I'm not even sure I can afford the house. It may disintegrate before anyone can inherit it."

"Please do not construe anything I've said as legal advice. I'm simply explaining the terms of the will and the possible ramifications of it being contested. There is one more thing."

Kat raised her head and looked into Larry's brown eyes. "What? There's more?"

"You might want to talk to Louise."

Kat groaned. "Why? She hates me. I mean she *really* hates me. It's bordering on bizarre."

"Just do it. She has lived in Alpine Grove for her entire life. You may find she has… information. But again, I'm not giving you legal advice."

"Okay, Larry. I'll give it a shot. I suppose she couldn't possibly hate me more than she already does."

Larry smiled brightly again. "If you talk to Maria, please tell her I'm looking forward to this weekend!"

Kat stood up and shook his hand again. "I'll do that."

∼

Kat went home and related the legal details from her meeting to Joel. After listening to Kat's long monologue, Joel sat in silence.

She raised her eyebrows. "Well?"

"That was a lot of information. I'm thinking."

"Think louder."

He shrugged. "It sounds like with no proof that Abigail really divorced the Lumberjack, you're screwed."

"Thanks. I got that."

"What do you want me to say?"

"Is there anything I can do?"

"Larry said you should talk to Louise. Maybe she knows something that could help?"

Kat rolled her eyes. "Right. That's gonna be a fun conversation."

He got up from the table. "Sorry, that's all I have right now." He reached to take her hand. "I've got to work on setting up my computer. Are you okay?"

Kat squeezed his hand, then slumped in her chair and flopped her arms on the table. "Yeah. I guess so. I'll see if I can meet Louise somewhere with no pet hair. It would be nice to have a conversation with her when she's not sneezing or yelling at me, for once."

Joel laughed. "Good luck."

Kat called Louise, and after an uncomfortable conversation, they agreed to meet at the Alpine Grove diner. Kat went downstairs to tell Joel she was heading out.

He was hunched over a computer manual. Looking up, he said, "You're off the phone. Good."

"I'm meeting Louise at the diner."

"Great. I'm getting my computer modem hooked up, so I can get on the Internet. I need to do some research. And check my email."

"Okay. Happy nerding."

"Takes one to know one."

Kat stood up straighter. "I beg your pardon. I am not a nerd. I just associate with them."

He grinned. "So it seems."

As she got into her Toyota, Kat tried to think about what she could say to Louise that could possibly change anything. "Hi, Louise. As it turns out, I probably don't own the house after all, so your wish that I never see one cent of Abigail's money will come true." Okay, that probably wasn't a good opener. Kat was just going to have to wing it.

At the diner, Kat slid into a booth and ordered a cup of coffee. She looked up at the old pictures of Alpine Grove that were scattered across the knotty-pine-paneled walls. She thought about what it must have been like for her aunt to live here for forty years and the changes she must have seen.

Kat's historical daydreams were interrupted by Louise, who bustled into the diner and slid into the booth across from Kat. "Hello," she said primly as she settled into her seat.

"Thank you for meeting me. Larry Lowell suggested that we talk about what's going on with the house and Abigail's inheritance. I know you don't like me much, but perhaps we can put that aside for the moment."

Louise touched her blue curls with her hand. "You may be a fine person. I simply do not think you are a good steward of Abigail's estate. That is all. Abigail loved her animals and wanted them taken care of properly. I want her wishes to be honored."

"Actually, it's possible her wishes won't be honored at all if she didn't actually divorce Jack Palmer."

"Who is Jack Palmer?"

"The Lumberjack."

Louise waved a hand at Kat and exclaimed, "Oh, that awful person. Good heavens yes, she was rid of him years ago."

"Are you sure?"

"Of course I'm sure! Abigail had some rather choice words to say about that man. She absolutely detested him, particularly after he walked out on her. He left her with a half-built house. It took years for her to scrimp and save to finish it off."

"He's here. And he wants the house. Not to mention the trees. I found him passed out in the yard last night."

Louise looked across the table more closely at Kat. "What? He's alive? And here in Alpine Grove?"

"Yes. Quite alive, although I'm not sure how many brain cells he has left. Apparently he's staying at the Enchanted Moose. He heard Abigail died and came up here. Now he wants the place. He said he knew she wouldn't have ever sold it."

"No. She never would have."

"Oh, and by the way, just to be clear, I did not poison my dog. The Lumberjack did it. He thought he was poisoning a bear. It was an odd story."

Louise looked slightly mollified. "I see. That makes me feel a bit better. After the dogs running wild everywhere and the cat in the wall, Lord knows what you could have done."

Kat looked down and shook her head. "I guess I don't really have anything else to say. I just wanted you to know what was going on. And that I have tried. Really tried. I truly do want to take over the house and care for the animals. I love them, and it will break my heart to leave them. I had plans to fix up the place and start a business."

Louise shook her finger at Kat. "I know that horrible man was not married to Abigail. I just know it."

"But we have no proof. There is no record of any final divorce paperwork at all. Larry said it might have burnt up in a fire, though. But I've gone through just about all of Abigail's things, and I haven't found anything."

"Where has that man been all these years?"

"Apparently, he's been living in Las Vegas. He says his plan is to take over the property, cut down all the trees, and sell it to a developer."

Louise looked horrified. "That's dreadful."

"I agree. If you can remember anything that might help, let me know. Since the Lumberjack just talked to Larry about filing papers, I think I can still live there for a while and continue taking care of the animals if it's okay with you."

Louise nodded. "Yes, please do."

"I'm not sure how long this type of thing takes. And it's possible I still could inherit. Larry said that my relationship with Abigail is distant, particularly compared to a spouse. And the Lumberjack may be able to claim that there's no rational reason she'd will something to me. He may claim she was too sick to know what she was doing."

"That's ludicrous! Abigail was as sane as you or I until the day she died."

Kat shook her head. "Everything is really up in the air right now. Thanks for meeting me and letting me stay in the house. I should go now. I'll be in touch if something changes."

Kat handed Louise some money for her coffee and left the diner. She slowly walked to her car with her hands in her pockets. She'd learned a few things from Louise, anyway. The woman was convinced Abigail had divorced the Lumberjack and apparently her aunt's mental health was fine before she died. Maybe Louise would be willing to testify to that. But it might not be enough to make a difference. Even if Kat inherited half the property, it could be difficult to keep the Lumberjack and his chain saw away from those profitable cedars.

Chapter 12

Multi-tasking

When Kat returned to the house, Joel was still downstairs doing nerdy things with his new computer. He certainly was focused. Kat smiled. When his attention was on her, that level of focus could be a good thing.

She stood in the doorway of the office and tapped on the open door. "How goes the exciting journey into the World Wide Web?"

Joel looked up and smiled. "I got into my CompuServe account and surfed a few Web sites. I am connected again and my inner geek is rejoicing."

Kat walked over to his chair and bent down to put her arms around his neck. She looked deeply into his green eyes with mock seriousness. "Wow, how sexy."

He pulled her down into his lap and wrapped his arms around her, poking her playfully in the ribs. "It could be." After she stopped squirming, he kissed her deeply. He paused and raised his eyebrows suggestively. "Have you noticed there's a bed in here? I've never had an office with a bed before."

Kat giggled. "And here I thought all you cared about was your new computer."

"Not at all. I'm very good at multi-tasking." He grabbed her around the waist and raised her out of his lap. Taking her two hands in his, he stood up and walked backwards until he fell on the bed, pulling her on top of him.

Kat looked into his eyes. As she inclined her head to kiss him, her long, dark hair cascaded around his face. He pushed her hair back, gathering it into one hand to keep it out of the way. Looking at her for a long moment, he drew her back down to him so he could kiss her more thoroughly. Kat's body began to relax and she lost herself in his warm embrace. The phone rang and Kat pulled her head back suddenly. "Owww! Let go!"

"Oops. Sorry about that."

They both sat up and stared at each other for a second as Joel disentangled his fingers from her hair. Kat grinned at the distressed look on Joel's face. Noting the twinkle in her eye, he burst out laughing. "Okay, that was definitely *not* sexy."

Kat gave him a quick peck on the lips. "I know you'll make it up to me." She got up off the bed and ran upstairs to answer the phone.

Kat got to the phone and picked up the receiver as the answering machine picked up. She jabbed her finger on the button to turn it off. "Hello. I'm here. Sorry."

Maria said, "Hey, girlfriend, you sound all out of breath. What have you been doing?"

"Uh…nothing. Larry said you're coming up this weekend. He's looking forward to seeing you. When do you get here?"

"I was going to come up Saturday night to see Larry, but work is stupid."

"That's nothing new."

"I was wondering if I could crash at your place later tonight."

"Do you mind sleeping downstairs? I cleaned out the bedrooms. It's a lot better."

"I don't care. I'll be in pretty late, though. Just tell the sexy engineer not to be walking around naked or something."

"I'll try and keep him under control."

"Maybe we can do something tomorrow morning. I want to go get close to nature. I read an article that said the trees exhale and give you more oxygen. It's supposed to be good for you. I want to be feeling extra healthy and have my stamina at its peak in case Larry makes a big move."

"Do you want to go hiking somewhere? I can ask Joel if he knows about trails around here."

"Can I wear my heels?"

"I don't think that would be a good idea."

"Why do they put the trees in places we can't get at? Stupid trees."

"There are plenty of trees here at the house. We'll think of something else to do. I'm looking forward to seeing you."

"I need to get a good look at the sexy engineer for myself. If he's another loser, I'm going to need to have a conversation with you."

"I've never known you to hold back."

～

Maria arrived late that night after fighting Friday evening traffic out of the city. She was grumpy and Kat suspected her friend might be disappointed that Joel wasn't wandering around naked, after all. In fact, he had been sleeping quite naked in the bedroom, but it probably wouldn't be a good idea to mention that.

The next morning, Kat and Joel were sitting at the kitchen table when Maria emerged from the stairwell, wearing a frilly pink baby-doll nightgown that appeared to be a few sizes too small. She walked into the kitchen and stretched out her arms. "I feel good! I think it's the trees. I'm oxygenating! And I think the big dog down there just felt me up with his nose. I feel a little violated now."

Kat said, "He's just friendly. You remember Joel, right?"

Maria walked behind Joel, wrapped her arms around his neck and gave him a loud smacking kiss on the cheek. "Hey, roommate! Any friend of Kat's is a friend of mine. It sounds like you two are waaay better friends than you were the last time I was here. Did you have lots of fun last night?"

Looking uncomfortable, Joel slowly peeled Maria's arms off his shoulders and turned his head to look at her. His eyes widened at the sight of Maria's nightwear. "I'm fine thanks. Kat said you had a long drive last night."

Kat giggled at Joel's obvious distress at Maria's touchy-feely ways. When she had met Maria, it had taken a while for her to get used to how physically affectionate her friend was. Joel might need a little time to adjust, too.

Maria patted Joel on the shoulder. "Yeah, but work and stupid traffic are behind me now. I'm going to get me some lawyer action tonight. So it will all be worth it."

Joel glanced quickly at Kat, who grinned back at him. He said, "I hope so."

Maria flopped down in a chair and slapped her palms on the table. "So what do you guys do for fun up here? We tried the night life last time, and I hate to tell you this, but there isn't any."

Kat looked at her. "True. We usually just hang around here."

Maria waved her hands at them. "What? Are you 90 years old? You guys aren't really that boring, are you?"

"Well, the other day we had to take Linus to the vet. That was something. And then the other night, there was the old weird dude we found lying in the weeds."

"What? There was a dude? Was he dead? Was there gore?"

Joel volunteered, "He was alive. Just passed out."

Maria raised her eyebrows. "I thought all the drunks lived near my apartment. I guess they're expanding their territory."

Kat said, "He claims he owns the house. Remember the pictures where the Lumberjack was whited out?"

"Yeah."

"That was the guy in the yard."

"Wow. You met White-Out Guy? There's way more action here than I thought."

Kat and Joel explained the situation with the inheritance and the Lumberjack's potential claim on Chez Stinky to Maria. By the end of the story, she was shaking her head.

"That's just wrong. He walks out on the woman and this place and 30 years later he wants it back? You can't let that happen."

Joel got up from the table. "I hope it won't. If you'll excuse me, I need to go check on something on my computer."

Kat and Maria watched in silence as he descended the stairs. Maria turned and looked at Kat. "I've never seen anything like that."

"What? Is this where you give me the lecture about my taste in men? We've been over that before. A lot of pinot noir grapes have given their lives in the never-ending quest to analyze my romantic failures."

"No. It's freaky to hear you and Joel talk together. It's like you're connected at the brain."

"What? We just talk."

"No. You don't talk like that with anyone else. Except me sometimes, I guess. But then occasionally I'm just too fabulous for you and you get all quiet."

Kat raised her eyebrows. "I think you may be mistaking quiet for me not being able to get a word in."

"Whatever. This guy rocks your world, doesn't he?"

Kat blushed and lowered her eyes. "Pretty much."

"So what are you going to do about it?"

"Do?"

"You're in this weird limbo thing with him living here. What if you lose this place? Do you move in with him? Move somewhere else? Go your separate ways? What if he gets a job somewhere? Or you get a job? Would you move with him? Would he move to be with you?"

Kat giggled. "So you're asking me what my intentions are with this man? You're like a stern parent in some nineteenth-century novel."

"I prefer to think of it as getting the real dirt on the situation."

"That, too. Who knows what will happen? As you point out, my life is a disaster area. I have no idea."

Maria put her elbows on the table and rested her chin in her hands. "So here's the million-dollar question: are you in love with him?"

"I don't know. Maybe. Probably. We've only known each other a few weeks. I can't be sure how he feels about me. It seems like he cares, but I told you he dated a super model before me. He might need to think about it for a while before jumping into anything."

"Figure it out, girlfriend."

~

After spending the afternoon exploring the shops of downtown Alpine Grove and watching Maria buy things, Kat returned to Chez Stinky. She rummaged in the kitchen for food while Maria got ready for her evening with Larry.

Maria hauled her suitcase up the stairs and put it by the front door. She was dressed in a tight black dress that emphasized her curves.

Kat looked at her. "Larry will like that outfit. But can you walk in it?"

"I'm working on it. I'm practicing. By the time Larry sees me, I'll have worked out the issues." She reached out her arms to hug Kat. "You behave. Or not." She raised her eyebrows. "Remember what I said about the sexy engineer. Figure it out."

After the little red Miata pulled out of the driveway, the house was oddly quiescent without Maria's effervescence. It was a bit of a relief. Although Kat loved Maria, it was nice to return to her normal peaceful existence. She went downstairs to see what Joel was up to and let him know Maria had hit the road. He'd undoubtedly been trying to stay out of the way.

Joel looked up from his computer as Kat walked in the room. He had an odd look on his face. Kat stopped in front of him. "Maria is off on her date now."

"I hope it works out for her."

"You never know with Maria. Poor Larry doesn't know what he's in for." Kat turned to leave.

"Wait. I need to talk to you for a minute."

Kat turned back toward him with a questioning look. "Okay."

"I need to go on a trip for a couple days. I don't think that the Lumberjack is going to be sneaking around here anymore, so you should be okay, right?"

"I'll be fine. Where are you going?"

"Just a quick flight south. It's a family thing."

The expression on his face indicated he was probably lying. Even if he wasn't, he certainly wasn't offering any details about the trip, which was irritating. She shrugged. "You don't have to ask my permission. You can leave any time you like."

A flash of anger or disappointment flashed in his eyes. Kat wasn't sure what that look meant, but it wasn't good. After a long pause, he said, "Fine. I should probably pack. I have to leave here early in the morning to get to the airport." He stood up, navigated around her without touching her, and walked out of the room.

Kat turned and stared at the empty space where he had walked by. That was strange. What had just happened? She went up the stairs into the bedroom and stood in the doorway. "What's going on?"

Joel looked up from the suitcase he'd pulled out of the closet. "Nothing. I just have to go on this trip. That's all."

Kat walked over to him and looked up into his eyes. "Are you sure? You're being weird."

He smiled and reached out to take her in his arms. "I am sure. And no I'm not."

"If you say so. But can you tell me something? Are you looking for another job?"

"No, I'm not. I'll call you when I get there."

"I'm going to miss you again, you know."

"I know." His expression relaxed and he gently eased her down to the bed with him. "Maybe we should make up for the time we'll be apart in advance."

"Way to plan ahead."

∼

After getting very little sleep, Joel left at three the next morning to drive to the airport. Kat wished him a safe trip and went back to sleep, trying not to think about how large and lonely the bed felt without him in it. Or about all the deer out on the darkened roads that might leap out in front of his truck.

Later Kat rolled out of bed, made some toast, and then wandered downstairs in her nightshirt to feed the dogs. She was determined not to spend the entire day moping and worrying about Joel again. Been there; done that. Of course, the next obvious possibility was that he was meeting Allison somewhere. What if they were getting back together? Kat shook her head. *No. Don't go there again.*

The dogs all gathered around expectantly. "Hi, guys. Yes, it's that magic moment you've all been waiting for."

She went through the routine of dispensing and delivering the food, causing much canine joy and reveling. Life was so simple for a dog. Eat. Walk. Dump. Nap. Eat. Dump. Sleep. And then do it all over again the next day. There was beauty in simplicity.

Walking into the bedroom that she now considered Joel's office, Kat pondered the idea of looking for Abigail's divorce papers again. When she had been cleaning out stuff, she hadn't seen anything that looked like important papers. But then again, she hadn't been looking for that type of thing. She had just been trying to make the rooms fit for human habitation.

She opened up the closet, sat cross-legged on the floor, and pulled out the closest cardboard box. Murphee walked into the room and sat next to her to supervise as she riffled through the contents of the box. Deciding that it was time for some managerial input, the cat put her paws up on the side of the box and daintily hopped inside.

"Thanks Murph. You're not helping."

Murphee meowed proudly, obviously pleased with her accomplishment.

Kat lifted the cat out of the box and folded the flaps back up. "This isn't getting me anywhere."

She went back upstairs, took a shower, and got dressed. After taking the dogs for a walk, she decided to go to the reference section of the library to look through the *Writer's Market* and take notes on possible magazines that might want articles she could write. Maybe Joel would let her use his new computer to write some query letters, since she couldn't afford to get her own computer right now. It wouldn't hurt to ask.

When she returned home, her answering machine light was flashing madly. The first message was from Joel. She smiled as his voice came from the machine. "Hi. I'm just letting you know I'm here. I'll call you later." Good thing he was going to call back, because he didn't leave a number. How annoying.

After the beep, Louise's voice said, "Hello, Kat? This is Louise Johnson. I'd like to talk to you again if you have an opportunity."

Kat raised her eyebrows. Maybe Louise had good news. She picked up the phone and called Louise's number. "I got your message. When would you like to meet?"

"As soon as you can. I need to talk to you. Could you come to my house? It's in town, not too far from the diner."

Kat got directions and promised to be there after she walked the dogs.

Later, she parked her Toyota in front of the house at the address Louise had given her. The compact bungalow sported a meticulously manicured garden with an arbor covered with pink climbing roses. She got out of the car and knocked on the door.

"Kat, I'm so glad you're here. I've been thinking about our conversation, and I think there are things you need to know. I'm not sure any of it matters now, but I feel I must share something with you." She wrung her handkerchief nervously in her hands. "Please sit down. Would you like something to drink?"

As she sat on the sofa, Kat looked at Louise more closely. Her eyes were red, and it looked like she had been crying. "No, I'm fine, thank you."

Louise cleared her throat. "Well, I'm sure you know that your grandmother's name was Florence."

"Yes, she's Abigail's sister."

"And your grandfather was a banker. They had a lovely little house where they raised your mother."

"Yes. I've heard all about that. I think my mother wishes it were still 1958."

"Abigail was...let's just say, she was a bit more of a free spirit than Florence. She didn't get along with the family very well. She ran away from home when she was quite young."

Kat raised her eyebrows. "I had no idea. I thought she lived here."

"No, she came here later. That's when I met her. I'm getting to that. I don't know how much you know about the early fifties, but Greenwich Village in New York was rather a hip place to be. It was the beatnik era. Abigail got involved with some of those people and traveled around the country in an old school bus. They ended up in New York. I don't really know all the details. Abigail didn't talk much about it, but I think it was a crazy time. In any case, she got pregnant."

"What? So she did have children!"

"Well, yes. But there's more." Louise twisted her handkerchief more vigorously. "She was scared and young and called her parents. They flew her back home and she was in confinement until she had the child. Her parents insisted that she put the little girl up for adoption."

Kat stared at her. "I had no idea. Do you know who adopted the baby?"

Louise smiled. "Well, yes I do. I adopted Abigail's baby. She was my daughter Kelly."

"I didn't know you had a daughter."

A tear slid down Louise's cheek. "I don't anymore. I'm getting to that."

"I'm sorry."

"Please let me finish. This is a bit difficult for me. Anyway, Abigail was not happy about giving up Kelly. It was a private adoption that her parents arranged with my husband. Somehow Abigail found out that the baby was adopted by someone in Alpine Grove. So she ran away again and came here."

"Wow."

"As you might imagine, Alpine Grove in the early fifties was even smaller than it is now. It was quite easy to find out who had a new baby girl that was exactly the same age as Abigail's child."

"So is that how you met?"

"She got a job in the old cafe in town. I met her there. We became friends. Kelly got to know her, but it wasn't until much later that Abigail actually told me who she was. Kelly loved going to her house. Abigail was so young when Kelly was born. And they were so alike."

"Kelly is the little girl in the photos I found?"

"Yes, that's her."

"So what happened?"

Louise sniffed "Kelly was more like her mother than I thought. She was a rebellious teenager and it was the sixties. We started to fight. Horrible arguments. You've probably heard about the Summer of Love and all that. It was a difficult time."

"I've read about it. I was born in 1967."

"Yes. I know. I'm getting to that."

"What?"

"At that time, many people were hitchhiking around the country. Many strangers came through Alpine Grove. Truck drivers, hippies. All sorts. There were many parties and I believe a lot of drugs."

"What happened to Kelly?"

"She got pregnant when she was 17."

"You mean history repeated itself?"

Louise sighed. "Very much so. Needless to say her father and I were furious. Since she was adopted herself, she knew all about the options. We insisted that she give up the baby, but she refused."

"What happened to her? Who was the child?"

Louise began to cry. "Kelly died having her baby. The baby was you."

Kat's eyes widened. "Me?"

Dabbing at her eyes, Louise continued. "Yes. You. We were devastated about Kelly. And then a week later, my husband Harold, rest his soul, had a massive heart attack. I was a wreck. I couldn't handle taking care of a new baby while my husband was an invalid. So I arranged to have you adopted. At the time, I couldn't deal with an agency and all the paperwork. Abigail suggested her niece Mary."

"My mother?"

"Yes. I've regretted my decision ever since. I didn't try hard enough. But I hope you've had a good life. Your mother used to let you come up here to visit. But then she and I got into a major argument. Words were said. She never let you come back to see Abigail."

Kat rested her chin in her hand. "So Abigail was actually my grandmother. Not my aunt."

"Yes. And you are so much like her. And Kelly. You remind me of them, and it makes me miss them both even more." Louise started weeping.

Kat sat in silence for a moment trying to digest this information. Like most kids, she had wondered occasionally if she was adopted. But there was a family resemblance, so she never really put much stock in it. "Thank you for telling me. It actually explains a lot."

"I'm sorry I was horrible to you. Because I felt guilty for giving you up, I've never gotten along with your mother. And then I took that out on you."

"Well, my mother is not the easiest person to get along with."

"Just please don't run away. I know your mother loves you."

"I think it's a little late for me to run away from home."

Louise smiled. "Yes, I guess that's true. I forget how old you are now. You remind me so much of Kelly. Time goes by so quickly."

Kat didn't know what else to say and Louise looked exhausted. Kat stood up. "I should probably go. I appreciate you explaining what happened. I don't know that it will affect the inheritance, but I suppose it could."

Louise stood and walked Kat to the door. She awkwardly clutched Kat and hugged her. "I'm so glad I talked to you. Abigail would roll over in her grave if that horrible Lumberjack ends up with her place. She loved her trees and land so much. And I know she loved you, too. I will do whatever I can to help you stay in Abigail's house."

Chapter 13

Movie of the Week

Kat's mind was a jumble of new information and she barely remembered the drive back to Chez Stinky. She walked in and her answering message light was frantically blinking again. After pressing the button, Joel's voice came on the line. "Hi, Kat. I'm just trying to reach you again. I hope everything is okay. I'll be busy most of tomorrow and then I have a late flight out of here. I should be back there around 11 p.m. I miss you."

Kat gave the machine a dirty look. It was annoying that she'd hadn't been here to take the call. And that Joel didn't leave a number...again. She was bursting with information she needed to share. Just hearing his voice would make her feel better.

After the meeting with Louise, Kat was mentally and emotionally exhausted. She flopped down into a chair at the kitchen table and her stomach growled. When had she last eaten? She got up and stared into the refrigerator for inspiration.

She looked up from her quest for food as a car rumbled down the driveway. Maria's little Miata was slowly navigating the potholes. She walked outside to greet her friend.

Maria jumped out of the car and waved. "Hey, girlfriend! I forgot to give you your money!" She ran up the stairs holding an envelope and came inside.

Kat took the envelope from her peeked inside at the bills. "Money? I need that. Thanks for coming back out here to give it to me."

"I've got to head out now, but most of your furniture is gone. And your last paycheck is in there, too. After I extracted it from Mark, I decided not to mail it, since I figured I'd see you first."

"How was your date?"

"It was good. We went to the Italian place. Larry really likes Italian food."

"I noticed."

"He likes it when I talk about my grandmother's recipes, too. I told him about her lasagna, and I thought he was going to faint."

Kat smiled. "I didn't know your grandmother made lasagna."

"She usually doesn't. Actually, she mostly eats TV dinners. I embellished a little. Food talk makes Larry horny. I need to get some Italian cookbooks and find more recipes."

"He's going to be disappointed if he ever meets your grandmother."

"Oh, that won't happen. He thinks she lives in a little village in Tuscany."

"Wait, doesn't she live in New Jersey?"

"Larry doesn't know that."

Kat smiled. "If he wants to honeymoon in Italy, you're going to have a problem."

"Give me a break. I'm not getting married for a long time. I'm still sowing my wild oats. I don't know what sowing is exactly. But I know I've still got a lot of oats that need to get sowed."

"Is it sowed or sown?"

"I don't know. Whatever. Speaking of sowing, which we all know is just a fancy word for getting it on, how's the sexy engineer?"

"I don't know. He went on a trip."

"Where?"

"I have no idea."

Maria frowned. "I'm not going to have to have that chat with you, am I?"

"No. I'll deal with it. His sister calls it 'clamming up' when he shuts down and won't talk. I think he might think he's protecting me or something."

"I guess that's sweet. Sort of. No. Not really. That would piss me off."

"I'm trying to retain composure, particularly after I melted down about his ex-girlfriend."

"Yeah, I don't think that was your finest moment."

Kat nodded. "Plus, I had a weird day. Do you have to leave right away? Or do you want to hear about how I'm adopted and my aunt is actually my grandmother."

Maria raised her eyebrows. "What?" She walked into the kitchen to look at the clock on the wall. "I definitely have time for that. Maybe I'll just go in late to work tomorrow. Mark will just have to deal with it."

"Okay. I'm going to have a glass of wine. You can't have any because you're driving."

"Yeah, yeah. So come on, spill it."

Kat related the story Louise had shared earlier. By the end, Maria was sitting up straight in the chair staring at Kat. "That's like an ABC movie of the week. You need to sell the film rights about your family to a TV network."

"I'm not sure my mother would be up for that idea."

"That doesn't matter. She's just a supporting character."

After Maria left, Kat fed the animals and collapsed into bed. Thanks to the wine and information overload, she was asleep moments after her head hit the pillow.

~

The next morning, Kat had a headache and a sick feeling in her stomach. Was she hung over? Yuck. Maybe the wine hadn't been such a good idea. She moved slowly feeding the dogs and dealing with her morning routine. Taking a shower sounded like way too much work. For the unemployed, Mondays weren't particularly different than any other day. She was at loose ends wanting to talk to Joel about everything that had happened, but unable to reach him.

After the morning dog walk, she went outside with Linus. She stopped and leaned on the fence of the garden area, which was still filled with six-foot-high grasses. She looked through the welded wire fence. A small purple flower was reaching up through the thick weeds to find some light. Seeing the little plant struggle to grow shifted something in her mind.

She went out to the Tessa Hut and dug through various dusty and rusty things on the shelves until she found an old trowel. Even if she wasn't going to live here in the end, she wanted to see if there was anything left of the garden Abigail had cared for and loved so much.

Linus settled in for a nap under a tree and watched as Kat dug, scraped, yanked, and pulled in her effort to uncover any flowers and herbs Abigail might have planted. After about an hour of effort, one small corner of the garden was clear. Kat sat on the ground with her back against a fence post, pleased at having unearthed some feeble thyme and sage plants. With a few breaks for water and dog walks, Kat continued digging for hours while Linus supervised with his eyes closed from his shady spot under the tree. As the big dog's fur ruffled in the breeze, Kat worked until she was too exhausted to think about anything anymore.

That night, Kat awoke to the sound of a dog bark. Linus woofed once from downstairs. A few minutes later, Joel's snuggled his warm body next to her and wrapped his arms around her. She rolled over in his embrace and looked into his face. The moonlight was streaming in through the window, glinting on his eyes. She smiled at him. "Welcome back."

"It's good to be back." He nuzzled his face in her hair and kissed her neck. "I missed you. You smell like Thanksgiving dinner and wine. What have you been doing?"

Kat giggled, enjoying the feel of his body next to hers. "I fell asleep before I took a shower. Sorry about that. I found some herb plants in the garden. And Maria stopped by last night to give me my last paycheck and the money from all the furniture she sold. Apparently, she's a hard-nosed negotiator. She was motivated by the prospect of shoe shopping. Then we talked for a while. It has been a weird couple of days."

"Really?" Joel sat up and looked down at her. "The Lumberjack didn't come back, did he? Is everything okay?"

Kat pulled him back down to her. "Relax. It's nothing like that. And I'd like to know where you were first."

He sighed. "Okay. I went to Las Vegas."

"Vegas? Why?"

"I wanted to see if I could find the records of the notification of your aunt's divorce. I have a friend there who went to engineering college with me, so I stayed with him. I spent most of the day looking at microfilm of old newspapers. I know more about the Las Vegas news of yesteryear than I ever wanted to know. That's one strange place."

Kat smiled. "I don't think anyone would argue that point. Why didn't you tell me?"

"I didn't want you to worry or get your hopes up about it."

"Sorry, but that plan failed. I did worry. I had no idea where you were. You said if I had questions about you, I should ask you. I think you need to do your part to provide answers when I ask questions."

He looked into her eyes. "I know. You're right. I'm not used to telling people what I'm doing. Then you said I didn't have to ask permission, and I didn't want to talk about it. Anyway, the trip was a failure. I didn't find anything. But I didn't have time to go through everything. A lot of little newspapers have come and gone over the years. I asked a librarian for help before I left, and she said she'd keep looking into it. She looked really bored, so I think she was excited about having something else to do."

Kat sighed. "That's too bad. I can't believe you went all the way down there. I think that's the nicest thing anyone has ever done for me." She reached out toward his face, caressed his cheek and smiled. "I think I forgive you."

"I tried, anyway. One good thing happened, though. My friend works for a company that supplies slot machines for casinos."

"I guess he got out of engineering?"

"No. He is an engineer. Slot machines have gone high-tech. He said his company might be interested in some consulting work." He grinned. "You don't want to have programming errors on the circuit boards that would lead to too many payouts. He wants me to send an email tomorrow."

"If you figure how the slots work, maybe you can give me some of that extra cash they spit out, since I could be homeless again. I seem to have bad luck with housing lately."

Joel propped his head on his hand and looked down into her eyes. "You could always stay with me. I could add on to the shack. Maybe make it less of a shack and more of a house."

"You'd do that?"

"Of course I would. I don't want you to go anywhere."

"You know I have all these dogs and cats, too. They go where I go."

"I know. It might be a crowded shack. I just want to be with you."

Kat breathed a sigh of relief. "I want to be with you, too. I thought you might be going on the trip to get a job or something."

"I said I wasn't. I love you. I'm not going anywhere."

Kat's eyes widened. "I love you, too. I don't care where I live as long as it's with you."

Joel leaned down and kissed her slowly and tenderly. The tension Kat had stored up for days evaporated from her body and then there was nothing but the warm sensation of his touch.

~

The next morning, Kat and Joel slept in later than usual, entwined with one another in the bed, unwilling to break the cocoon of warmth they had created. Kat lay in his arms and explained her newly discovered family history.

When she was done retelling the tale, he gazed at her thoughtfully. "That's quite a story. I think I see why your aunt's, or I guess your *grandmother's*, nightstand is so well stocked."

"Abigail was late to the safe sex game, but apparently she made up for it."

"So it seems."

"Given my family predilection for extreme fertility, I'm glad I've always been a little hysterical about birth control."

"Better safe than sorry. And speaking of that…"

Kat rolled her eyes. "If we don't get out of bed soon, there's going to be a canine citizen uprising."

Joel nibbled on her earlobe. "Mmm. Maybe. Maybe not."

Kat giggled. "They'll be okay. It's not *that* late."

Later that morning after feeding and walking dogs, Kat was downstairs lying on the bed in Joel's office, staring at the ceiling. "I'm tired."

Joel looked up from his computer. "I think I know why."

"I did a lot of gardening."

"That, too." He looked back at his computer monitor. "Hey! I got an email from the librarian! It looks like she found something."

Kat sat up on the bed and looked over at him. "Really?"

"Yes. She found the newspaper notification. In some small obscure paper in Nevada. Impressive."

"Librarians do love a research challenge."

"She's going to scan it and email it to me. Then I can print it out."

Kat jumped up off the bed. "This is good news!"

"Have you seen any paper anywhere? I need to set up the printer."

"I think there was some in the closet."

Kat opened the door and bent over, looking around on the floor and rummaging through the boxes in the closet. She'd seen copier paper somewhere. Joel walked up behind her and touched her back, startling her. She jerked upright and hit her head on something metal that was jutting out from one of the shelves at the side of the closet. "OW! Not again!" She rubbed the top of her scalp. "What *is* that? This is the second time I've hit my head on it."

Joel maneuvered around Kat and pulled out a large metal box. "Looks like a fireproof box."

Kat raised her eyebrows and met his gaze. "Like the kind of box you'd use for storing important documents?"

"Exactly."

They put the box on the floor and quickly discovered it was locked. Joel got up. "I'll be right back." He returned with his toolbox, crouched down next to the box, and pulled something from his toolbox that looked suspiciously like lock picks.

Kat looked at him. "Do you have a life of crime I don't know about?"

"No. I locked myself out of the shack so many times, I got a set. You'd be surprised at the ads you can find in the back of geeky magazines."

"You are a man of many talents."

Joel grinned up at her. "You know it." He looked back down at the lock and continued fiddling with the picks.

At last the lock released and he opened the box. They both peered inside. Kat picked up the pile of papers sitting within, sat down on the floor and started going through them. "I found a copy of the will. That's good, I guess." She kept flipping through papers and then stopped. She looked up at Joel. "I think I found it." She handed the papers to him. "What do you think?"

"I think it's time to give Larry a call."

Kat squealed, grabbed the document, and ran up the stairs to the phone. "Woo hoo!"

Chapter 14

Epilogue

A month later, the leaves on the aspen trees were starting to change color and the forest was beginning to smell like fall. Louise, true to her word, had given her blessing for Kat to inherit Chez Stinky and receive the money from the trust.

Before the Lumberjack returned to Las Vegas, Joel had agreed to go out into the forest with him to help the old man finally find his gun. Kat kept Linus in the house, just in case. She didn't want the Lumberjack to mistake her dog for a bear again.

Kat and Joel set to work refurbishing the roof and the rest of the house, so it would survive the winter. Kat was also having plans drawn up to build a boarding kennel the next spring. And she bought a new computer, which she set up in the second downstairs bedroom.

One sunny fall day, Kat was outside digging more weeds out of the garden when Joel stepped out of the front door onto the landing. He had rebuilt the front entryway to the house, so the stairs were now under cover and no longer sported blue carpet. Joel stood with his arms crossed. "Cindy wants to talk to you about something."

Kat looked up from her digging. "Cindy? Why does she want to talk to me?"

"Who knows?" He turned and went back inside.

Kat brushed the dirt off her hands and went up the stairs into the kitchen to answer the phone and find out how Joel's sister had managed to annoy him this time.

"Hi, Cindy. What's up?"

"Joel told me you're going to board dogs. Like as a business."

"Yes, that's the plan. We're building a kennel this spring."

"One of my friends needs to board a dog now. Right now. It's an emergency and it's too far for me to drive out to her place every day. Can she leave her dog with you?"

Kat raised her eyebrows. "I'm not really set up with the business yet. But Joel fixed up the Tessa Hut. It was leaning and he straightened it out, so it looks a lot better than the last time you saw it."

"Great! She'll be there in an hour. 'Bye!"

Kat hung up the phone slowly and looked over at Joel, who was leaning on the kitchen counter.

"Apparently, I'm in the boarding kennel business now."

He walked over to her and wrapped her in his arms. He tilted her chin up and looked into her blue eyes. "You might be pretty busy with all those dogs."

She smiled and put her arms around his neck. "Not *that* busy. We'll figure it out."

Joel bent down to kiss her and whispered, "Yes we will."

Thanks for Reading

Thank you for dedicating some of your reading time to *Chez Stinky*. I hope you are enjoying Kat's adventures and I wanted you to know that I'll be writing more books that will feature Kat, Joel and various other residents of Alpine Grove who bring dogs to the new boarding kennel. The second book in the series, *Fuzzy Logic* is available now. Also be sure to keep an eye out for third book, *The Art of Wag* too.

If you would like to be notified by email when I release a new book, you can sign up for my New Releases email list at SusanDaffron.com.

I know that not everyone likes to write book reviews, but if you are willing write a sentence or two about what you thought of *Chez Stinky*, I encourage you to post a review at your favorite book vendor site or share a message with your social networking friends.

If you would like to share your thoughts about the book with me privately, you can reach me through the contact page on the SusanDaffron.com web site.

I look forward to hearing from you!

~ Susan C. Daffron

Acknowledgements

Writing a novel is not a small task and I'd like to thank my husband James Byrd for his support and encouragement throughout my first foray into fiction. If he hadn't written his first novel *Vaetra Unveiled*, I never would have been inspired to write *Chez Stinky* so this book wouldn't exist.

I'd also like to thank my beta readers for their eagle-eyed reading and great feedback:

- Cynthia Daffron
- Dian Chapman
- Kathy Goughenour
- Kate Turner

Posthumous thanks to my mom Margot Daffron for finding a typo on a preliminary cover printout and to Carolyn Daffron and Rich Weishaupt for answering a few last minute questions. (I take full responsibility for any errors.)

About the Author

Susan Daffron is the author of the Alpine Grove Romantic Comedies, a series of novels that feature residents of the small town of Alpine Grove and their various quirky dogs and cats. She is also an award-winning author of many nonfiction books, including several about pets and animal rescue. She lives in a small town in northern Idaho and shares her life with her husband, two dogs and a cat—the last three, all "rescues."

31224254R00189

Made in the USA
Middletown, DE
22 April 2016